"Something's wrong here."

"Yeah. I feel it, too," Jak said, a concealed knife dropping into his hand from his sleeve.

"Better stay in the mat-trans," Ryan said. "If we come back with a droid on us, we'll need backup."

Turning away, he saw that J.B. was already at the oval hatch, looking for traps.

"Clear," the Armorer reported.

"Okay, friends, triple red." SIG-Sauer at the ready, the one-eyed man pressed down the lever and the hatch swung open silently. Then with a snarl, Ryan instantly stepped backward, dropping into a crouch.

In the next room, several men in Navy uniforms operated the controls of the humming comps....

Other titles in the Deathlands saga:

JAMES AXLER

DEATH LANDS®

Moonfeast

A GOLD EAGLE BOOK FROM

WORLDWIDE®

TORONTO • NEW YORK • LONDON
AMSTERDAM • PARIS • SYDNEY • HAMBURG
STOCKHOLM • ATHENS • TOKYO • MILAN
MADRID • WARSAW • BUDAPEST • AUCKLAND

Recycling programs
for this product may
not exist in your area.

First edition November 2010

ISBN-13: 978-0-373-62605-2

MOONFEAST

They sang the song eternal, and strove to drums infernal. Then marched-marched-marched to the edge of the world. The damned fools sang as they marched to the edge of the world.

—Private A. B. Hassan,
Confederate Army 1861

THE DEATHLANDS SAGA

This world is their legacy, a world born in the violent nuclear spasm of 2001 that was the bitter outcome of a struggle for global dominance.

There is no real escape from this shockscape where life always hangs in the balance, vulnerable to newly demonic nature, barbarism, lawlessness.

But they are the warrior survivalists, and they endure—in the way of the lion, the hawk and the tiger, true to nature's heart despite its ruination.

Ryan Cawdor: The privileged son of an East Coast baron. Acquainted with betrayal from a tender age, he is a master of the hard realities.

Krysty Wroth: Harmony ville's own Titian-haired beauty, a woman with the strength of tempered steel. Her premonitions and Gaia powers have been fostered by her Mother Sonja.

J. B. Dix, the Armorer: Weapons master and Ryan's close ally, he, too, honed his skills traversing the Deathlands with the legendary Trader.

Doctor Theophilus Tanner: Torn from his family and a gentler life in 1896, Doc has been thrown into a future he couldn't have imagined.

Dr. Mildred Wyeth: Her father was killed by the Ku Klux Klan, but her fate is not much lighter. Restored from predark cryogenic suspension, she brings twentieth-century healing skills to a nightmare.

Jak Lauren: A true child of the wastelands, reared on adversity, loss and danger, the albino teenager is a fierce fighter and loyal friend.

Dean Cawdor: Ryan's young son by Sharona accepts the only world he knows, and yet he is the seedling bearing the promise of tomorrow.

In a world where all was lost, they are humanity's last hope....

Chapter One

Pretending to scratch his belly, Ryan Cawdor loosened the 9 mm blaster at his side. A seasoned veteran of hundreds of fights, the man knew when the blood was about to hit the fan. It was chilling time, that much was certain. Death was close. He just wasn't sure from which direction. Not yet, anyway.

A tall man with broad shoulders, Ryan had long curly black hair, and a badly scarred face that rarely knew a smile. A wicked heavy eighteen-inch blade called a panga was sheathed on his thigh, a holstered SIG-Sauer 9 mm blaster balancing the oversize blade on the other side. A bolt-action Steyr longblaster hung from a shoulder. Spare ammunition filled the loops in his leather gunbelt, marking him as a wealthy man, and also a deadly killer. Brass was better than gold, as the saying went, and the Deathlands was filled with the unmarked graves of strong men who had been brutally aced for a single live round. To display that much live brass meant that you were tough enough to keep it, and thus served as a clear warning to anybody smarter than a stickie to stay away—or else.

Crude alcohol lanterns hung from the overhead wooden beams, filling the tavern with a murky blue light, and swirling clouds of pungent smoke filled the air of the Busted Axle like a morning mist on distant mountains. Everybody seemed to be puffing on home-made cigs, or corncob pipes, and the roaring blaze in the brick fireplace was leaking smoke out the sides to add a rich woodsy smell to the mixture of tobacco, maryjane and a local favorite called coot, hemp rope cigars soaked in sweet shine.

Most of the people in the tavern were eating dinner at their tables, hunched over the hubcap plates as if they were afraid somebody might try to jack the horse meat stew, which was highly unlikely. Uniformed sec men were playing dominoes at a large table near the front door, their scarred faces scowling in concentration. Each man had a handblaster tucked into his belt, and a flintlock longblaster hanging from the back of his chair, shiny chunks of flint jutting out from the cocked hammers. The museum pieces were in perfect working condition, and in a world where a single round of live brass bought a person a few days of food and bed, the black-powder rifles were the standard weapons for many ville sec men. No other table in the tavern was close enough for another patron to try for a grab. A drunken outlander had tried anyway, and his corpse was cooling outside, waiting for the loser of the game to bury the triple-stupe fool.

Small piles of live brass lay in front of each sec man, and everybody seemed to be playing with one hand hidden under the table clutching the handle of a knife. Just in case, as Baron Harrison always liked to say. The only cure for stupidity was a hot dose of lead in the head. True words, indeed.

In the corner, a young boy without shoes was playing a dilapidated upright piano with considerable skill, but there was no jack in the tip jar perched on top. On the second-floor balcony, a host of gaudy sluts leaned over the battered wooden railing, their bare breasts openly on display to entice new customers upstairs for fifteen minutes of sweaty delight.

Telling jokes and pouring shine behind a plywood counter, the bartender was a tall man named Mark Michalowski, a thin man with a shaved head and a wide, easy grin.

Gathered along the counter were a couple of sluts and a dozen burly men. Mountain men from the looks of them, Ryan guessed, remembering a friend of his from a long time ago. The hunters were dirty, unshaved, and dressed entirely in clothing made from animal hides: griz bear boots, deerskin pants and shirts, beaver coats and coonskin caps, minus the tails. They looked friendly enough, but machetes hung at their backs and muzzle-loading longblasters hung across their shoulders. The men looked so similar to one another that Ryan knew they had to be close kin, and from a pretty damn small gene pool, at that. Which only made them that much more dangerous. The only true law in the Deathlands was that kin helped kin, especially in a fight.

The mountain men were talking low among themselves, drinking shots of shine from cracked plastic tumblers and stuffing their bearded faces with handfuls of salted popcorn as if they'd never encountered the stuff before. Ryan knew that the locals used the stuff to feed their pigs when it got stale, but when it was fresh, Big Mike the bartender gave it away free, the heavy coating of rock salt a mighty inducement for his customers to drink more shine, and eventually end upstairs where their pockets could really be emptied. The one-eyed man knew that there was no such thing as a free lunch. That phrase had never been so nuking true than in the desert ville of Hobart where everything had a price. Baron Felix Harrison was so crooked that he could eat soup with a corkscrew, and the sooner Ryan and his companions were out of this rad pit the better he'd like it. But for the moment, they were trapped. Nobody could leave Hobart without a signed pass, and those were damn near impossible to get from the baron. However, Ryan knew one of the ville sec men from his days riding shotgun with the Trader, and the man was going to meet Ryan here at any moment.

"Ya wanna refill?" a serving girl asked, the wooden tray expertly balanced on an outthrust hip as if it was nailed there.

The teenager was shapely and well proportioned, with a lot of cleavage showing over the top of her tight leather bodice. Unfortunately her face was horribly scarred from once being caught in an acid rain storm, and her features were nearly destroyed. What little there was remaining had twisted into a permanent scowl as if she hated the whole nuking world and wished it to die screaming, as had her youthful beauty. Even her long auburn hair was sprinkled with white from the ravages of the acid rain. Only her full breasts seemed to have been spared. They were pink and plump, and damn near perfect.

Ryan had heard several of the customers call the teenage girl Crate, and guessed that was a short version of Crater-face, the nickname given because of her ghastly resemblance to the moon. Unconsciously touching the disfiguring knife scar that crossed his own face, Ryan felt a tug of camaraderie for the disfigured girl.

"Just some more beer and bread," Ryan said, tossing over a .22 cartridge. "And lean over more when you bring it, honey." He had no real interest in bedding the girl, but Doc always liked to say that good manners cost nothing. Which was true enough, the man supposed.

Making the catch with a free hand, Crate seemed startled by the crude pass, then clearly warmed to the idea. "This much brass will get ya the best beer we got, and some time with me in the back room, if ya like," she whispered, a suggestion of a smile appearing briefly on her distorted lips. "I'm good. Damn good, and I don't mind facing the wrong way, if you know what I mean."

Clearly hearing the need in her voice, Ryan understood that in spite of working in a tavern situated under a gaudy house, the girl had never shared a bed with anybody before. The local boys had to be feebs. The fruit of the desert cactus looked like a brain tumor and was covered with more barbed needles than a mutie porcupine, but inside was the sweetest damn pulp a person ever tasted. Mother-nuking-ambrosia. Ryan knew that ugly didn't tell you drek about what juicy treasures waited for a smart man on the inside of an apron.

"So what do they call you?" Ryan asked, looking directly into her face. Her eyes were bright and alive with intelligence.

"Crate," she muttered, both cheeks turning bright red.

"Short for Catherine, eh?"

The girl blinked in surprise at that, then smiled broadly and leaned over to rest an elbow on the table, both breasts nearly spilling out of her bodice. "You can load that into your blaster," she said in a throaty purr. "Short for Catherine." Impulsively she reached out to touch his face. "I'll bet the other guy lost a lot more in the fight."

"Damn straight he did," Ryan muttered, adjusting the leather patch covering the empty socket that had once held his left eye. His own brother had taken the eye in an effort to chill Ryan and claim the throne of their home ville, Front Royal. However, in the end, Harvey was breathing dirt, while Ryan was still walking the shattered earth, so there was no question to him who won that fragging knife fight.

In fact, Ryan and the companions had been on their way from Ohio to visit friends at Front Royal when an avalanche had closed off the only pass and they had been forced to circle around through Hobart. Now all they wanted to do was to get out again, as soon as possible.

"Well, what do ya say?" Catherine asked eagerly.

But before Ryan could answer, the front door swung open and Derby Joe Schwartz sauntered inside. Tall and slim, the man appeared to be made out of nothing but bones and darkly tanned skin. His scraggly hair hung to his shoulders, and a battered old derby rested on top, an eagle feather sticking out of the leather band. Blasters rode on each hip, and a cloth star was sewn onto his shirt, showing he was the sec boss for the entire ville.

Whistling sharply, Ryan caught the man's attention, and Joe nodded in greeting, already heading over.

"I'll have to put a timer on that ride, Catherine. My friend is here, and biz comes first," Ryan said, patting her on the rear. It was nice, warm and well-rounded. The man didn't finish the offer because soon he would be long gone, but Ryan never saw the profit in hurting somebody weaker than yourself just because you could.

"Anytime, anywhere, Blackie," Catherine stated, her damaged face alive with raw sentiment. The girl unexpectedly leaned in to kiss him hard on the mouth, then turned to rush away through the smoky tavern and disappear into the steamy kitchen.

"Hey," Joe said, pulling out a chair and sitting in it backward to keep a clear and fast access to his blasters. "How drunk are you to be sucking face with Crater?"

"The name's Catherine," Ryan replied, a rare smile coming and going just as fast. "And, brother, the man who corrals that mare is in for the ride of his life."

"That so?" Joe asked, tilting back his derby to expose a large bald spot. "A fellow could forget that face, if she could really cook." Then he smiled lewdly. "Who knows, mebbe she even knows how to do stuff in the kitchen!"

Slapping their palms together into a shake, the old friends shared a mutual laugh. Then the men jerked their hands back and clawed for weapons. The subtle sound had almost been lost in the sea of conversations filling the tavern, but somebody somewhere had just worked the pump-action on a scattergun. The noise was unmistakable.

"Nothing behind you," Ryan growled, easing the SIG-Sauer into his lap.

"Look south by southeast," Joe answered softly, both of his hands out of sight below the table.

Risking a glance sideways, Ryan saw a bearded man eating stew at a small table in the corner of the tavern. A fat gaudy slut was lounging alongside, smoking a cig and drinking shine.

"Nuking hell that was good!" the man said, stuffing the wooden spoon into a pocket, then lifting the plate to lick it clean.

"Honey, if you bed like you eat, I'm not going to survive going upstairs," the gaudy slut drawled, lifting a glass of shine in mock salute. She was a plump blonde wearing a thin cotton dress, and it was plain to see that she wasn't wearing anything under the clothing but a lot of bare skin.

"Hungry. Ain't eaten for a week," the man replied, wiping his mouth on a sleeve. The gesture made his coat part, showing that he was carrying a brace of handcannons tucked into a gunbelt, with two more riding in a rope shoulder holster.

"And now you've eaten enough to last for a week." She laughed, leaning back in her chair to spread her legs wide. That made her dress ride high, exposing a lot of smooth thigh and a host of lewd tattoos.

The man looked where he was supposed to, and grinned. "No need to prime the pump, darling." He chortled, hitching his gunbelt higher. "Just let me drop some ballast, and I'll ride you till dawn!"

"About time!" she answered, lifting the glass again, and this time draining it completely.

Moving quickly, the big man lumbered toward the side door of the tavern marked with a small half-moon.

But just as he cleared the last table, a scattergun roared, blowing the door off its hinges in an explosion of lead and splinters.

"Hold it right there, Brinkman!" a gruff voice bellowed, and there came the sound of a scattergun being worked.

Instantly the entire tavern went still, until the only sound came from the crackling log in the fireplace.

His hands only inches away from the blasters on his belt, the man stopped moving, then slowly turned his head to see the bartender aiming a predark 12-gauge in his direction.

"What's the jam in your breech?" Brinkman demanded, puzzled, his fingers itching to reach for iron. "I paid for the meal already, and the fat slut, too!"

"Don't know, don't care," Mark replied, leveling the scattergun. His friendly smile was gone, replaced with a grim expression of raw hatred. "But last summer I was in a convoy that got jacked by some coldhearts. My wife got shot in the belly and took a week to die."

"Nothing to do with me," Brinkman answered, sweat appearing on his brow. "I ain't never been to the Great Salt."

Both Ryan and Derby Joe grunted in disgust at the amateurish gaff. The feeb had just confessed to everything.

"Didn't say where it happened, Brinkman," Mark whispered, moving the barrel of the weapon down a little to point at the stomach of the other man. "Hey, Joe!"

"Right here, Mark," Joe, replied, easing out his weapons. The blasters were big-bore Ruger .44 Magnums, the muzzles pitted and worn from constant use.

"You want him?" Mark asked, his sight intent upon the coldheart.

"I'd be happy to have him dance in the air for ya, but the outlander ain't done anything wrong in Hobart," Joe answered truthfully. "So if you shoot him cold, then I gotta take you in. The baron won't stand for it." Then he smiled coldly. "Unless it's a fair fight, of course."

"Understood," Mark stated, dropping the primed weapon and immediately going for the small blaster holstered behind his back.

Instantly, Brinkman went for the blasters on his hips, then both men drew and fired in unison. The double explosion of the black-powder weapons filled the smoky tavern with dark fumes so thick that it was nearly impossible to see what had happened.

Chapter Two

A cold breeze wafted through the shattered door, thinning the acrid gunsmoke in the tavern until the air was relatively clear. With a low moan of pain, Brinkman crumpled to the floor, the twin Colt .45 blasters tumbling from his limp hands to clatter on the wooden floor.

Standing behind the counter, Mark looked down at the red stain spreading across the sleeve of his shirt and grunted. "Crate! I need you to take over the bar!" he shouted, shifting the smoking S&W .38 revolver to his left hand and awkwardly tucking it back into the holster. "I gotta go see the healer!"

"No prob!" she called back, stepping out of the kitchen, sliding a .22 zipgun into the pocket of her patched dress. "And the name is now Catherine."

Clutching the bloody wound in his arm, Mark merely raised an eyebrow at that, then shrugged in acceptance and shuffled away through the muttering crowd.

"All right, boys, divvy up his possession," Joe commanded, holstering his weapons. "The baron gets any live brass, I want his knife, and you can keep everything else."

"Then find something to block that damn door," Catherine added tying on an apron, "and get that garbage out of here!"

Grinning in avarice, the sec men abandoned their game of dominoes and pushed their way to the corpse to start stripping off his weapons and boots.

"That was a nuke of a good shot, old buddy," Joe said, sitting.

"Nothing to do with me," Ryan muttered, putting away the warm SIG-Sauer.

Fanning himself with his derby, Joe smiled tolerantly. "Now that's funny, because Mark couldn't hit the ground if he fell off a mountain. That's why Crate...er, Catherine, bought him that scattergun last winter."

Taking a sip of his warm beer, Ryan said nothing, waiting to see where this line of questioning would eventually end.

"How much do you want to gamble that if I was to dig the slug out of that coldheart," Joe continued, "it would be a nine, the exact same caliber of your blaster?"

"Lots of 9 mms in the world," Ryan said, lowering his arm so that his hand rested on the checkered grip of the blaster. "Think that's gonna happen?"

"Nope," Joe said amiably, laying the hat on the table. "But it's just another good reason to get you the frag out of my ville." Fumbling inside the hatband, he removed a small piece of folded paper and passed it over. "Okay, you saved me from stickies when Trader passed through Broken Neck, and now we're even. That pass is good until nightfall. So, use it right quick. Because I'm suppose to arrest you at midnight."

"Arrest me for what exactly?" Ryan asked, tucking away the paper.

The sec boss scowled. "For using too much air.

Spitting on the sidewalk. Treason, murder, the charge doesn't matter, Ryan. Hell's bells, Baron Harrison wants your fancy blaster more than a jolt addict wants another fix!" he stated forcibly. "So go far, and fast, old friend. I swore an oath to obey my baron, and if he sends me after you, I'll have to hunt you down." He frowned. "I won't like it, but I'll put you on the last train west."

"You can try," Ryan answered coldly, pushing back the chair to slowly stand. "For old times' sake, it was good to see you again, Joe."

"Same here." The man sighed, wiping the inside sweatband of his hat with a cloth. "Now make sure it never happens again."

Since there was nothing more to add, Ryan simply grunted in reply and strode from the tavern. But the man somehow felt that he was leaving behind more than just a friendship. A small piece of his life with the Trader had just died, and that disturbed him more than expected.

Stepping onto the brick sidewalk, Ryan looked around the busy ville and soon found three of his friends across the street leaning against a battered old school bus that had been converted into a crude war wag. Cobbled together from a dozen other wags, it was a formidable little brute. Barbed wire covered the roof and sides, spikes lined the bumpers, and steel plates had been welded over the tires to protect them from bullets or arrows. The glass was gone from the windows, replaced with louvered shutters that protected the passengers from attacking muties, while still letting them shoot at any coldhearts who attacked. The bus was short, but looked more than ready to handle anything the Deathlands threw its way. The sec men and civies passing by gave the group of heavily armed outlanders a wide berth, some of the wiser people actually crossing the street to stay as far away as possible. He headed that way.

Built from the ruins of a mining town, Hobart had paved streets, although the roads were now so heavily patched it was damn near impossible to tell which sections were the original pavement and which were the replacement. Ryan had heard that the baron sometimes sent out gangs of slaves to rip up other roads and bring back the slabs of asphalt to use in his town. That sounded like mighty hard work for a pretty small return, but then, Ryan had met several barons who had more than a touch of madness.

"Hey, lover, how did it go?" Krysty Wroth asked, her arms casually crossed with hands on her elbows.

"I got the pass," Ryan replied

She smiled. "Thank Gaia." Almost as tall as the one-eyed man, Krysty possessed an abundant wealth of flame-red hair that oddly seemed to always be stirring by an unfelt wind, almost as if the filaments were alive. She was dressed in an old olive-drab jumpsuit and a bearskin coat. A canvas gunbelt was slung low across her hips, a S&W .38 revolver holstered in the front for easy access. A knife was strapped to one of her shapely thighs.

"How long got?" Jak Lauren drawled, a touch of his bayou ancestry softening the words.

"It expires at dark," Ryan said, glancing at the darkening sky. "So we better haul ass."

"Good, I don't like this place," Krysty said, openly

scowling in distaste at a group of armed sec men walking by with a prisoner in chains. The old man had been badly beaten and he was dragging a twisted leg that would probably never work correctly again.

"Damn straight," Jak agreed, both hands resting on his belt buckle to stay close to his blaster. A true albino, the lean teenager was pinkish-white, as if the savage Deathlands sun never reached his pale skin. His long hair was the color of fresh snow, his eyes as red as the dawn after a storm. A pair of sunglasses poked out of his shirt pocket for when needed, the bridge repaired with a piece of duct tape. A knife was sheathed at his side, another at the small of his back, and a third jutted from the top of his left boot. Several others were hidden all over his body. A big-bore Colt Python .357 Magnum blaster rode in a leather holster at his side, the brass in his gunbelt an odd combination of both .38 short rounds and the slightly larger .357 Magnum Express rounds.

"Then let us make haste, Hermes, and outrace the golden apple of yore!" Doc Tanner rumbled in a deep bass.

"Come again?" Jak asked, blinking.

"Let's blow this pest hole before nightfall," Ryan said by way of translation.

The albino teen smiled. "Fucking A."

"Quite so, my young friend. Quite so," Doc stated in agreement, dourly watching the sec men shove the prisoner into a tan brick building. The faded lettering on the side proclaimed that the place had once been the Hobart Public Library, but now it served as the city jail, an internment facility from which few, if any, ever departed still requiring air to breathe.

Tall and slim, Theophilus Algernon Tanner was neatly dressed in clothing from another era: a frilly white shirt with a black string tie, and a swallowtail frock coat. Everything he wore was patched, but clean, and his fingernails were neatly trimmed, which set him apart from most people in Deathlands. His long face was heavily lined, but not from age, and his luxuriously thick hair was a deep silver in color. A massive Civil War blaster called a LeMat rode on his hip, the pouches of his gunbelt bulging with black powder and other items needed to feed the monstrous handcannon. A small eating knife was sheathed behind the revolver, and an ebony stick with a silver lion's head was thrust into the gunbelt like a Japanese war sword.

Born in the nineteenth century, Dr. Theophilus Tanner had been an unwilling participant in a time-trawling experiment. Ripped from the bosom of his family into the late twentieth century, Doc had been deemed too difficult a subject and was sent one hundred years into the future to what had become Deathlands. Alone and confused, Doc had nearly gone insane struggling to survive in the savage reality of the shockscape until Ryan rescued him from the slave pit of a sadistic sec chief named Cort Strasser. Sometimes, Doc's mind slipped a little, and he briefly imagined that he was safely back home in the loving embrace of his wife, but he always rose to the occasion if there was trouble. Doc was a valuable member of the group with his mental encyclopedia of arcane knowledge, and a deadly fighter. However, the companions knew for a fact that the man would abandon them in a heartbeat if he ever got a chance to go back home to his children and beloved wife, Emily.

Going to the folding door of the bus, Ryan yanked it open and climbed inside. The wag was empty. "Where are J.B. and Mildred?" he growled, sliding into the driver's seat. The man had fully expected them to be asleep in the back.

"Just down the street," Krysty replied, slipping into the gunner seat opposite the man. "There was a commotion down at the local healer's, so Mildred wanted to see if there was anything she could do to help."

"And J.B. went along to guard her six."

"Exactly, my dear Ryan," Doc stated, taking a place alongside Jak. "He is the Daemon to her Pythius."

Understanding the obscure literary reference only because the time traveler had used it many times before, a brief flood of anger filled Ryan, then he forced it aside and accepted the simple bad timing. There was nothing else to do in the matter. Dr. Mildred Weyth, a freezie from the twentieth century, had her own set of priorities, and helping folks in need of medical attention was at the top of that list.

"All right, let's find them fast, then roll," Ryan said, pulling the lever to close the door. It cycled shut with a hiss of working hydraulics.

"No prob," Jak said confidently, cracking open the cylinder of his Colt Python to start removing the .38 rounds and replace them with the much more deadly hollowpoint .357 Magnum cartridges. One reason the teenager carried this particular model blaster was that it could use both size brass, a unique feature that had saved his life many times.

Working the throttle and gas, Ryan fought the old diesel engine into life, then rumbled away from the curb and started down the middle of the road. Kids and barking dogs scattering at the advance of the rattling vehicle while adults went to hide inside homes and stores, and mounted sec men fought to control their frightened horses at the sound of the sputtering engine.

"Rad-blasted bastards," Krysty muttered, reading the lips of a passing guard. "These local boys really hate us."

"We not slaves. Of course hate," Jak stated, closing his blaster. "They try capture, we fight. Easier ace drunks and crips."

"How true, lad," Doc agreed, thumbing back the hammer on the single-action LeMat. "Too long have these cowardly poltroons feasted upon the flesh of the weak, and the taste of an honest fight fills their bowels with Hobbesian turpulence."

"They still outnumber us fifty or sixty to one, Doc," Ryan reminded him, turning the wheel sharply to take a corner. "So stay razor, people!" Then he added almost as an afterthought, "And if a man wearing a derby hat comes at you, chill him fast."

"Isn't that your friend who got us the exit pass?" Krysty asked, her animated hair curling in confusion.

"He was," Ryan growled, going around a huge pothole before angling into the parking lot of a large brick building with a lot of tiny windows set high off the ground.

Once, long ago, the place had been a carpet warehouse. But now the ville used it as the slaughterhouse for the animals they raised to feed the baron and his army of sec men. Supposedly, it was also what passed locally for a hospital. There was a strong smell of blood and excrement in the air, and from somewhere inside the building came the agonized squealing of a hog that abruptly stopped, only to be followed by the dull thuds of a butcher's hatchet.

"By the Three Kennedys, this is an abattoir!" Doc said in utter repulsion.

"Not our business," Ryan stated, braking to a halt. Briefly, the man checked the plastic mirrors to make sure nobody was lurking outside the wag, before cycling open the door. "Let's just find our people and jump out of this rad pit."

"Agreed, lover," Krysty said, removing the tape from the handle of a gren. Gaia, the Earth Mother, said that all living things were precious, but the woman also knew that sometimes the only way to save an innocent life was to chill an enemy. She saw no contradiction in this. It was merely common sense, a question of balance in maintaining the circle of life.

After checking their weapons, the companions dutifully clambered out of the vehicle, and Jak went behind the wheel.

"I stay," the teen announced, slipping on his sunglasses. "Keep engine hot in case we run fast."

"Just remember the codes," Krysty warned, and the teen scowled in reply as if such an event was beyond impossible.

Heading past a low corral full of bleating sheep and a couple of three-eyed goats, the companions walked into the slaughterhouse and were instantly assaulted by the nearly overpowering reek of bodily fluids. The concrete floor was covered with a mixture of sand and sawdust clotted with feces and spilled blood. Clattering chains hung overhead, the dressed carcass of a cow going by, the warm meat steaming slightly in the afternoon chill.

Lining the walls were tiny stables of assorted animals waiting to be aced, rough trenches were cut into the flooring to drain away their urine to be used in the tanning process.

Scurrying around were teams of young children carrying plastic buckets full of blood, probably to be made into sausage, while somber adults pushed along wheelbarrows piled high with raw animal skins. The hides were covered with thick layers of salt as a preliminary step to becoming cured, then tanned and turned into various useful forms of leather.

Off to the side was a claw-foot bathtub full of slimy animal brains, and right alongside was an open hole in the floor that a squatting man was using as a toilet.

"Mildred must have gone ballistic over these filthy conditions," Krysty muttered, trying not to breathe through her nose. Outside the slaughterhouse, the combinations of ripe smells was horrendous, but inside the building they were beyond description, almost becoming a tangible force.

"You got that right," a familiar voice said.

Turning, the companions saw a short, wiry man step out of the shadows. He was in a worn leather jacket, a battered fedora and fingerless gloves. An Uzi machine gun was slung at his side, and a strip of damp cloth was tied across his nose and mouth.

Called J.B. by his many friends, John Barrymore

Dix was also known as the Armorer, a nickname given to him because there wasn't a firearm known that the man couldn't repair. Hanging at his side was a bulging leather bag, a stiff piece of fuse and the end of a pipe bomb sticking out from under the protective flap. A S&W M-4000 scattergun was strapped across his back, the nylon strap lined with fat, red, 12-gauge cartridges.

"Here, try this," J.B. said, tossing over a plastic bottle.

Catching the container, Ryan removed the cap then pulled out a handkerchief to liberally douse the cloth with the murky fluid. He passed it over to Krysty, then tied the makeshift mask around his face. Instantly the reek of the place eased noticeably, to be replaced with the sharp, antiseptic sting of witch hazel. It made his nose tickle, but the urge to vomit was seriously reduced.

"Millie hated to waste the witch hazel, but there was no other choice. This place stinks worse than a stickie's underwear," J.B. said, adjusting his wire-rimmed glasses. "So, did we get the pass?"

"Yes, but we have to leave right now," Ryan stated, covering his mouth with a hand. "Where's Mildred?"

"This way," J.B. said, walking deeper into the reeking building.

Just beyond a pile of rock salt that reached almost to the ceiling was a curtain of red velvet that had probably been salvaged from a movie theater. Pushing it aside, the companions saw only smooth concrete floor and canvas cots. Most of them were filled with limp bodies lying perfectly still in a way no living being could ever duplicate.

At the sight, Doc was stunned speechless. This was also the ville morgue? Reaching into a pocket, the man extracted some beef jerky he had purchased from a street vendor and surreptitiously threw it away. He would rather starve than consume anything processed from this house of horrors.

In the center of the room, several large wooden spools used to carry cable had been tipped over sideways to be used as makeshift tables. Old-fashioned glass lanterns stood on each of them, the alcohol flames turned up all the way to give the maximum amount of light. Surrounded by the tables was a sec man firmly strapped into a chair, and a black woman was standing nearby running the flame of a butane cigarette lighter over the end of a pair of ordinary pliers.

Short and stocky, the woman's beaded plaits hung to her shoulders and occasionally clattered when she moved. She was dressed in denim jeans and a long-sleeved shirt, and a lumpy canvas satchel hung at her side, the worn fabric bearing the faded lettering M*A*S*H. A police-issue gunbelt circled her waist, the holster supporting a Czech-made .38 ZKR target pistol.

Born in the twentieth century, Dr. Mildred Weyth had gone into the hospital for routine surgery, but something had gone terribly wrong and the attending doctors desperately attempted to save the life of their friend by putting her into an experimental cryogenic freezer unit. A hundred and some odd years later, Mildred awoke to find the nuclear war long over and herself trapped

in a never-ending battle for survival in the nightmarish world of what had once been the United States of
America.

"Now this is going to hurt," Mildred said, cutting
off the lighter and waving the pliers to cool them down.
"But there's no other way if you ever want to eat meat
again. Understand?"

Dumbly, the man nodded, his muscles visibly tightening.

"I don't know about this," said a stocky man wearing
a bloodstained carpenter's apron. The loops were filled
with different types of knives, homemade probes and
car mechanic tools. "I've never been able to transplant
the teeth from a corpse into a living man before."

"That's because you probably waited too long," Mildred admonished. "Or washed the teeth first. Never do
that. Teeth are alive, but if the roots are cleaned of blood
they die in moments. You have to remove the bloody
teeth from a warm corpse, and hammer them into the
gums of the patient as fast as you can. Then lash his
mouth shut to keep him from using the teeth for a week.
After that, he should be okay."

"'ow eat wid no 'eeth?" the sec man mumbled.

Mildred smiled tolerantly. "We'll leave a gap in the
front for you to drink soup and water."

"'hine?" he asked hopefully.

"Absolutely," she said. "All the damn shine you
want."

"Sorry to interrupt, Millie, but we have to go," J.B.
said, resting a hand on her shoulder.

She shook the man off, intent upon the forthcoming

surgery. "In a minute, John," she answered, examining the bowl of freshly extracted teeth.

"Now, Mildred," Ryan stated gruffly, stepping closer.

Hearing that tone in his voice, the physician sighed and passed the sterilized pliers to the ville healer. "Wash them with shine afterward. Wash everything with shine, before, after and during."

"Understood," he said, touching the pliers with a dirty finger to test their cleanliness.

Sighing deeply, Mildred quickly stuffed the rest of her instruments haphazardly back into her med kit, wished the patient good luck and followed the other companions out of the building. Her instruments, such as they were, could be cleaned and organized later. But first and foremost, the physician had to stay alive. It was a sort of sidestep to the ancient Hippocratic medical code: first, do no harm.

Reaching the bus, the companions checked for anybody loitering nearby, then Ryan rapped on the bumper with the barrel of the SIG-Sauer.

"Hey, Albert," Ryan said, using the code for all-clear.

"The name's Adam," Jak replied, working the handle to open the folding door. As they entered, the teenager wrinkled his nose. "Who-wee! What all been doing? Skinning week-aced-old stickies?"

"I would not at all be surprised if that exact scenario occurred here on a daily basis," Doc rumbled, taking a seat. "Immediately followed by a dung-fire barbecue." Rummaging though his backpack, he extracted an MRE food pack and found the tiny lemon-scented moist

towelette that came with each U.S. Army meal-ready-
to-eat. Removing his handkerchief, the man wiped his
face and hands thoroughly, then did it again. Better.

Since Jak was already behind the wheel, Ryan went
to the seat directly behind the teenager and settled into
place with both of his weapons at the ready. Everybody
else took similar positions, and for a moment the wag
was filled with the mechanical sounds of bolts being
worked and safeties being disengaged.

"Nice and slow," Ryan advised, placing the Steyr out
of sight and pulling out the pass. "Remember, we have
the baron's permission to leave."

"If only it true," Jak said, shifting gears and easing
in the clutch. The clouds were thick overhead, but they
could still see that the masked sun was starting to dip
behind the western mountains. One heartbeat after that,
the pass would become only a piece of paper again, as
useless as a eunuch in a gaudy house.

Rolling along the paved streets, the teenager kept the
pace of the wag steady, as if they had all the time in the
world. A wrinklie with a crippled leg hobbled along the
sidewalk, using his lantern to light the pitch torches set
on the corners. The workday was nearly done, and the
crowds of ville people were going into the ramshackle
huts to start the evening meal.

Passing a group of sec men standing on a corner,
Doc tried to smile affably, but they scowled in return,
one of the women going so far as to hawk and spit at
the vehicle.

"The age of courtesy is dead, and so shall we be, if
our egress is long delayed," Doc muttered, hefting the

massive LeMat just below the louvered window. "Make haste with thy chariot, Hermes!"

"For once, the old coot is right," Mildred said unexpectedly. "Better move it, or lose it!"

"Hear that," Jak muttered in agreement, shifting into a faster gear.

"J.B., do we have any explos?" Ryan asked, scanning the rooftops.

"Some," the man replied. "Want me to make some bombs?"

"Just a big one," Ryan countered grimly. "We'll try blowing a hole in the wall before we go into the chains."

"We don't have enough to breach the ville wall," J.B. stated honestly.

"Make it anyway," Ryan ordered, pulling out a butane lighter and setting it on the seat.

The rumbling storm clouds were turning lavender as the bus turned the corner at the barracks and headed for the main gate of Hobart. The wall was massive, as it needed to be this deep in the Deathlands, well over ten feet tall, and made of everything and anything the locals could get their hands on: bricks, pieces of smashed bridges, concrete slabs, wooden logs, cinder blocks, thousands of pieces of broken glass and endless coils of barbed wire. Armed sec men walked patrol along the wide top, and guard towers were situated every hundred feet, the wooden platforms equipped with machine guns. There was no way of knowing if the baron had any brass for the military rapidfires, but only a feeb would put them on the wall otherwise. The gate itself was a composed of railroad beams bolted and chained together into a formidable mass, the outside surface studded with thousands of sharp nails.

Set directly in front of the gate was a sandbag nest blocking the path of any possible invaders. The nest contained armed sec men and two shiny brass Civil War cannons that Doc called Napoleons. Nearby were small wooden barrels of black powder and several low pyramids of dull gray cannon balls.

"They set for war," Jak said, going around the nest and braking to a halt directly in front of the deadly cannons. He hated to park there, but it was the only way to leave. The baron was a triple-cursed bastard, but not a fool.

Impatiently the companions waited for a sec man wearing sergeant stripes to leave the others and saunter their way. The man was clearly in no hurry, and deliberately took his sweet time crossing the scant few yards.

Somewhere in the ville, a bell began to toll.

"Nobody can leave," the bored sergeant said as a greeting.

"We got a pass," Ryan countered, lifting the window to hold out the paper.

Scowling in disbelief, the sergeant took the slip and unfolded the paper, reading it carefully. His cocky smile slowly vanished. "Son of a bitch," he muttered. "It's real!"

"Mind getting a shake on there?" J.B. added, resting an elbow out the window. "We got some business to handle for the baron. And you know how he hates failure."

"Sure, sure, no prob," the sergeant replied, then

looked up and cupped his hands. "Ahoy, the wall! Open her up!"

"Say what?" a guard yelled down. "Nobody ever leaves, Sarge. You know that!"

"You been smoking wolfweed again, sir?" Another guard laughed.

"I said, open the fragging gate!" the sergeant boomed, a hand going to his blaster. "They have a pass from the baron himself! So move your asses, or you'll go to the mines!"

That threat clearly startled the sec men, one of them dropping a smoking cig from his slack mouth.

"Yes, sir!" the first guard replied loudly, snapping off a proper salute. The second guard merely dashed into the thickening shadows.

A few moments later there came the sound of a gasoline engine sputtering into life, then rumbling gears, and the titanic gate slowly scraped aside, moving slower than winter ice.

"Be back soon," Jak cheerfully lied, and shifted gears to casually drive through the widening crack between the gate and the wall. They were less than halfway through when somebody unexpectedly shouted for them to stop.

"Fake!" a sec woman shouted. "The pass is a fake!"

"Chill them!" the sergeant shouted at the top of his lungs, spittle flying from his mouth.

Instantly, Ryan triggered the Steyr, and the woman flipped over backward, her red life spraying into the air. As the rest of the companions opened fire at the sec men behind the sandbags, Jak stomped on the gas pedal and shifted into high gear. The engine paused as it revved to full power, then the armored bus shot forward with a roar, black smoke pouring from the exhaust pipes.

Releasing the handle on the gren, Krysty threw it backward over the bus and it hit the ground to roll a few feet then violently detonate. A score of screaming people clutched their faces, blood gushing from the hundreds of tiny shrapnel wounds.

Twisting the steering wheel hard, Jak guided the wag at an angle where the cannons couldn't reach. One of the Napoleons thundered anyway, the cannonball humming past the rear of the vehicle and missing by the thickness of an atheist's prayer.

"Move this heap!" Doc bellowed, holding down the trigger of the single-action LeMat and fanning the hammer with the palm of his other hand. The big-bore blaster fired a fast three times, and two more sec men tumbled into eternity, one of them discharging his own handblaster impotently into the sky.

"It's a break!" somebody shouted on the wall, and a blaster boomed, sending out a thick cloud of dark smoke.

Something zinged off the roof of the bus, and J.B. responded with a short burst from the Uzi. A man cried out in pain and fell back into the ville.

"Hug the wall!" Mildred shouted, snapping off shots from the ZKR. "The machine guns in the towers can't reach us there!"

However, a flurry of arrows shot down from the sec men on the wall and something crashed to the ground just behind the bus and exploded into flames.

"But their Molotovs can," Krysty cursed, her hair flexing wildly. "We can't risk going all the way around to the pass with those raining down."

"No choice then. Head for the trees!" Ryan growled, acing a dimly seen figure brandishing another Molotov. The man fell and the bottle shattered, whoofing into a fireball. Standing upright, the man shrieked insanely, his entire body covered with flames. Ryan tracked the man as he dashed around madly, but didn't waste a brass on acing an enemy who was already on the last train west. Hopefully, the pitiful screams would discourage the other sec men from following his example.

"That'll put us into range of the machine guns," Mildred reminded, hastily reloading.

"Got better plan?" Jak asked over a shoulder.

"No!"

"Then hold on to ass!" the albino snarled, and banked away from the safety of the wall.

As the wag streaked across the open grassland, everybody braced for the arrival of machine-gun fire. Nothing happened for almost a full minute, and the speeding bus was nearly at the trees when the ville gate began to lumber aside and out poured a dozen sec men on galloping horses, closely followed by a dozen more.

Chapter Three

Just then, the rapidfires in the guard towers cut loose with a rattling cacophony, the leaves in the trees over the bus exploding in an emerald blizzard.

"Keep the riders between us and the machine guns!" Ryan shouted, firing his longblaster twice. "They're not going to ace their own people!"

With a cry, a sec man clutched his arm while the horse next to him buckled with a wounded knee. The riders were so tightly packed, the horses collided with one another, sending three more riders down in a tangle of limbs and cursing. However, the rest of the hunting party arched around their fallen brethren and kept coming, bent low over the necks of their horses, now even more grimly intent upon reaching the hated runaways.

As the companions sent hot lead at the sec men, Jak steered the jouncing bus into a swatch of shadows thrown by the ville wall from the setting sun. Once inside the darkness, he hit the headlights to see, then cursed and aced the lights. Their glow would only silhouette the wag and make them a perfect target. The teenager would have to do this the hard way. Shaking his head, Jak sent the sunglasses flying away, then squinted hard into the darkness ahead, starting to zigzag around what seemed to be bushes and tree stumps. Most villes kept the area around their walls completely clear so that an enemy would have nothing to hide behind during an attack. However, one good-size rain gully, or a tree stump, and the bus would be smashed, leaving them stranded and helpless at the mercy of the brutal ville sec force.

Reloading her blaster, Krysty started to aim at the riders once more, when she had the oddest sense of danger from ahead of the bus. Acting on impulse, she flipped on the headlights again, the beams showing a large griz bear sitting directly in the path of the racing vehicle eating a wiggling rabbit with too many legs. Triggering her S&W a fast five times, the woman wounded the giant beast, as Jak arched around it from the other side.

"Why do?" the teenager demanded angrily. A seasoned hunter, the albino teen didn't chill animals for fun, only for food.

"Watch," Krysty replied, reloading once more.

Seconds later, the riders encountered the bear. Bellowing a strident roar, it reached out with both paws and slammed two of the sec men out of their saddles to start mauling them. The other riders slowed for only a moment, then resumed their pursuit of the outlanders in the bus. But the gap between the two was significantly wider now.

The rapidfires in the towers spoke again, louder and longer this time, then stopped as the thick greenery of the forest closed over the companions, removing them from sight.

"Okay, give some cover, Doc," J.B. snarled, biting

the fuse on a pipe bomb in two, then flicking alive a
butane lighter.

Surging to the rear of the vehicle, Doc yanked aside
the locking bar and lifted the rear shutter, then fired
the LeMat twice, the booming reports vomiting forth
a dark cloud of gunsmoke. Safely out of sight of the
riders for a single instant, J.B. quickly lit the fuse and
simply dropped the bomb in their wake. Then both
men ducked as a fusillade of blasterfire came from the
riders, their assortment of handblasters, predark blasters, longblasters, scatterguns and zip guns making them
sound like an army. The lead hit the louvered shutters
like a hailstorm, rattling them hard and chewing the
green wood into splintering ruination. More than one
slat broke apart and simply fell away, leaving a wide
gap in the protective shield.

"Bah, wooden armor," Jak snorted, swerving around
a tree stump and crashing through a bush to just avoid
slamming into an oak tree. There was no road, or even
a path, in this direction through the forest, which was
both good and bad. The companions would have thicker
cover faster, but it also meant they would be traveling a
lot slower. Jouncing over a hole, Jak heard a headlight
shatter, but kept his boot pressed hard against the rubber
floormat. Speed was their only hope now.

"Herd them in!" Ryan yelled, and started shooting
from the right side of the bus. Krysty was close behind
him doing the same thing, and everybody else went to
the left.

Assailed from the sides, the sec men rode their horses
a little closer together, then a sec man shouted a warning
and they began separating once more. But it was already

too late. In a thunderous blast, the pipe bomb violently detonated, throwing aside ragged pieces of men and horses in a boiling hellflower of fiery destruction. A dozen sec men were aced in the explosion and several more thrown from their mounts to slam into the nearby trees, their bones breaking.

Whinnying in terror, the remaining horses reared high, throwing additional sec men to the ground before bolting away, leaving their former masters sprawled unconscious among the dead and the dying. Then the bushes parted as the griz bear arrived, its long teeth shining brightly in the dappled forest.

As the bus rattled away into the greenery, the screaming began and didn't stop.

"Okay, that should do it," Ryan stated, working the bolt on the Steyr to clear a spent brass from the breech. "But keep a watch for any stragglers. There were too many of the bastards to count. I have no idea if we got them all."

"Not catch," Jak said confidently, turning on the remaining headlight. "They on horseback, we in wag!"

The blue-white light of the halogen beam stabbed into the murky forest, brightly illuminating the trees and bushes. A score of inhuman eyes blinked in surprise at the intrusion, then quickly disappeared, leaving the wag to rattle through the wild greenery in relative peace.

"Hatred always makes a man fast," J.B. countered, pulling an empty clip from the pocket of his leather jacket to start thumbing in live rounds from the loops on his gunbelt. "And these boys have a real hate-on for us."

"Then more the fools they," Doc replied, his hands already busy in the laborious process of reloading his black-powder blaster. A stiff brass brush first purged each chamber in the cylinder, the spent powder sprinkling down like black snow. Next, he began to carefully charge each chamber.

"We're probably the first people to ever leave the ville in ages," Krysty added, leaning back in the seat, her hair moving against the wind blowing in through the louvered shutters. She was still rather tired from the single instant of mentally sensing the unseen danger of the bear. Gaia offered her followers many gifts, but afterward the woman was always exhausted. Krysty really wanted to catch some sleep, but that would have to wait until they were inside the underground redoubt, safe behind the nukeproof blast doors.

"Yeah, we're gonna have to do something about Hobart one of these days," Ryan stated, taking down a canteen and unscrewing the top to take a long drink. The water was warm, but it cut the tang of the gunsmoke from his throat.

"Derby Joe?" J.B. asked, holding out a hand.

Nodding, Ryan passed over the canteen. If Baron Harrison was turning into a slaver, that was bad enough, as Hobart was fairly close to Front Royal. However, Joe had also run with the Trader, the same as Ryan and J.B., and the man might know where their former boss had hidden his caches of predark supplies—weapons, wags, fuel, even some nerve gas. Front Royal was heavily defended, but those predark mil supplies could easily tip the outcome in favor of Harrison if the man ever decided to expand his territory.

"Don't want to ace Joe," J.B. said, taking a drink, then putting the cap back on with a twist. "But if we have to make a choice, my vote goes to Front Royal."

"Indeed, sir, as does mine," Doc intoned, finally holstering the LeMat. "Blood must be defended. Your nephew, my dear Ryan, is family."

"Speaking of blood, is anybody hurt?" Mildred demanded, looking over the companions. They were slumped in their seats, loose brass rolling on the floor-mats under their boots. But nobody was showing any red, or seemed to be cradling a wounded limb. Good enough.

Softly a wolf howled in the distance, and then quite unexpectedly the forest ended. Flat grassland stretched ahead of the wag, the single halogen beam bobbing along to illuminate tufted tops of the low weeds and reeds.

"Where now?" Jak asked, relaxing slightly in his chair.

"Tell you in a sec," J.B. answered, pulling a compass out of his munitions bag. Impatiently the man waited for the spinning needle to settle down. "Okay, we're heading due west toward the Sorrow River, so head to your right. We should see the foothills in about fifty or sixty miles."

It was closer to a hundred miles, and dawn was tinting the eastern sky when the tired companions encountered the foothills of the Rockies. Before sky-dark rearranged the topography of much of the world, these mountains had dwarfed the Darks. But the rain of nuclear bombs had hammered the Rockies down to merely rolling hills, occasionally adorned with a live volcano.

Retracing their original route down from the hills, the companions found the small section of predark road that still existed along the edge of a ragged cliff. The crevice was deep, the bottom lost from sight by the mist of a nameless river not on J.B.'s predark map. Just more nuke-scaping, as Mildred liked to call it. A hundred cars and trucks were piled in jumbled heaps on the road, some of them in fairly decent condition, the all-destroying acid rain cut off from reaching them by an overhang of solid granite that extended from the hills like the eager hand of a beggar.

This was where the companions had found the necessary parts to assemble the bus in the first place for the long journey to Front Royal. Now, it was where they had to leave it. If Baron Harrison sent more sec men after the companions, or worse, those mountain hunters, the tire tracks could easily lead them someplace the companions didn't want anybody else alive to know about—a redoubt.

Buried deeply underground and powered by nuclear reactors, the massive military bunkers were proof to the killing radiation of the ancient bombs, but more importantly were interconnected with a series of mat-trans units, top secret machines that allowed people to jump from one redoubt to another in a matter of seconds, no matter how far apart they were located. Sometimes Ryan and his people found clothing, tools or edible food in the rooms of the subterranean bases. Occasionally there were caches of condensed fuel and working vehicles, or even better, military weapons, a vital necessity for maintaining life. But most importantly, the mat-trans units gave the group mobility, the ability to quickly escape a dangerous area as they searched for some small section of America that could someday again be called home.

"Everybody out," Jak said, pulling the lever to open the door.

It resisted at first, the frame bent slightly from the ride through the forest, but the albino teen put some muscle into the task and the door finally yielded, squealing loudly as it cycled aside for the very last time.

Gathering their belongings, the companions clambered outside, adjusting their clothing against the morning chill. Winter was coming soon, even though it was early August.

"Hate to let her go," Mildred said, affectionately patting the battered machine. "Took us a week to build her."

"Can't leave it for the others to use," Ryan said, his breath visible in the cold air. "Remember when we were attacked by the Leviathan? I'm not going to let that happen again." Lifting a louvered shield, the man reached in through the window and yanked the gearshift into neutral, then released the handbrake. The bus rolled back a few inches, then stopped.

"Okay, put your shoulders to it, people!" Krysty ordered, flexing her hands.

All together, the companions started pushing and soon got the wag creeping along. Slowly, it began to build some speed along the slight incline, and they promptly let it go. Steadily gathering speed, the homemade war wag rattled and clattered as it jounced along the cracked pavement until reaching the end of the cliff. Sailing off the edge, it began to tumble end over end, and they watched as it vanished into the white mists below. If there was an explosion when the wag crashed, nobody could hear it over the murmur of the unseen river.

"Now we walk," Ryan said, shifting his backpack to a more comfortable position.

It was noon by the time they reached the small arroyo set amid a craggy span of outcroppings. There was nothing to mark any of them as special in any way.

Drawing their weapons, the companions assumed combat formation and eased into the arroyo, half expecting to be ambushed at every step. It had happened once before, and they were grimly determined that it would never happen again. Jak stayed in the rear and used a tree branch to erase their footprints.

At the end of the arroyo a huge black door towered more than twenty feet high, the metal as smooth and perfect as the day it had rolled out of the foundry more than a hundred years earlier.

An old enemy of the companions had boasted that nothing known to modern science could damage the blast doors of a redoubt. Ryan and J.B. had no reason to doubt the statement, but privately they had discussed whether an implo gren might do the trick. However, that was an experiment neither man wished to try unless it was absolutely necessary, and even then they'd want to be very far away from the event.

Going to a small keypad set into the jamb, Ryan tapped in the access code. There was a pause, then the colossal door rumbled aside to the sound of smoothly working hydraulics. Now exposed was a long, dark corridor, the terrazzo floor clean of any dust or dirt, much less scratches or wear.

A warm breeze wafted over the companions as they stepped through the opening, and at the touch of their boots on the floor, the overhead lights flickered into life bathing the entryway and showing the first of many turns. Ryan quickly pressed the required code to close the blast door.

Warily, the companions watched for the strings they had rigged just before leaving the redoubt to see if anybody, or anything, had gotten inside the subterranean fortress. But the strings were intact.

"We are alone," Doc said with a sigh, holstering the LeMat. "It would seem that the only real danger in this redoubt is hunger."

Ruefully, the others agreed. The contents of each redoubt were different, and this one had been particularly annoying. The arsenal had been well stocked with automatic rifles, but no ammunition whatsoever. There were hundreds of pairs of combat boots, without laces, while the pantry was full of condiments—salt, pepper, catsup, mustard and such—but no actual food, and the freezers were working perfectly, endlessly making ice cubes.

"At least Millie didn't have to make some more of her infamous boot soup." J.B. chuckled, nudging the woman.

Trying to hide a smile, Mildred nudged him back. "Don't complain, John. It kept us alive long enough to find real food."

"Tasted like used sock." Jak snorted, then felt his

stomach flip at the realization that that was an accurate description.

Past the last turn, the companions finally entered the top level of the redoubt. The garage was huge, fully capable of parking dozens of civilian wags, or half that number of bulky military vehicles. Except that the rows of parking spaces were empty, devoid of even an oil stain. Workbenches lined the wall, the pegboard covered with the silhouettes of tools to show exactly where each one should go. But the board was empty, along with tool cabinets and drawers. There wasn't a spare fuse in the garage, much less any engine parts. Even the supposedly limitless fuel depot had proved dry. The pumps worked fine, but only delivered a stale air that smelled faintly of chems. Whether the stripping of the base had occurred when the military personnel departed, or long afterward by some intruder, nobody could say. It didn't matter. Empty was empty, the details of who and when were thoroughly unimportant.

"I was looking forward to a shower," Krysty said, stroking her flexing hair. "But we might as well jump, and then wash at the next redoubt."

"Sounds good to me," Ryan stated gruffly, rubbing his stomach. "Mildred, what's the food situation?"

"Nine cans of stew, one self-heat of hash, four assorted MRE packs and a couple of smoked gophers that should be good for another week or so," she replied, without even glancing into her backpack. "I was expecting to purchase more food at Hobart, but after seeing their slaughterhouse…" She gave a shiver and didn't bother to finish the sentence.

"Gopher." Jak frowned, putting a wealth of meaning into the single word.

"Agreed, my young friend. If our choices are gopher for dinner, or risk a jump, then suddenly a journey through the mat-trans sounds like an exceptionally fine idea," Doc declared, casting a sad glance at a soda machine standing mute in the corner. Just like the fuel pumps, it still worked, but the hoppers were empty. "I always did like the odd taste of Dr Pepper," he said unexpectedly.

"Me, too," Mildred said in surprise. "Good Lord, we actually agree on something?"

He shrugged. "It had to happen eventually, madam."

"Not had," Jak replied, dropping his backpack onto the floor in front of the elevator. "Taste like shine or caf?"

The man and woman exchanged glances, each completely unable to even vaguely explain the amazingly complex mixture of flavors of the delicious predark soda.

Tapping for the call button, Ryan was pleased when the elevator doors opened immediately, the cage having waited there patiently for them for the past few weeks. It was another good indication that the redoubt was totally deserted. Some of the underground bases had devices that provided protection from unauthorized intruders, and the companions were as unauthorized as they could possibly be. More than once they had encountered a sec hunter droid, a robotic guardian. The machines came in several different types, each more lethal than the next, and were hard to chill. True, J.B. had a stash of pipe bombs, but it was highly doubtful those home-made bombs would be powerful enough to stop one of the deadly machines. Running away was usually the best tactic. Except that this time, the companions had nowhere to run but another redoubt.

Stepping over the threshold, Ryan waited until the rest of the companions had hurried inside before hitting the button for the middle level. The ride down was smooth, silent and uneventful.

Leaving the elevator, they proceeded down a long corridor lined with doors and entered a room full of comps. On the other side was another door. Stepping through the doorway, the companions closed the portal behind them and walked across a small antechamber to the mat-trans unit.

"Okay, this time we each take a drink before leaving," Mildred directed, holding aloft a canteen.

The battered container sloshed as she removed the cap. There came a strong smell of coffee, shine and something sweet. For some time now Mildred had been working on a remedy for the jump sickness that always hit some of the companions after arriving at their destination. So far, the physician had achieved scant success, but she still tried.

"What is this, coffee and…honey?" Krysty asked, taking a sniff.

"Close enough. The best results I ever had against jump sickness was with a crude form of Irish coffee," Mildred said apologetically. "I figure the relaxing effects of the shine, combined with the mental stimulant of the caffeine in the coffee, is what does the trick. But since I don't know how these damn things work, it's just a guess." She gave a wan smile. "For all I know it could be the water content that keeps us from getting dehydrated, and the sugar."

"Credo qua ab, sur dom est!" Doc announced dramatically.

Mentally, the physician translated the garbled Latin into, "I believe you, because the idea is absurd." She wanted to snap back at the time traveler, but sadly, he was right.

One at a time, the companions took a drink, then stepped into the hexagonal chamber and found a spot to sit. There was an alphanumeric keypad set into the wall where a person could tap in the code for their next destination, but since they had never found a directory, Ryan, the last person in, closed the gateway door, which would automatically trigger a random jump.

White mist flooded the chamber, swirling around the companions, faster and faster. A powerful hum started to build as tiny sparks appeared inside the mist like a billion imprisoned stars, then the floor seemed to vanish and the companions dropped through infinity, accelerating beyond logic and reason. Each of them had related that it sometimes felt as if their skin pulled away from the bones, and that knives shot painfully through their bodies, piercing every organ. Other times there was no pain, but the companions experienced vivid jump "nightmares."

Slowly, the noise faded, and there was only the sound of the friends' harsh breathing. But a few minutes later a warm breeze started to blow from the wall vents, the sterilized air helping considerably to revive them.

"Eas...easy...jump." Ryan coughed, then stopped

talking as his stomach roiled, its contents threatening to leave.

Concentrating on his breathing, Ryan managed to ride out the usual wave of nausea and carefully sat up to inspect the others. Everybody else seemed fine, just limp and exhausted, but that was how they always arrived. Except for Doc and Jak. For some reason the jumps hit them harder than the others, and Doc was sprawled on the floor, clearly unconscious.

"At least…not bad sick," Jak panted, wiping some drool off his face. "New juice helped."

"Th-thanks. B-but I h-have no f-fragging idea if it h-helped or not…" Mildred wheezed, laying on her back to stare at the ceiling. She knew the unit was motionless, but it felt like it was spinning around and around, and standing at that moment was completely impossible.

It was often this way after a jump, and it took the companions several minutes to recover, during which they were almost completely unable to defend themselves. As a physician, Mildred thought this was a purely natural reaction, merely random synapses firing in their brains from being reduced to their component molecules being disassembled. Doc philosophically considered it merely a side effect of their disintegrated bodies being without a soul for a little while until it found them again at the new destination. Mildred considered that total nonsense, of course. However, as a scientist, she was forced to honestly admit there really was no way of knowing for sure which answer was correct. Or if the truth was somewhere in the middle, a sublime combination of both answers, with maybe another element unknown to either science or religion.

With a low groan, Ryan forced himself to stand, one scarred hand pressed to the smooth wall to help him remain upright. In a sheer effort of will, the one-eyed man took a shuffling step forward, then collapsed inadvertently on the lever that opened the door to the mat-trans unit. The portal opened, spilling Ryan into the antechamber. Blinking hard to clear his vision, he looked up to see that the armaglass walls of the mat-trans were colored a pale flesh tone with a diagonal black stripe. The theory was that each mat-trans was different so that a traveler instantly knew where he or she had arrived, but that was only a guess. The redoubts were as jammed full of the mysterious as they were advanced technology.

"Peach and black," Ryan muttered, brushing back his damp hair. "We've never been here before." A quick look showed no one lying in wait, but oddly the door leading to the control room was a closed oval hatch.

Sluggishly joining his friend, J.B. removed his glasses from the shirt pocket where he always put them for safekeeping during a jump.

"Yeah, this is a new redoubt," he said, a gloved hand resting on top of the Uzi machine pistol. The man wasn't sure if he had the strength to control the bucking 9 mm Israeli blaster, but it was better to have a blaster ready and not need it than the other way around.

Surreptitiously, Mildred made a note of the colors in her journal. Someday the information might come in handy.

"Something's wrong here," Krysty said with a scowl, a hand going to the blaster at her side. The woman seemed perfectly normal, but then she had always re-covered faster than anybody else.

"Yeah, I feel, too," Jak said, a knife dropping into his palm from a sleeve as his other hand drew the .357 Magnum Colt Python. "Sound wrong."

"Then let us…" Doc began but broke into a ragged cough that drove the old man back to his knees. "Pro-ceed…with care…" he whispered, using both hands to draw the huge LeMat and clumsily cock back the trigger.

"Better stay in the mat-trans," Ryan decided, feeling the strength returning to his body. "If we come back with a droid on our ass, I want a backup here."

"C-consider me…Balador on the…rainbow bridge…" Doc wheezed, then managed a smile. "None shall… pass."

"Crazy old coot," Mildred snorted, then passed the man the canteen again. "Here, finish it off, the coffee will do you a world of good."

Nodding his gratitude, Doc holstered his weapon and accepted the canteen to start sipping at the contents with obvious pleasure. Slowly, some color began to return to his pale face.

Turning away, Ryan saw that J.B. was already at the oval door hatch, checking for traps.

"Clear," he reported.

"Okay, friends. Triple red."

Pulling out his SIG-Sauer, Ryan pressed down the lever that operated the oval door and it silently swung aside. Then with a snarl, the man instantly stepped backward, dropping into a crouch.

In the next room several big men in U.S. Navy uniforms operated the controls of the humming comps, M-16 assault rifles slung across their backs.

Chapter Four

Ryan swung up his longblaster, but before he could fire, the sailors at the work stations began to sag, then shrivel, their bodies wasting away in moments until there was nothing left of them but some grinning skeletons in perfectly preserved uniforms.

Giving a low whistle, Ryan waited until J.B. took a position behind him, his Uzi at the ready. Moving slowly forward, Ryan eased into the control room, his eye sweeping the interior for anything suspicious. But everything was as it was supposed to be, aside from the uniformed skeletons.

While the air vents sucked away the swirling cloud of dust, Ryan studied the comp. He had no idea what the twinkling lights on the console meant, but after so many jumps, he could tell when they took on a new pattern, which always meant trouble. Thankfully, it was the standard sequence.

Going to the opposite door, Ryan listened for any movement in the corridor. Hearing none, he tapped the standard code into the keypad. The door slid open and he sneaked a peek outside. Dozens of corpses wearing Navy uniforms were on the floor, each in the process of crumbling from the infusion of fresh air coming from the vents.

Ryan then turned to find the rest of his companions

already in the control room. Krysty and Jak were standing guard, while Mildred and J.B. checked the clothing and blasters.

"This man…excuse me, this woman, was a lieutenant in Navy Intelligence," Mildred said, fingering the rank insignia. "While this fellow was a corporal in the Navy SEALs and the other man was a pilot in the Navy Air Corps."

"If this isn't a bastard ship, then we must be at a Navy base," Ryan stated, thoughtfully rubbing his jaw. "Or at least, damn close to a base." That was good news. The Navy always stored tons of extra supplies in their bases. With any luck, dinner would be beef stew, not gopher surprise—surprise, it's gopher again.

"These weapons are in fine shape," J.B. noted, working the arming bolt on one of the M-16 assault rifles to cycle a round out the ejector port. "The springs in the clips are weak, but still functional, and aside from that these rapidfires should work without any trouble. There's no rust at all on the brass from the dry air."

"Dead air," Mildred corrected him. "I suspect that in this redoubt, when the sensors don't detect anything alive inside, the computers flood the base with inert gas to retard any corrosion or chemical decompositions."

"Which is why the bodies were in such good shape until we activated the life support system," Ryan guessed.

"Quite so," Doc rumbled from the other side of the oval door. "Apparently even the conqueror worm is humbled before the iron law of science."

"Amen to that," Mildred said with a half smile.

Bemused, Doc grunted in reply.

"Any spare clips?" Krysty asked.

"Plenty," J.B. replied, opening an ammo pouch on the belt. "Five, no six. Mixed rounds, solid lead, HEAT and tumblers."

"Expecting trouble," Jak stated, holstering his Colt Python. "Still might come. I take."

After adding a few precious drops of homogenized gun oil to the rapidfire, J.B. passed two of the rapid-fires and ammo pouches to Jak and Krysty, then gave another to Mildred. With sure hands, the three companions checked the assault rifles for themselves. The action was a little slow, and the trigger kind of stiff, but aside from that the weapons were in fine shape and ready for battle.

"Damn, barrel blocked," Jak said, looking through the weapon at the ceiling lights. Shaking the assault rifle, he saw a slim roll of tightly wound paper fall onto the floor. Why hide cig? the albino teen wondered, then took a sniff. This wasn't tobacco, but maryjane! Jak started to tuck the joint into a shirt pocket, but the pressure of his fingers made it crumble into loose leaves and ancient dust.

"No loss. It would have tasted awful," Mildred said with a knowing wink. "Wine and whiskey age well. Weed does not."

"And exactly how do you know that, madam?" Doc asked accusingly.

"Ah…I had glaucoma in high school."

"What?"

"Never mind."

"Dead air, or not, we still need to do a sweep of the base to make sure that we're alone," Ryan stated, entering the code to open the door, as it had automatically closed behind him. He entered the corridor again. As expected, the vents had finished their task and the clouds of desiccated human flesh were gone. Now, only loose clothing and skeletons dotted the entire length of the corridor. One figure lay blocking an open doorway, a petrified doughnut in his hand with a single bite taken.

"These folks died fast," Ryan stated, scowling at the grim sight. "Think it was some sort of plague?"

"No disease I know kills this quickly," Mildred said, hefting the assault rifle to try to find a comfortable position. "Not even the genetically created plagues."

"Rad leak?" Jak asked nervously.

Both Ryan and J.B. checked the rad counters clipped to their lapels.

"Clear," J.B. announced. "Not even a trace of rad."

Mildred bit her lip. "My guess would be that a gas of some kind did this."

"Nerve gas took out an entire redoubt?" Doc asked, shocked. "Is that even theoretically possible, madam? I mean, with all of the automatic safeguards of a redoubt?"

"It's the only thing that makes sense," J.B. added, pushing back his fedora to scratch his head.

"Well, the gas must be long gone by now, or else we'd be facedown on the floor," Krysty stated, the rapidfire balanced in her hands. "Where next, lover?"

"Armory," Ryan stated, heading for the stairs. "If this was done by nerve gas, that's the most likely storage place. We better make sure that whatever leaked is completely empty."

"Before we, too, join the choir invisible," Doc rumbled, glancing nervously at a wall vent.

Nobody commented on that dire possibility as they followed Ryan along the corridor. The skeletons were everywhere, and the companions had to exercise care to not tromp on any of the bony hands. Every room they passed had more bones, some of them merely scattered piles, while others were lying neatly tucked into their beds, holding a clipboard or working at a comp or listening to music.

Once, very long ago, the companions had found a redoubt with eerie sounds playing over the intercom. But instead of a half-crazed survivor, it had proved to only be a music CD still trying to play reveille after a century. But this redoubt was disturbingly still. Quite literally, the quiet of a grave.

In the ward room, five sailors in pants and T-shirts were sitting around a table, a game of poker in progress. Several more were on a sofa watching a TV monitor now showing only static. One fellow wearing glasses was reading a paperback novel, while another died on the toilet, a yellow newspaper lying nearby bearing the precise date of the nuclear doomsday.

"Brass by ton," Jak said happily, noting the countless array of sidearms worn by the skeletons. Most of the officers seemed to carrying 9 mm Glock blasters, but the guards were armed with Colt .45s, the regulation gunbelts holding a standard four spare clips. Those were the best; the Colt was a brutal little manstopper that could blow the head off a stickie at fifty yards.

Unfortunately the stairs were choked with uniforms, or rather, loose piles of bones that were still tumbling down the steps now that the last vestiges of flesh holding them in place were gone. With no choice, the companions took the elevator to the armory level. Two of the cages were full of skeletons, but the third was empty.

"This is rather unnerving," Mildred said, watching a sec camera in the corner of the ceiling steadily move back and forth. The people were all aced, but the machines continued to function on whatever was their last setting.

"Be a lot worse if somebody had activated a sec hunter droid before collapsing," J.B. countered, pulling out a pipe bomb and tucking it into his belt for fast access.

Without comment, Ryan reached up and yanked out the power cord of the vidcam, the red indicator fading to black.

"How many of those do we have, John Barrymore?" Doc asked pointedly, gesturing at the explosive charge with the barrel of his LeMat.

"Just the one."

"Then pray, make it count, my friend."

"That was the plan, Doc."

Reaching the fifth level, Ryan and the others found the main hallway clear of bodies. But that was only to be expected. Combat personnel didn't lounge around the armory for fun.

Located at the end of the hall was a massive armored door, a truncated cone of layered steel and titanium that not even a laser could burn through. Luckily, the formidable barrier was ajar, a skeleton lying across the threshold, holding a clipboard of ancient papers, a CD player clipped to his belt.

"Hmm, he had good taste in music," Mildred said, reading the title through the clear plastic.

"Beethoven?" Doc asked curiously.

"Billy Joel."

The companions stepped over the bones and into the armory.

"Good God!" Mildred gasped.

Turning fast, Ryan had his blaster out and ready, but then he blinked in surprise and slowly smiled. *Jackpot.*

Many of the armories the companions found were completely bare, not even a scrap of paper remaining behind. Sometimes they found a few loose rounds under a shelf, or a single live gren left behind when the base personnel departed before or after skydark, heading for, well, wherever they had gone a hundred years earlier. None of the companions had ever discovered where all of the people had gone, or even had a plausible theory. But this armory seemed to never have been touched. It was completely full, literally stocked to the rafters.

The companions couldn't speak for a minute at the miraculous sight of dozens of pallets filling the room, the wall shelves jammed full of supplies. There were also endless racks of M-16 assault rifles, M-203 combination assault rifles, 40 mm gren launchers, M-60 machine guns, even bulky .50-machine guns too heavy for a person to carry, much less fire and remain standing. There were entire rows of plastic drums marked as containing ammunition, and pallet after pallet of sturdy plastic boxes that the companions knew contained grens, and even LAW rocket launchers. It was the military might of the predark world spread out in front of their astonished eyes like a holiday feast.

"Nuke me, this redoubt was never emptied after skydark!" J.B. cried happily. "The people must have died just before the evacuation order came."

"Fully stocked redoubt," Jak muttered. "More than we dream finding!" For the normally laconic teenager, that was an extraordinarily long speech.

"Thank you, Gaia," Krysty whispered.

"Not even that deep storage locker in New Mex had this much ordnance," Mildred agreed, already looking around for any medical supplies. Sometimes, field packs were stored in the armory along with the weaponry.

"All right, fill your pockets, but nothing more," Ryan ordered brusquely, resting the stock of the Steyr on a hip. "Krysty and I will stand guard. Don't weigh yourself down for the rest of the sweep. We can come back later and take what we want."

Instantly the rest of the companions separated, walking swiftly through the stocks and piles, checking the numbers on the countless sealed containers and mentally translating those into descriptions. Boots, combat, size ten, for use of. Milk, powdered, vitamin fortified, for daily consumption. HazMat suits, Level 10, hazardous materials: antinuclear, antibacteriological, antichemical.

Going to a wall cabinet, Mildred pulled it open to find a stack of boxes full of MRE food packs. Grinning widely, she went to a nearby pallet and grabbed a nylon duffel bag, then returned to start packing the shiny Mylar envelopes. There was beef stew, veal parmesan, meat loaf and mac and cheese. Pausing for only a second, the woman removed the smoked gopher from her backpack and unceremoniously deposited it into a waste chute.

Eagerly, Doc went in search of trade goods. Among the thousand and one things stored in the redoubts, the predark government had considered the fact that some sort of crude civilization might arise from the nuclear ashes of America all by itself, so the base personnel would need trinkets to trade with the survivors outside. The companions had found such things before and they were always tremendously useful, such as unbreakable pocket combs, Swiss Army knives, Bowie knives, plastic mirrors, pots and pans, rain ponchos, fishing hooks and, of course, lots of weapons. Mostly battle axes, shields and swords. The Pentagon had clearly expected civilization to fall all the way down to true barbarism, but sometimes there were also black-powder weapons, which was what Doc wanted. Especially the tiny copper nipples full of fulminating mercury that the Civil War– era .44 LeMat used as primers. He never had enough of those.

Unfortunately, Doc was unable to find any such items on this initial pass, and consoled himself with a Webley .44 revolver and a cardboard box containing fifty live rounds.

Meanwhile J.B. was having trouble restraining himself from taking everything in sight, and was snagging only a few choice items, several sticks of TNT and a box of detonator caps, a small coil of primacord, a fistful of waterproof timing pencils and items for pipe bombs. Then the man paused at the sight of a wall safe. A safe inside a vault?

Mentally crossing his fingers, J.B. went to work on the combination lock and soon it yielded with a soft click. Turning the handle, J.B. opened the door and stopped breathing. A portable lockbox filled the safe, and he removed it as gingerly as if defusing a land mine. Placing it on the floor, J.B. used his knife to trick the lock, then lifted the lid. There nestled in the soft, gray foam, were six implo grens, the most powerful predark weapon invented by the human race. It worked just like a regular gren: pull the safety pin, release the arming lever and throw. But instead of an explosion, the gren created a gravity whirlpool, an implosion that could condense an Abrams tank to the size of an orange in less than a microsecond. With these at their command, the companions no longer had to worry about sec hunter droids, or much of anything else, for that matter.

Quickly rummaging in his munitions bag, J.B. found some duct tape and securely attached the arming lever of each gren before transferring it to his bag. The weight was considerable, but the man had never seen this many implo grens.

Affectionately patting the leather bag, J.B. proudly started back to find Ryan when he saw something twinkle out of the corner of his sight. Twinkle? *Oh shit.*

Frantically grabbing for an implo gren, J.B. sniffed hard for any trace of ozone, but the air in the armory was warm and flat, sterilized and purified until it was completely without any taste or flavor.

With the gren clenched tight in a fist, J.B. crept around a pallet stacked high with plastic boxes containing M-4 rifles, to stop dead in his tracks. There was a small alcove directly ahead of the man, thick

metal bars sealing it off from the rest of the armory.
Set into the metal was an alphanumeric keypad similar
to the type used to open the redoubt's door, and behind
the bars were a dozen crystalline containers, inside of
which was a swirling white cloud filled with sparkling
lights. The sight almost made him drop the gren.

"Cerberus clouds," J.B. whispered, the soft words
somehow sounding louder than thunder.

Backing away slowly, J.B. tried not to breathe, the
terrible sight of the inhuman slayers filling his world.
Just for a second, the man looked at the implo gren in
his hand, then realized in cold reality that if the charge
didn't chill all of the clouds at once, he and the rest
of the companions would be in for the fight of their
lives.

When their old boss the Trader had first discovered
the existence of the redoubts, the entranceway had been
guarded by a cloud that bit, and chilled. Over time, the
companions learned the inhuman guardian of some of
the redoubts was called a Cerberus cloud, and aside
from an implo gren, the friends knew the things were
virtually indestructible. The clouds were sentient, or at
least they acted that way, but if it was only a software
program running into their vaporous minds, or if they
were truly alive, who knew? Certainly no one alive
in Deathlands. What was known for a fact was that
they ruthlessly aced unauthorized personnel inside a
redoubt.

Going back around the pallet full of M-4 rifles, J.B.
never took his sight off the crystal jars while he softly
whistled like a nightingale. Immediately everybody else

in the armory stopped talking, and soon the others were alongside the man, their weapons primed for combat.

"Trouble?" Ryan asked, looking around.

"See for yourself," J.B. whispered, indicating a direction with his chin. The implo gren was still in his fist, the tape removed from the arming lever, a finger in the safety ring.

Starting forward, the companions paused at the first twinkle of light. While Ryan and Jak sniffed hard, Krysty tried to sense anything unusual, Mildred held out a mirror to see around the stack of boxes, and Doc stepped onto the pallet to sneak a peek over the top.

"By all that is holy, a Cerberus cloud!" Doc whispered in a strained voice. "No, by thunder, it is six of the Hellish constructs!"

"Jars of Cerberus clouds," Mildred said in awe. "This must be how they transported the damn things."

"Use implo gren," Jak suggested. "Use all."

"And what if there are more of these things that we haven't found yet?" Mildred asked, trying to ignore the tingling sensation on the back of her neck. The physician knew it was only a psychological reaction to the tense situation, but her hackles still wanted to rise in preparation of immediate flight.

The teenager scowled at the possibility, and hunched his shoulders as if getting ready to charge the clouds.

"Okay, people, fall back by the numbers," Ryan commanded softly, walking backward on the toes of his combat boots, trying not to make any noise.

The rest of the companions closely followed his example, and the group carefully retraced its path through the massive armory until reaching the entrance again.

Quickly, Ryan and Krysty removed the old bones from
the threshold, and anxiously waited while the massive
door cycled shut then rotated slightly to firmly lock.

"All right, if those clouds come alive, this'll buy us
some time," Ryan said, slinging the Steyr over a shoulder. "But we better haul ass out of here, just in case."

"Jump?" Jak asked succinctly.

"No," Ryan decided. "We'll check outside first. See
where we are before we do another blind jump."

"A wise choice, my dear Ryan," Doc said. "To be
honest, I am still feeling somewhat queasy from our
last impromptive sojourn through the ethereal void."

"And without any more of Millie's juice, we'll probably arrive puking out our guts this time," J.B. added,
glancing at the ceiling. "Mebbe we can drive out of
here. Should be lots of wags in the garage upstairs just
waiting to be used."

"Wherever the nuke we are," Krysty retorted, starting for the elevator banks in a long stride.

Along the way, J.B. passed an implo gren to each of
the others. That way, in case he got chilled, they would
still have a fighting chance to survive.

Piling into the cage, the companions started for the
top level of the redoubt, each of them feeling slightly
more at ease the farther they got from the armory. Six
Cerberus clouds. They would have been happier finding
a roomful of rampaging stickies.

Arriving at the garage, the companions were delighted to find the place full of vehicles: civilian wags,
vans, trucks and some motorcycles. There was even
a score of military wags: trucks, Hummers, several
armored-personnel carriers, and even a couple of LARC

amphibious transports. Even better, the worktables were covered with equipment, the pegboard walls festooned with tools of every description. Unfortunately, each APC seemed to have been undergoing some serious maintenance on the transmissions. There were numerous skeletons in greasy coveralls bent over the exposed diesel engines, tools and spare parts scattered across on the floor.

Over by the fuel pump, skid marks on the floor revealed that a big GMC truck had clearly come out of the tunnel too fast and lost control, desperately trying to brake to a halt before crashing. However, the driver failed, and the big Jimmy had plowed into an SUV, the two vehicles then smashing a Hummer into the wall.

"And there is the source of the nerve gas," Mildred stated, running stiff fingers though her beaded plaits.

In the rear compartment of the crashed Hummer was a large equipment trunk securely strapped into place. But the crash had snapped the restraining straps and popped the locks, allowing some of the containers inside to tumble out. Their broken valves lay nearby, the concrete severely discolored from the escaping contents. The containers were small, hardly larger than a fire extinguisher, and painted a very bright yellow with a black skull and crossbones painted on the side, along with the universal logo of a biohazard.

"I stand corrected. It wasn't nerve gas, but some type of a plague." Mildred scowled in open hatred. "It must have been airborne to spread so quickly through the entire redoubt before the scrubbers cleaned the air."

"Germ warfare," Doc snarled. "The most foul and cowardly of weapons!" Doc had read hundreds of books during his stay in the twentieth century, and he had been astonished by man's inhumanity to his fellow man.

"We safe?" Jak asked in an even tone. If the teen was frightened, there was no sign of it in his calm demeanor.

"Safe? Oh, absolutely," Mildred stated, her shoulders easing. "There's not a plague in existence that could survive a hundred years in such a sterile environment."

"That you know about," Krysty countered, her hair coiling protectively around her face.

Without comment, the physician shrugged. The world was full of unknown dangers. That was just part of life.

"Any way to check, see if the plague is still live?" J.B. asked, taking the stub of a cigar from his shirt pocket and tucking it into the corner of his mouth.

"No, John. Afraid not."

"Damn," the man muttered. In spite of Mildred's disapproving look, he used a butane lighter to light the cigar and take a deep drag. "Frag it then. We're still standing, and that's good enough."

"Agreed," Ryan declared. "Krysty and Doc, find the least damaged APC, see what needs to be done and start the repairs if you can. Jak and Mildred, start filling gas cans, and find some extra engine oil. Those wags burn it like crazy. J.B. and I will go outside and see where we are."

Everybody began to hustle, but as the two men headed for the exit tunnel the elevator doors unexpectedly closed and the cage began to nosily descend. That caught everybody by surprise as there was nobody else in the redoubt to summon the elevator…

Chapter Five

"Gaia, the clouds must be loose!" Krysty cursed, pulling out an implo gren.

Spinning, Ryan raced toward the elevator bank. "Forget the outside recce! Doc, grab some fuel! Everybody else, find something that rolls, any mother bastard thing, and let's haul ass!"

Everybody exploded into action. Bitter experience had taught them that a Cerberus could move faster than a running man, so a wag was their only hope of escape. However, the garage was full of vehicles, most of them in pitiful shape despite the inert gas that had filled the redoubt. The civilian wags were the worst with flat tires that had deflated over the years, and many were situated over dark puddles that might once have been engine oil, but now was closer in consistency to tar. Those vehicles were ignored and the companions concentrated on the mil wags, each choosing something different.

Reaching the working elevator, Ryan rammed his panga into the rubber seal between the two doors and managed to force them apart by sheer strength. Instantly the cage stopped moving. That bought them a few moments, and every second counted now.

Scrambling to the workbench, J.B. grabbed a welding torch and wheeled it over to the stairwell door. It took him a few tries to get the equipment working, then the rod gushed out flame. Narrowing that into a white-hot stiletto, J.B. expertly moved the torch along the edge of the metal door, feeding in a melting iron rod to try to create an air-tight seal.

Risking a glance down the shaft, Ryan heard nothing moving inside the cage, but then caught a faint twinkling of reflected light through the ventilation grille. Fireblast, it was a cloud, all right. Mebbe even several of them, or even all six. The weight of the implo gren in his pocket was sorely tempting, and he thrust in a hand to touch the charge, but then decided to save it for an emergency. The cloud seemed to have stopped for the moment, but the man knew that it could simply float to the shaft if it wanted, so there was no sense clearing a direct path for it that lead directly to the companions.

Lying sideways inside the cab of a Mack truck, Jak tried to hot-wire the engine. It struggled to start, then coughed hard and roared into life, only to immediately bang and stop cold. Hot rads, it blew a rod!

Extracting himself from the wiring, the albino teen yanked open the rear door of an APC to try for better luck there. Kicking the skeletons of the sailors out of the way, Jak headed straight for the driver's seat and started flipping switches.

Turning away from an ambulance in disgust, Mildred next yanked out a grinning skeleton from behind the wheel of a Hummer. The physician desperately longed to raid the medical supplies stored in the back of the ambulance, but that was impossible right now, so she forced those thoughts from her mind. Run away, and stay alive, was her mantra for today.

Leaning dangerously far into the shaft, Ryan used the

curved blade of his panga to slash at the control wires until he was satisfied that the cage would never work again without extensive repairs. Then he stepped back and let the door close again. When nothing happened, Ryan grunted in satisfaction and went directly to the next elevator to repeat the process.

"John Barrymore, please extinguish that cigar!" Doc barked, dragging a pair of sloshing cans across the garage, the nozzle of the fuel pump dripping slightly onto the floor. "How are we going to detect the dulcet smell of ozone with you puffing on that reeking cheroot?"

Accepting the logic of that, J.B. spit out the precious cheroot and crushed it under a boot, but his hands never stopped in their desperate work. Sweat was running off the man from the staggering heat of the acetylene torch, but J.B. was more than halfway done, the door nearly welded shut. Whether that would stop a Cerberus cloud he had no idea, but it was the best plan he had.

There came a whirring sound and an engine sputtered into operation, then settled into a steady roar of power. Whistling sharply for everybody's attention, Krysty waved from inside the tiny pilothouse of a LARC amphibian transport. Resembling a flat-bottom boat with wheels, it looked about as speedy as a wheelbarrow, but this was the first wag they found that worked, and that was good enough for today. Checking over the small control board, Krysty saw that both of the fuel tanks read empty, and she quickly killed the V8 diesel engine to save what gas was still lingering in the ancient fuel lines.

Finished with the elevator bank, Ryan turned just

in time to snarl a curse at the sight of twinkling lights
coming from a wall vent. The bastard clouds were inside
the ventilation system! Now pulling out the implo gren,
the man backed away to a safe distance, ripping off the
duct tape and curling a finger into the arming pin. Ryan
would only get one chance at a chill, and he couldn't
miss.

Tossing the spare gas canister over the gunwale of
the LARC, Doc went to the rear fuel port and used the
butt of his LeMat to hammer off the rusty gas cap. With
no concern for his own safety, the man simply turned
the canister upside down, to quickly pour as much as
possible into the amphibious transport. A lot of the fluid
splashed onto the sloping side of the vehicle, staining
his pants and shoes, but Doc never slowed for an instant
in his task. Clothing could be replaced, but not that
elusive state of existence colloquially known as life.

With a dry mouth, Ryan watched as the Cerberus
cloud flowed from the grille of the wall vent, growing ever larger. Released from its jar, the thing was
twenty feet across, the sharp smell of ozone filling the
garage.

Rushing over to the LARC, Mildred tossed in an
M-60 machine gun yanked from a Hummer, and Jak
heaved two more gas canisters into the middle span.
Then everybody yanked out an implo gren and clawed
off the strip of duct tape.

"Done!" J.B. announced, stepping back triumphantly.

But then he cursed as he saw a tiny glowing spot in
the middle of the door. That wasn't his work, he had
been nowhere near the center. As J.B. watched, the spot

got a little bigger as it changed color from a dull red, to bright cherry red rapidly escalating to orange, then yellow and finally white. Then the door would melt, and the cloud on the other side would flow through. He had spent ten minutes welding the fragging door shut, and the Cerberus cloud would get through in only a few moments. Not knowing what else to do, J.B. shoved the welding torch at the orange splotch. The white-hot flame instantly cut through the softened metal and there came a sound from the other side, almost as if the cloud had experienced pain.

Trying to keep his hand steady and pointed at the same location, J.B. watched for the formation of any other burns, knowing that he was now trapped. If he dropped the welding torch, the cloud would pour though the hole like escaping steam. The implo gren was in the pocket of his leather jacket, the tape removed and ready to go. But that might as well be on the moon for all the good it would do him right now. There were more iron rods on the workbench, but by the time he got back, the cloud would be through. Not that any of that really mattered, because the pressure gauge on the acetylene tank was rapidly approaching zero. Suddenly the man was filled with the overwhelming urge for a smoke.

Gunning the diesel of the LARC, Krysty wheeled the long vehicle around to point toward the exit tunnel. She reached for the horn, but like most military vehicles, the amphibious transport didn't have one, rush-hour traffic being one of the few problems for sailors storming an enemy beach.

"Time to go!" she yelled, the muscles standing up on her back from the sheer force of the cry.

Wheeling over a tool chest, Doc set it directly in front of the door, and J.B. arranged the welding torch into position, then used a heavy wrench to hold it there. Releasing his grip, the man stepped back to check the work, then turned and bolted for the waiting half-track with Doc close behind, the tail of his frock coat flapping behind him.

As the cloud started to move away from the wall, Ryan yanked the pin and gently rolled the gren along the floor, then turned and raced away. Reaching an APC, he grabbed onto a stanchion set into the armored hull and held on for dear life. His skin began to prickle from the close proximity of the Cerberus cloud, then there came a musical ting and the gren activated.

Instantly the garage was effused with a blinding white light, the Cerberus cloud emitted an inhuman noise that might have been a scream, and then a violent wind filled the inside of the underground garage as the gravitational vortex began dragging every loose item toward its epicenter. Dust streamed toward the powerful implosion, papers went flying, bones rattled across the floor, and small tools pelted Ryan as they hurtled by. The ceiling lights swayed, a motorcycle toppled over, an empty jumpsuit sailed through the turbulent atmosphere like a kamikaze ghost—then the wind stopped as abruptly as it had begun.

Releasing his hold on the APC, Ryan glanced at the circular crater where the air vent had existed. Yards wide, a huge section of the floor and wall were gone, vanished, compressed into an allotropic state beyond comprehension. Shuffling toward the LARC, Ryan could see the internal plumbing and wiring, the ventilation shaft a wide gaping mouth, the edges mirror-bright. There was no sign of the cloud, even the smell of the ozone was gone, every trace annihilated by the staggering power of the deadly implo gren.

Clambering over the low gunwale of the LARC transport, the Deathlands warrior nodded to Krysty in the pilothouse, then saw her face contort with fear, and knew the truth. Turning fast, Ryan saw another cloud rising from the open ventilation shaft. Only this one began to move across the garage before it finished rising from the shaft. Fireblast, Ryan thought, the fragging things learned from their mistakes!

"Me this time," Jak snarled, standing in the vehicle and yanking out the arming pin.

Flowing over some of the disorganized skeletons on the floor, the cloud paused for a few moments, the bones vanished, and the mass of the cloud grew slightly larger.

"Eat dead?" Jak snarled. "Try eat this!"

Throwing the gren against the distant pegboard, the albino youth banked the shot, and the mil sphere rolled toward the cloud from behind. As the cloud turned at the noise, Krysty slammed on the gas and the LARC lumbered into operation, the four huge tires squealing in protest.

Angling fast around the first corner, Krysty heard the gren activate, her hair fluttering from the wind of the implosion.

"Dark night, I saw the torch go out!" J.B. stormed, adjusting his glasses. "That means another cloud is on the way."

"The three heads of Cerberus, eh?" Doc rumbled, yanking the pin from his gren.

"Save that bastard gren until you see the thing!" Ryan commanded, grabbing the side of the gunwale with both hands and holding on tight.

At the best speed possible, Krysty raced the cumbersome LARC along the zigzagging tunnel, the steel hull throwing off sparks as it scraped along the walls. In the backseats, the companions were thrown around helplessly. Once, there had been safety belts, but implacable time had reduced those to a gossamer thinness more suitable for a bathroom than a restraining harness. As the LARC careened off a sharp corner, the M-60 bounced over the side. Jak tried for a save, but the weapon tumbled away, a sacrifice to the god of speed.

"The sixty!" Doc cried out aghast, then the man used a word that normally he pretended didn't even exist.

Reaching the blast door, Krysty slammed the transport to a brutal stop, the old brakes grinding in protest. The exit door didn't have a massive lever. Hopping over the side, Ryan ran to the keypad set into the wall, then with a pounding heart the man made himself slowly and carefully enter the exit code. A single mistake now would mean he would have to start again from the beginning, and that would bring the next Cerberus straight down their bastard throats.

As Ryan entered the last digit, there was a brief pause and then the blast door began to slowly move aside with the customary low rumble of heavy machinery from below the floor. A dry wind blew through the widening crack, carrying the faint tang of the sea. But then that was overpowered by the sharp reek of ozone.

"They're here!" J.B. snarled, turning to see a sparkling white cloud flowing around the corner, the interior filled with beautiful fairy lights.

"Move!" Ryan shouted, vaulting over the gunwale.

Stomping on the gas, Krysty threw the LARC into gear just as Doc yanked the safety pin on his implo gren, and the mil sphere knocked from his grip to go wild and hit the wall—only to bounce right back into the departing LARC. Moving with adrenaline-fueled speed, Mildred snatched the charge and whipped it backward, uncaring of where it landed as long as it was far from the vehicle.

Still accelerating, Krysty rammed the LARC into the opening between the blast door and the wall, becoming momentarily stuck when there came a brilliant flash from behind, closely followed by a reverse hurricane. Anything loose in the LARC was sucked away by the implosion, the companions nearly losing their seats from the sheer force of the wind, with J.B. grabbing onto his fedora with both hands.

Continuing to pour on the power, Krysty forced the LARC ever forward, the Navy transport advancing in screeching protest until the last curve of the hull squeezed past the blast door.

In a surge of speed, the LARC rocketed outside, nearly crashing into the side of a rocky tunnel before the woman regained control and headed pell-mell into the darkening gloom. Beyond the slice of illumination coming from of the redoubt there was Stygian blackness.

As the artificial wind eased, Ryan staggered into the pilothouse and took the navigator seat to start flipping switches. Running lights appeared along the gunwale, then a GPS unit came alive on the control board, but finally he found the headlights. Set at cockeyed angles, the halogen beams were pointed at the ceiling and the floor of the tunnel, but they threw back enough light for the two companions to see that this wasn't a predark tunnel built for vehicles. It was some sort of a circular tube, the smooth walls shiny with tiny flecks of a reflective material. Built to carry enough supplies for a platoon of U.S. Marines, plus the Marines, the wide LARC just barely fit into the tube, the tires cantered oddly on the curved bottom while the stubby radio antenna constantly scraped along the arched ceiling.

"This is a lava tube!" Doc gasped in horror. "We're inside a bedamned volcano!"

"Watch out for steam vents!" Mildred shouted from the distant rear of the transport. "They'll cook us alive!"

Busy working the controls, Ryan didn't respond, but Krysty half turned her head to nod in understanding. Now that her vision was growing accustomed to the gloom, she could see that there were numerous other tunnels shooting off at crazy angles. It was taking her constant attention to keep the LARC from crashing into one or lurching off into the unknown. Krysty didn't know much about volcanoes, but what the woman had heard was that the main lava tube was usually the largest. Usually. With luck, this one would empty somewhere on dry land instead of ending at a river of molten rock, or worse, a mile under sea. If either of those was the case, the companions would have to drive backward and try another tube, then another and another, until they reached the outside world or ran out of fuel and were forced to return to the redoubt for one last confrontation with the Cerberus clouds.

Releasing the steering wheel for a moment, Krysty grabbed Ryan by the shoulder and squeezed hard. He replied in kind, the man and woman speaking volumes to each other without ever saying a word.

Behind the LARC, the blast door was slowly closing, the ceiling lights narrowing quickly into a mere sliver. Then the light went murky for a moment, before the nukeproof door closed with a muffled boom.

"Cloud, six o'clock!" Jak yelled through cupped hands to the people in the pilothouse.

Turning, Ryan squinted his good eye, but there was only darkness behind them.

Rummaging in his munitions bag, J.B. unearthed a road flare and scraped it alive, the bright red magnesium flame hissing loudly. Tossing it over the end of the LARC, the man saw it hit and nearly go out, but then the flame sputtered alive, the red light clearly silhouetting the Cerberus cloud as it flowed over the flare and back into the darkness.

"How long do you think it will chase us?" Krysty asked, trying not to notice how low the gas gauge was. The ten gallons Doc had poured in were almost gone, and stopping to refuel was clearly out of the question.

"Fireblast, I don't know," Ryan replied truthfully, glancing over a shoulder. "But I once had a sec hunter droid follow me for close to a hundred miles before I got away."

"No choice then, eh, lover?"

"None that I can think of," the man stated grimly, and put two fingers into his mouth to loudly whistle.

In the rear of the transport, the rest of the companions looked up at the man, and he pointed at Mildred. The woman tilted her head in a silent question, and Ryan drew a thumb across his throat. Swallowing hard, Mildred nodded.

"My dear doctor, you cannot be serious!" Doc cried aghast. "We are inside a lava tube. The use of an implo gren here could easily trigger a full-scale eruption."

"Which will certainly chill that damn cloud!" Mildred growled, removing the tape and wrapping a finger around the arming pin. "They're tough, but not indestructible!"

"Well, if I am to die in a volcanic eruption, then at least stop the wag for a moment so that I may carve three notches into the wall first!"

Recognizing the literary reference, the physician almost smiled. The man might be crazy, but he had certainly guts to spare, and then some, she'd give him that much.

"Give me some light, John!" Mildred shouted, leaning over the stern. The wind was ruffling her hair, and the rushing walls were only a couple of feet away. The running lights shone brightly to the sides, but there was only darkness behind. The cloud might be only inches away from her face, and she would have no way of knowing.

Scraping another road flare into life, J.B. held it out as far as he could. For a fleeting moment, there was a twinkling cloud dimly visible just outside the radiant nimbus of the sputtering flare, then it was gone, pulling back to merge into the shadows once more.

Utterly furious, Mildred cursed at the sight. The cloud was deliberately staying out of sight to hinder any further attacks. Perhaps it understood that three other clouds had been aced, neutralized, whatever the correct word was, she had no idea, and it was being cautious. Perhaps it didn't comprehend the concept of death and was acting purely on instinct, or digital programming loaded into the matrix of its vaporous memory.

The technical details didn't matter. The result was that the cloud was staying just out of sight, as if trying to make the companions waste their small supply of implo grens. The only way to counter that move was to do the one thing an artificial construct couldn't do: gamble everything on a single throw of the dice.

"Hit the deck!" Mildred yelled, yanking out the arming pin.

As the three men dived for cover, Mildred held tightly on to the ticking gren, slowly counting to six before releasing the sphere, and then throwing herself to the floor.

Exactly two seconds later, there came a musical chime and a terrible illumination filled the tube, overwhelming the running lights until it seemed that it had winked out. There came an inhuman noise of pain and surprise, then a ferocious wind buffeted the LARC, the incredible vacuum caused by the gravitational vortex ripping away loose pieces of the hull. Contained inside the lava tube, the implosion was magnified a hundred times, steadily increasing in force until the racing machine actually began to slow, the tires slipping on the smooth tube and threatening to lose their grip.

The military diesel sputtered and coughed, almost failing from the inability to draw in any air and maintain internal combustion. Then Ryan went flying from the pilothouse to slam against the floor. His head hit the wood with a crack, and he went limp, rolling along the floor toward the rear gunwale. Moving fast, Doc and Jak grabbed their friend, then J.B. and Mildred held on to them, the four companions struggling to stay inside the fleeing LARC against the buffeting wind currents.

For one long moment it seemed that they might fail, their tired hands weakening rapidly from the awful strain, then the vacuum dissipated, stopping just as quickly as it had been created. Set free once more, the LARC surged forward, the big diesel roaring with renewed power. Then the engine faltered and died away, the LARC coasting through the lava tube from sheer inertia.

"We just ran out of gas!" Krysty shouted in weary relief, taking both hands off the wheel to flex her aching fingers. Then the woman paused, her hair flexing wildly.

Over the soft crunching of the Navy tires, she could distinctly hear a low rumble that seemed to be coming from every direction. Steadily, the noise increased in volume and power, until the rock walls began to visibly shake, loose dust sprinkling down from the ceiling, and there came a strong whiff of raw sulfur.

Chapter Six

Carrying the smell of the open sea, a cool wind blew over the busy people on the mountain plateau. Coated lightly with a yellow dust, the men and women working there greatly appreciated the brief relief from the awful stink of the sulfur pit, and momentarily paused to breathe in the fresh air and refill their lungs.

Stripped to their waists, the muscular torsos of the men gleamed with sweat, the big men swinging their sledgehammers and matlocks at a steady pace, the tools falling in unison. Sitting on a water barrel, a young girl was beating a tempo on a rabbit skin drum to help them keep pace. Rhythm was the key to efficiency in such an endeavor, rhythm and sheer muscle.

Older people, both men and women, pushed along homemade wheelbarrows, with shovels strapped to their backs like a sec man did a longblaster. Their wrinkled faces were caked with the precious yellow dust, sweat cutting ravines through the sulfur to stain their clothing golden. Rags served in lieu of gloves, and some of them were barefoot. However, nobody was wearing chains, leashes or tethers, and most of the men were wearing dark blue uniforms, and heavily armed with blasters. Even the little drummer girl carried a brace of knives, and a homemade bolo, small rocks lashed together with leather thongs to create a particularly deadly weapon for chilling small game, such as coneys or cave bats.

When the debris on the ground got deep enough, they would scoop it up and fill the wheelbarrow, then push it over to the ville guard to be inspected. Some loads were accepted and piled in boxes filling the back of a battered wag, while others were rejected as too impure. Those would be dumped unceremoniously over the side of a tall cliff overlooking the beautiful azure Cific Ocean. The orange-and-black toxic clouds overhead were reflected in the gentle waves, making the waters seem dark and ominous. However, the salty Cific teemed with life; there were fish of every description, most of the creatures good eating, and only a few of them mutie enough to chase a norm onto dry ground. There were no other islands in sight for a thousand miles, only the vast and empty ocean.

Standing guard over the precious cargo of dust was the ville baron and his wife, both carrying rapidfires and watching the nearby rock for any suspicious movements. The plateau was the secret source of sulfur for Sealton ville. It was a vital ingredient for making black powder, which was the only thing that kept away the Thunder Kings and the coldheart army run by that Captain Carlton.

Oddly, there were no clouds directly over the people working in the sulfur pit of the rocky plateau, and a clear bright sun shone down upon them. Removing his hat to beat some of the yellow dust off the brim, Baron Carson Jones appreciated the fact that there was always clear sky above Clemente Island, and attributed it to the heat rising from the mouth of the Cannon, the largest of the Twelve Volcanoes in the Cesium Mountains. Smoke moved away from fire, any feeb could see that in a campfire with their own eyes. Obviously, clouds were just a kind of smoke, and they kept far away from the nuking heat of the bubbling lava boiling inside the mouth of fire mountain.

Baron Carson Jones was huge, easily the tallest person on the entire island, and covered with enough curly black hair for him to get a lot of jokes as a small child about being a griz bear. Then the teenager learned how to break bones, and the jokes stopped. There was a jagged scar on his forearm from the explosion that had aced both of his parents and made the young man into a baron, and a tattered paperback book was tucked into a specially designed pouch on his gunbelt, with another tucked into the pocket of his fringed vest.

"How about a song, boys?" the baron shouted, fanning himself with the hat. "I know one about a bow-legged gaudy slut whose titties tasted like sugar beer!"

A ragged laugh erupted from the workers.

"That old clunker!" Lady Veronica Jones countered, resting the stock of her blaster on a well-curved hip. "How about the one about the sec man who had a very special gift in his pants for the ladies, one for every day of the week, and two for the holidays!"

There came more laughter, mostly from the women this time.

Taking that as her cue to stop drumming, the girl laid aside her sticks and began to relay a leather bag full of spring water to the workers. As per regulations, everybody took a sip to first slosh the dust out of their mouths, and then spit, before drinking.

In stark contrast to her burly husband, Lady Veronica was a stately beauty with curly black hair that reached to her trim waist. Her eyes were almond-shaped, giving her an almost catlike appearance. Nobody on the island was faster than the lady with either blaster or blade. She was a chilling machine, as beautiful as lightning and every bit as deadly.

"Your decision, my lord!" a sec man shouted with a chuckle, but then his smile disappeared as there came a dull boom from the ground and a faint vibration was felt by everybody. The loose dust on the ground danced like beans in a fry pan.

"What the frag was that?" Lady Veronica demanded, twisting her head around to try to catch the dim sound again. But the source of the noise was gone, lost amid the general clatter and cacophony of the excavation.

"I don't know, my love," the baron replied uneasily, watching in the opposite direction.

As always, his first thought was that this was some sort of a trick from Captain Carlton, but if the mutie-loving freak had discovered the location of the sulfur mine, he would have simply blown it off the face of the island. No sulfur meant no blasters, which meant that Carlton could take over everything with those triple-damn crossbows. Their range was fantastic, and the accuracy of his coldhearts was just short of frightening.

"My lord, is Cannon gonna blow?" Sec chief "Digger" O'Malley asked, nervously licking dry lips. The matlock in his hands was worn and heavily patched, but it also had several notches in the wooden handle where the man had taken off the heads of stickies with the digging implement. His arms rippled with muscles, and his barrel chest was so huge that it seemed to hint at some mutie blood in his ancestry. But the first, and only, feeb to ever ask that question had quickly become the second notch in the handle.

"By the lost gods, I hope not," the baron replied, a hand scratching his hairy chest.

Holstered under his left arm was a massive predark weapon called a Desert Eagle. It was a nuke-storm of a blaster, the .50-caliber cartridges bigger than his thumb, and the recoil was damn near impossible to control. However, the Desert Eagle was the only known weapon to ever deter a thunder king. Not chill it, of course, nobody believed that was even possible. But the colossal handblaster at least gave the excavation team a fighting chance for life outside the safety of the thick stone walls of Sealton ville.

Anxiously, the group waited, straining to hear anything else. Minutes passed, and just as they began to relax there came a second explosion from under the ground. This time louder and more powerful. But also strangely hollow, almost as if it was a reverse explosion.

"Something is happening underground," Lady Veronica growled, looking down, as if trying to see through the solid rock.

"My lady, do you…do you think that Carlton might be trying to steal our powder?" an old man asked, tugging at the bandanna tied around his neck. "You know, digging up while we be digging down?" Below the sweaty cloth was a gnarled scar that completely encircled his neck, the classic scar of the rare survivor of a Thunder King attack.

"By the coast gods, I have no damn idea," the baron growled, pulling out the Desert Eagle and dropping the clip to check the load. Then he slammed it back in and worked the slide to chamber a round for immediate use. "But I think that we damn well better find out!"

"Davis, Johnson, Coulier, McFinny!" Lady Veronica yelled. "Stay with the dust! Keller, Furstenberg, guard the littles! Svenson, Dumas, start rigging the traps around the excavation!"

"Everybody else with me!" the baron commanded, striding toward the rope ladder leading down the side of the mountain.

THE CRATER in the lava tube caused by the implo gren was enormous, extending halfway up the curved walls and almost beyond the fluttering light of the dying road flare.

"Well, there is no way we are getting across this back to the redoubt." Krysty sighed, her hair flowing around her shoulders.

"Bust up floorboards in LARC, make bridge," Jak stated simply, running stiff fingers through his snowy hair. "But not want to go across first."

"Indubitably," Doc said in somber agreement. "I am often foolhardy, but never a fool. Such an endeavor would be tantamount to suicide."

"Maybe we can walk across the bottom and simply climb up the other side using a rope," Mildred said, rummaging in her med kit. "I mean, how deep can it be?"

Pulling out a survival flashlight, she started pumping the handle to charge the battery. A redoubt in Colorado had yielded the amazing device. It was getting harder to charge the ancient battery every time she used the flashlight, and there were no more spare bulbs. But the device was still infinitely better than a candle, torch or road flare.

Clicking on the flashlight, Mildred got a strong white beam that she swept along the edge of the crater, marveling at the razor-sharp smoothness of the edge. There was no need to measure the diameter. The spherical emptiness would be exactly thirty feet wide, just large enough to completely take out a front-line tank or sink a medium-size battleship.

"Seen bigger," Jak drawled, but it was clearly just youthful bravado.

Snorting, Mildred played the light into the crater and ruefully saw that there was no bottom. The implo gren had breached the side of another lava tube. Sluggish yellow fumes flowed along the passageway, and there was a dull reddish glow coming from somewhere below. Waves of heat radiated upward, carrying along a pungent smell of sulfur, and something else, something flat and metallic.

"Molten iron," J.B. stated with a scowl.

"Which means lava," Ryan translated grimly. "We must have come awful close to triggering an eruption. Or, at least, a breakthrough."

"Come again?" Jak asked, confused. Born and raised in the swamps of Louisiana, he had never even imagined such a thing as a volcano until encountering one in the South Sea Islands.

"What would happen if you stabbed a knife into the side of a whistling teakettle?" Krysty asked, glancing sideways at the teen.

Pursing his lips in thought, Jak started to answer then paused as he got the image, and then deeply frowned. "Best leave fast," he stated.

"I agree, my dear Jak," Doc rumbled. "Our best hope is a swift departure."

"Yeah, and go where?" J.B. asked, adjusting his fedora. He wasn't a fan of tightly enclosed spaces. The darkness of the lava tube was starting to get on his nerves and he was determined not to let it show.

"We're breathing air," Ryan stated, brushing back his hair. "Which means there must be some sort of a break to the outside world. All we have to do is find it before the juice runs out."

"Which doesn't give us very long," Krysty countered quietly. "Doc and I emptied every last drop of juice into the gas tank, almost fifty gallons, and it barely even registers on the fuel gauge in the pilothouse. That means the tanks must be huge, and the only reason for that has to be—"

"It gets drek lousy mileage," Ryan finished. "Okay, we leave behind everything we can—spare tires, radio, radar, rip out the bastard floorboards! Only take the essentials. Less weight means we can go farther and faster."

"Although, I would strongly suggest that we maintain a watertight hull," Doc added. "By their very nature, most volcanoes are located near water, and it would behoove us to keep the ability to float."

"Fair enough," Ryan relented when a blistering wave of heat rose from the crater, the searing temperature driving the companions back to the cool safety of the U.S. Navy LARC.

"I think the lava may be rising," Mildred said in a strange voice, both of her hands tight on the strap of the med kit.

"Then let's move with a purpose, people!" Ryan commanded, hastily climbing back on board the LARC.

Since she was familiar with the controls, Krysty took the wheel once more and started the wag along the tube, deeply thankful that J.B. had fixed the headlights with some duct tape. Now they pointed relatively straight ahead, which made driving a massively easier job.

Joining the woman in the pilothouse, Ryan got busy ripping out the advanced electronics. There was a lot of it, some of the devices completely unknown to the man, which puzzled him for a moment, before he remembered that although the LARC had been invented for the First Nuke War, which the old-timers called World War II, the amphibian transport had still been in use up to the end of the twentieth century. Ryan guessed there were some things that simply couldn't be improved, like the revolver, hardback book, can opener, pocket comb or the common hammer. Mildred called it the fork level of engineering. You could paint a fork different colors, but it was impossible to improve on the basic design. The one exception to that rule would be a nuke, which was easily upgraded by smashing it flat with an anvil until it could no longer detonate, thus improving the bastard thing a million fragging percent.

In the rear of the lumbering transport, the rest of the companions started tossing everything they could, beginning with the empty gas canisters, a toolbox, a fire extinguisher and then closely followed by long, heavy chain that ended with an anchor.

Locating a brace of spare tires, J.B. got to work on the lug nuts. As each one came loose, he tossed it cavalierly over the side, closely followed by both tires and then the hydraulic jack.

Encountering a crack in the wall of the lava tube, Krysty slowed the wag to look for any signs of access to the surface, but Ryan urge her onward. His rad counter was registering near the danger levels, clearly indicating that the passageway had been made by a nuke explosion, possibly during skydark itself.

Finding a fire ax, Jak got busy chopping free the excess seats, and disposed of a squat electric winch. It took three of the companions to get it over the side, and the machine crashed to the ground shattering the lava and releasing a small geyser of steam. That disturbing sight made the companions redouble their efforts. Soon the LARC was stripped to the gunwale and moving noticeably faster.

In short order, the pungent reek of sulfur and hot iron was left behind, and the companions clung to the cushioned gunwales, straining to see into the darkness up ahead, hoping for a glimmer of daylight.

Reaching an intersection of several tubes, Krysty slowed the wag to a crawl, listening for any sound of the surf or perhaps the call of a gull. But there was nothing, only the powerful hum of the big diesel, echoing slightly in the rocky passageway.

"Look, there on the wall!" Ryan stated, thrusting out a hand. "Those are chisel marks!"

"Somebody was down here, probably looking for a sulfur deposit to make black powder," J.B. said in obvious relief. "Well, if they got in, then we can get out!"

"Only one way to be sure," Krysty said, shifting gears to back the LARC down the tube a little ways before angling into the side opening.

This tunnel was a lot smaller than the main lava tube, and the rubber bumpers alongside the LARC began to rub along both of the walls. In only minutes they were worn away, and now the bare metal gunwale started to scrape across the congealed lava, throwing off sprays of bright sparks. The noise canceled out any attempt at conversation. J.B. wisely moved away from the sides of the amphibian transport and threw his leather jacket over the munitions bag for some extra protection.

Rubbing a hand across the inside of the windshield, Ryan scowled into the gloom ahead, unsure if he had just seen something. Dragging out a handkerchief, he spit onto the rag and tried rubbing the glass clean, but it was simply covered with too many scratches for his crude ablutions to have any real effect.

"Spot something, lover?" Krysty asked, downshifting the gears to try to keep the wag moving. If the walls got any tighter, that would become impossible and the companions would find themselves on foot.

"Not sure," he replied, tucking away the damp rag and drawing the SIG-Sauer. Flipping the blaster, he grabbed it by the barrel and swung the handle forward. The glass shattered and fell away, offering him an unobstructed view.

"Ace the lights," Ryan ordered, holstering the weapon.

Turning off the headlights, Krysty then killed the running lights. Now a soft glow could be seen in the distance, the dim light almost too weak to spot even in the near pitch blackness.

"Trouble?" J.B. shouted from the rear.

"Tell you in a second," Ryan replied, brushing the hair away from his good eye.

Slowly the dull illumination got brighter, until another branch in the tunnel was discernable. The right passageway was a Stygian maw, impenetrable and absolute. But the left was definitely lighter, almost a cottony gray.

"Wait a moment, is that…yes, it is. I can hear surf!" Krysty said excitedly, throwing the LARC into gear once more.

"Careful of a cliff," Ryan warned, reaching out to flip on the headlights. The blue-white beams lanced forward to reveal a hanging curtain of flowery vines just a heartbeat before the LARC plowed through and into bright sunshine.

Instantly, Krysty cursed and slammed on the brakes, savagely turning the wheel as the LARC raced straight for a huge lake of mud, the thick sludge bubbling and steaming.

Banking hard, Krysty nearly tipped over the wag, but the other companions threw themselves in the opposite direction and she managed to skirt along the irregular shoreline, finally coming to a ragged stop only a few inches from a flaming river of molten red rock. The heat from the lava hit them like a physical assault, stealing the breath from their tortured lungs, and the aluminum prow of the LARC began to visibly melt.

Throwing the transmission into reverse, Krysty quickly rolled away from the lava river until reaching the relative safety of the boiling lake, and the oppressive temperature eased to a more tolerable level.

"Fireblast, that was close," Ryan muttered, patting the woman on the damp shoulder while glancing around.

The Deathlands warrior had assumed that the wag would come out of the lava tube on a cliff, possibly overlooking a sea. But the LARC was parked on a sort of plateau that jutted from the side of a tall mountain, or rather a range of mountains that stretched for miles. Several of the peaks were masked by thick clouds of fiery smoke, rivers of glowing red lava meandering down the sides. One flow had burned a path of destruction through a lush jungle, the plants withered on either side for hundreds of feet, while another thickly pumped into an ocean, the resulting nonstop explosion of lava mixing with the water creating a huge cloud of steam that blocked any further view.

Surrounding the Navy wag were countless small steam vents, hissing and bubbling like a self-heat ready to pop. Off to their left was the mud lake and straight ahead was the river of lava, the thick molten rock sluggishly flowing over a cliff to rain down into a river valley.

"Behold, the wrath of Vulcan," Doc stated, shrugging off his frock coat to fold it over an arm. "Unless we have perished in our Quixotic sojourn, and this is the demonic abode of Beelzebub!"

"Either way, it's hotter than hell," Mildred agreed, opening the front of her shirt. The heat was incredible, almost palpable, and she was already dripping sweat.

Peevishly, Doc arched an eyebrow. "That is what I just said, madam."

"Frag, how leave?" Jak demanded, slipping off his jacket. It clanked as the teen laid it on the floor.

"Over here!" J.B. shouted, pointing behind the wag.

Situated between the mud lake and the crumbling granite side of the volcano was a narrow bed of cooled lava, the rough black surface extending down the side of the mountain to another plateau alive with greenery. The abundant plant life continued onward to become a thick jungle, the trees alive with birds and tiny monkeys. In the far distance was a shimmering blue lake that looked deliciously cool and inviting.

"That'll do," Ryan stated, never happier in his life to see something that was not boiling or molten. The Great Salt was hotter than a frying pan, but this combination of heat and humidity was sapping his strength. He labored to draw in every breath, and his clothes were already soaked completely through with sweat.

"Agreed," Krysty panted, shrugging off her backpack, then dropping her bearskin coat to the floor. That helped a lot, but not enough, so the woman undid the buttons of her shirt to let it hang loose. Her sports bra was nearly transparent with sweat, her taut stomach glistening with tiny droplets, but she felt a whole lot cooler anyway.

Removing the cap, Ryan passed her the canteen and she took a long drink, then poured the rest over her head. If they made it to the lake there would be water to spare. If not, the fall would ace them, not dehydration.

"Here we go!" Krysty announced, passing back the

empty canteen. She nodded her thanks, then shifted the wag into reverse. There was nowhere near enough room to turn, so she would have to do the maneuver backward.

Inching along, the LARC eased onto the bed of cooled lava to start crawling down the jagged slope, the tires bouncing and jerking as the sharp lava spires shattered under the weight. The mil tires blew in the first few yards, but quickly sealed themselves, and Krysty continued onward. But each crushed spire now began to emit an endless snaking tendril of dull yellow smoke.

Chapter Seven

Stopping at a branching tunnel, Baron Jones scowled at the river of dark smoke flowing past. In so many ways, the heavy smoke acted like water, obediently following the tunnels and the grooves in the rock. The rush resembled a solid wall until a person looked closer and saw that it was actually speeding smoke. Deep inside there was a thin red line of lava flowing from one part of the rumbling mountain to another. Like blood in a body.

Mebbe the wrinklies were right, the baron thought, heading down the middle passageway. The Earth was alive in some sort of strange way.

Exiting the tunnel, the baron looked over the small plateau before whistling sharply. Seconds later his wife appeared from the darkness, along with a dozen of the sec men.

"Digger is taking the dust back to Sealton ville," Lady Veronica stated. "I wanted a shot at Carlton for myself."

"After me, my love," the baron returned, studying the western slope of Cesium Mountain. There were numerous steppes and plateaus in sight, most of them empty as a stickie's pockets. A few were masked completely in steam, while others... The baron blinked to clear his sight. There was some sort of machine moving along an old lava flow that connected two plateaus.

"That's a war wag!" Lady Veronica growled in open hatred. Her hair almost seemed to move at the words, but the ebony filaments merely fluttered in the humid breeze.

"That one-eyed bastard must be Carlton!" a sec man growled, raising a longblaster and working the arming bolt to chamber a round. "A pound of dust says I can put one into his good eye!"

"A splendid idea, Eccels," the baron stated, resting a hand on the barrel. "But the rest of us are too far away for our blasters to be of any use. Can you ace all six people in that wag with your five brass?"

"Three," the tall sec man sullenly admitted, lowering the weapon. "But I can get him, sire."

"We want them all, plus their wag," the lady said softly, unable to take her sight off the redhead driving the vehicle.

There was a strange tingling in her mind, very similar to the feelings Veronica used to get from her mother and sister, may Gaia greet them both to paradise. Then the redheaded woman looked up sharply and Veronica emptied her mind, thinking very hard about nothing, absolutely nothing. After a moment the redhead went back to her driving, the long wag jouncing and bouncing along the rough lava road.

Working the arming bolt on her stubby MP-5 rapid-fire, Lady Veronica allowed herself a small smile of contempt. It would seem that Carlton had found himself a witch somewhere, just not a very good one. Now she wanted the redhead aced even more than before.

"All right, we're gonna do this fast and silent," the baron said, opening the breech of his M-203 gren launcher and sliding in a 40 mm brass. Located under the fluted barrel of the M-16 rapidfire, the big gren launcher closed with a satisfying clunk. It was the only gren he had for the massive blaster, but it would be well worth the cost if he saw it blow Carlton off the mountain in a dozen small pieces.

"Hart, Billington, stay with my wife! Perriweather, Barker, head for the escarpment! Everybody else with me," the baron commanded. "Now, iron up! It's chilling time!"

As the sec men grimly rallied, the nearby Cesium Mountain gave a low and powerful rumble as if somehow anticipating the bloody slaughter to come.

THE VEHICLE CLATTERING and clanking off the irregular lava flow, Krysty gratefully parked in the middle of a smooth patch of grass growing on the small plateau.

Releasing the bent steering wheel, she then turned off the engine to save fuel and flexed her stinging hands. Fighting the ancient wag down the lava road had been like wrestling a kraken. Her whole body ached from the strain of trying to control the rattling wag. Even her temples were throbbing, almost as if somebody had tried to touch her mind with their thoughts. It had been an unnerving feeling, and her animated red hair curled and flexed unhappily.

"That was fun," Ryan said in a rare display of humor, tugging on his teeth to make sure they were still firmly attached.

Snorting in reply, Krysty dug an elbow into his ribs.

It was much cooler down here, away from the steam vents and mud lake, and the companions spent a few minutes just savoring the wonderful sensation of not sweating like a holiday pig being shown the final apple.

Ahead of the wag, or rather behind, since they were backward, was another lava flow, a lot more rough than the short stretch they had just traversed. Hardly a tempting avenue. However, off to the side was a much smoother dirt trail that led into a field of boulders, but those hid anything beyond.

"Not much choice," Jak stated gruffly, using a strip of cloth to tie back his sodden hair.

"Six apples or a dozen oranges, eh, Doc?" J.B. asked, drying the moisture off his glasses with a handkerchief.

Opening his mouth to correct the garbled expression, the old man paused and merely smiled. "Just so, my friend," he blatantly lied for the sake of camaraderie. "Just so!"

"Everybody remember to lick your arms," Mildred said, doing just that as an example. "I don't have any sodium tablets, and we have to maintain our salt level in this heat."

Leaning in close, J.B. whispered a suggestion to the woman about another possible source of sodium, and she fiercely blushed. Tactfully, everybody else turned away and pretended not to notice.

Stepping out of the tiny pilothouse, Ryan pulled out an antique Navy telescope and extended the device to its full yard length. When closed, it was about the size of a soup can, and the single lens was perfect for a one-eyed

man. Ryan had found the amazing device in an antique
store in the ruins of a nameless metropolis they called
Zero City. He had almost lost his son in that accursed
place, and suddenly Ryan felt the absence of the boy
as if he had just been standing alongside the man only
a second ago. He seldom spoke of Dean, but the boy
was often in his thoughts.

"Dean's fine, lover," Krysty said softly, recognizing
the expression. "Safe with Sharona." Reaching out a
hand, she squeezed the man's arm. It was like touching cordwood, but then the strength of the man was
incredible.

Nodding in silent reply, Ryan swept the horizon with
the Navy 'scope, and saw the ruins of a predark city to
the east and a major seaport of some kind across a bay,
the harbor jammed full of rusting Navy ships, aircraft
carriers laying on top of battleships, destroyers, subma-
rines and frigates. It was a hodgepodge of Navy vessels, now merely windblown trash gathered like autumn
leaves by the thermonuclear winds of skydark.

Spotting a vein of sulfur in the nearby rocks, Mildred jumped down from the wag to hurry over and
started scooping the dust into an empty plastic jar she
carried for just such a purpose. Sprinkled into an open
wound, sulfur helped fight infection, and mixed with
honey it made a wonderful poultice for a wide variety
of ills. Without a hospital pharmacy to draw vital supplies from, the predark physician was quickly becoming
adept at finding the basic ingredients of her trade under
rocks or scraped off machinery.

"No sign of any villes," Ryan said, collapsing the
telescope. "But a lot of ruins to the north and west."

"Mebbe chisel marks natural," Jak suggested, his voice betraying the fact that he didn't really believe the idea. "Seen gator tracks in mud damn near close to writing."

"No, my young friend, those were most definitely made by human hands," Doc countered, the gentle breeze from the jungle blowing back his long silvery hair. "Or, at least by some creature intelligent enough to use tools."

"Hunters are that smart," Mildred said, climbing back into the battered LARC. "But then, most bioweps are." Biowep, slang for biological weapons. Genetically designed, living weapons that were the bane of the Deathlands. Most redoubt droids were a century old, weak on power, malfunctioning and rusty. But the living, breathing, bioweps just bred new generations every year, each smarter and more deadly than their nightmarish progenitors.

"All right, let's see where the frag we are," J.B. said, pulling a minisextant from under his damp shirt.

But just then, there came the crack of a blaster and a window in the pilothouse shattered, spraying Krysty with glistening shards. A lock of her living hair fluttered away, severed at the roots, and the woman screamed in pain, tumbling limply to the floor. Instantly the rest of the companions turned and triggered their assorted weapons, the barrage echoing off the rocky walls of the cliff.

Two men stood in the mouth of a cave fifty feet above the plateau. They reared backward, blood spraying from riddled chests as they dropped from sight. Both had been wearing matching dark blue uniforms, vaguely resembling predark police, and the companions instantly tagged them as ville sec men.

"We're coming for you, Carlton!" somebody shouted loudly from a higher plateau.

Carlton? Looking up, Ryan looked directly into the face of a barrel-chested giant, a gold ring glistening in his left ear. Then they shot in unison. Ryan felt something hot graze his cheek, and the giant staggered, red blood appearing on his left shoulder. Fireblast, the big man was lightning quick with a handblaster! Faster than anybody Ryan had ever faced before.

Firing the Steyr again and again, Ryan stepped in front of Krysty to provide cover. He had seen this sort of wound happen before and knew that Krysty would be unable to protect herself for several minutes from the incalculable pain. Her hair was as alive as his fingers, and having them cut off would have stopped even him for a brief span. The human mind could only take so much pain before it retreated within itself for protection.

"Dastardly blackguards!" Doc bellowed, discharging both the LeMat and the Webley, the double explosions catching a short man in the face and blowing out the back of his head.

The rest of the sec men scattered for cover, then started firing back with a wide variety of black-powder weapons.

Shouting a war cry, Jak racked the cliff with a long burst from his M-16, the 5.56 mm rounds zinging off the rocks and kicking up a small storm of chips and dust. A section of the cliff broke away, and a sec man screamed as he fell all the way down to land on the cold lava flow, the hundreds of sharp spires piercing his body. Horribly alive, he twitched once, blood gushing in every direction, then mercifully went still.

Taking a position behind the gunwale, Mildred started snapping off shots from the ZKR, while J.B. rattled off a full clip from the Uzi. Another sec man went falling to his doom.

But now more sec men and women appeared, along with an Asian-looking woman with fluttering black hair. Expertly cradling an MP-5 submachine gun, she sent down a deadly halo of hot lead, the 9 mm rounds ricocheting off the hull of the LARC, smashing another window and blowing a tire.

Then the startled sec men on the cliff paused in their attack to stare as the mil tire stopped deflating and swelled back to normal size.

"Magic!" a sec man cried, turning to run away.

"No, they're fragging whitecoats!" the giant man roared, aiming the M-203. "Chill them all!"

The huge maw of the gren launcher belched black smoke and something slammed into the grass only a foot from the LARC to explode with amazing force. Shrapnel filled the air, ricocheting off the boulders and cliff. Doc gasped as he was hit in the face, blood pumping from his cheek, and Jak snorted as his hair jerked from the passage of a rock chip.

"Here!" J.B. shouted, thrusting the Uzi toward Mildred. She took the rapidfire and sent a burst skyward as the man swung around the S&W M-4000 scattergun. Which made no sense as the range was far too great for him to do anything more than merely annoy their attackers.

"Dodge this, Carlton!" the Asian woman snarled,

jerking her hands apart and then casting a small square object down the cliff.

Who the frag was Carlton? Swinging up the alley-sweeper, J.B. sent off three belching roars and the falling gren detonated high in the air, harmlessly spreading out a corona of flame and smoke.

As the snarling giant sent down a maelstrom of rounds from the stuttering M-16, another sec man stepped into view holding a glass bottle with a burning rag tied around the neck.

Switching targets, Mildred concentrated on the new danger, the 9 mm rounds shattering the glass bottle and dousing the sec man with the fiery contents of the Molotov cocktail. Covered with flames, the man just stood there, galvanized motionless and shrieking insanely.

Unexpectedly, the Asian woman shot the dying man in the head, tears appearing on her cheeks.

Using the momentary distraction, Ryan got behind the wheel of the LARC and started the engines. Without any kind of a roof, the bastard wag offered them about as much protection as a painted bull's-eye. It was time to leave. Throwing the wag into gear, Ryan started rolling for the field of boulders, zigzagging along the way to try to throw off the enemy snipers.

That only made the sec men on the cliff shoot faster, but his tactic worked and the incoming lead hammered the ground around the Navy transport, but never reached the companions crouching behind the gunwale.

"Cheap bastard should have given his troops more brass to practice shooting," J.B. snorted contemptuously, thumbing fresh cartridges into the scattergun. "Blasters are useless if you can't hit the fragging target!"

"Practice makes perfect," Mildred replied, reloading her blaster with nimble fingers.

Advancing to the extreme edge of the cliff, the giant man brandished a clenched fist at the retreating companions and loudly bellowed something in a foreign language.

That caught Doc and Mildred completely by surprise, and they openly stared at the dwindling figure until the LARC moved behind a boulder and blocked their sight.

"Madam, did you also hear that, or have I gone mad?" Doc whispered, the two blasters dropping in his hands. The words were slurred slightly, red blood still flowing from the gash in his cheek.

"Damn straight, I did," Mildred said, thumbing the safety on the Uzi and slinging it over a shoulder. "He cursed us in Latin!"

"Incredible, just incredible," Doc said, slowly standing to try to see the receding figure. There immediately came the report of a longblaster, and the man ducked back down again. A split second later, something zinged off a boulder.

"What say?" Jak asked, dropping the empty clip from the M-16 and starting to thumb in some spare rounds from his pocket.

"Revenge is a dish best served cold," Mildred said softly, an inadvertent chill running down her spine. A lot of coldhearts, cannies and slavers had shouted death threats at the companions over the years, but that simple Latin phrase made her feel incredibly uneasy. It was the sort of thing you shouted when revenge on the enemy was guaranteed.

"Indeed, madam, knowledge is power, and in these blighted days, anybody who speaks even a smidgen of Latin should be considered a most dangerous adversary," Doc said, swaying to the motion of the rattling LARC. The ground was starting to angle a little, and the Navy transport was beginning to increase in speed.

"Although his pronunciation was absolutely horrific," Doc added as an afterthought.

"And your grammar is any better?" Mildred retorted, pulling a sanitary pad from her med kit and ripping open the plastic packet to press the sterile material against the man's bloody cheek.

He winced from the contact. "My Latin is perfect!"

"Aybe-ma our-ya pig Latin," she countered, using duct tape to hold the crude bandage in place.

Unable to speak at the moment, Doc merely glared at the woman with marked disdain.

"He also called us by the name of Carlton," J.B. added. "So he must think that we're mercies, working for the man. Whoever the frag he is!"

Crashing through a dried thicket, the LARC bounded out of the field of boulders to crash into a dry riverbed. Or rather, what had once been a river. The bed was now a smooth strip of hard lava that flowed between the earthen banks like a long black highway.

"Make good time!" Jak said, pleased, then frowned. "No, get off! Lava road mebbe collapse under weight wag!"

"Working on it!" Ryan snarled in reply, frantically downshifting. The transmission seemed to have taken some damage in the brief fight, or more likely, from their bone-jarring ride down the lava field.

Following a curve in the riverbed, Ryan inhaled sharply as the ground suddenly dropped away on either side. The speeding LARC was now driving over a lava bridge, a dark river rushing underneath. The mud lake had to have overflowed its banks and dissolved the ground below the riverbed, converting the lava road into a makeshift bridge.

Maintaining an even speed, Ryan tried to do nothing that would disturb the delicate construct, then the wag hit a small dip in the lava and bounced. As it landed, Ryan heard the terrible sound of a cracking stone, and the bridge broke apart, sending the LARC straight down into the river.

However, the fall was only twenty feet or so, and the wag hit the river in a thick splash, some of the warm mud washing over the gunwales. Then the Navy transport buoyantly bobbed back up and was suddenly moving sideways down the swift currents.

"Forget this boat!" Jak laughed in relief as the LARC straightened and began to proceed along the river prow first.

Fumbling with the controls, Ryan switched the transmission from land to sea, and the mud behind the craft began to churn as the rear propeller spun into action. Their speed increased dramatically, so experimenting with some of the switches, Ryan got the transmission into reverse and the LARC began to slow to a more reasonable pace.

"This must be what the giant meant," Doc said, pressing a hand to his cheek, trying not to smile. "He thought we were in an ordinary war wag, and would sink like a rock once we reached the lava bridge… Is something wrong with the main engine?"

"Not that I can see," Ryan replied, checking the controls. Everything that worked was in the green.

Then he heard it. The sound was low at first, only a distant rumble, but it steadily increased until reaching deafening levels, and the LARC unexpectedly surged ahead, moving faster than ever.

Quickly, Ryan threw the wag into full reverse and stomped on the gas. The big Detroit diesel roared with power, and the craft slowed, but only for a few seconds. The dirty river was still accelerating, the banks beginning to flash by in a blur.

Now a churning mist was visible ahead of the craft, and they could hear the unmistakable thunder of a waterfall.

"Head for shore!" J.B. bellowed, tucking his glasses into a shirt pocket and buttoning it closed.

"The bastard current is too strong!" Ryan shouted back, the tendons standing out on his arms as he tried to force the craft toward land.

Hugging her med kit tight, Mildred started to order them to cast out the anchor, then remembered they had already tossed it away to save weight. What had saved them underground, now doomed them on the river. Even the lifejackets were gone.

A spray of muddy droplets pelted the companions with stinging force, and any attempt at conversation stopped as the sound of the waterfall became even louder, the noise filling their world.

Dashing forward, Jak lashed a rope around the

waist of the unconscious Krysty, then tied the other end around himself.

As the wag flashed into the dirty mist, Ryan couldn't see anything behind the partially melted prow. Then he felt a rush in his guts as the LARC sailed over the edge and began to fall. Releasing the useless wheel, Ryan scrambled out of the pilothouse and dived over the side, heading after Jak and Krysty. Just for a fleeting second, the plummeting man thought he saw a wide expanse of shimmering blue water very far away, then he was engulfed in chaos, noise and mud.

Chapter Eight

Erupting into a ragged cough, Krysty came awake fighting for air. She felt awful, every inch battered and bruised, as if she had been beaten by an overseer's whip.

As the cough came under control, there seemed to be something on her face, and she tried to brush it away, only to discover that it was sand. Still hacking, the woman weakly raised her head to see that she was lying upon a white sandy beach. It was night, and a full moon was bathing the world in a silvery light that made the still bodies lying nearby seem grotesque mockeries of her friends.

Struggling to get up, Krysty brushed the sand off her face, her animated hair flexing and moving to do the same. Dimly, she could recall the fight with the people on the cliff and the terrible pain of having her hair cut. Krysty shivered at the memory, then forced away the thought, concentrating on where she was at the moment.

It had been afternoon when they exited the lava tube, so clearly she had been out for a long time, and from the new location it was clear that the companions had gotten shipwrecked. Glancing around, Krysty saw the possible source. There was a huge black waterfall on the other side of the bay, the top and bottom lost in swirling clouds of mist. The fall was considerable, and the woman couldn't account for her survival until finding the knotted rope around her waist. Following it to other end, she found a sprawled Jak, the albino teen looking like he had drowned twice and then gone back to do it again.

Kneeling, she checked to make sure that he was breathing, then borrowed a knife and slashed the rope. Her longblaster was gone, but the S&W Model 640 was still in its holster, albeit with tufts of seaweed sticking out from under the flap.

Extracting the blaster, Krysty cleaned away the stringy plants, then removed the brass rounds to dry-fire the blaster a few times to make sure it was still in working condition. Satisfied, she reloaded the weapon.

Dragging Jak out of the shallows to a dry stretch of beach, Krysty started along the sandy coast, locating several of the other companions only a few yards away. The tide had to have washed them on shore like so much driftwood. Everybody was battered and bruised, J.B. with a clearly broken nose, and Mildred with her arm bent at an unnatural angle. Gingerly probing the swollen shoulder, Krysty sighed in relief that the joint was merely dislocated, and debated ramming it back into place. But on second thought, she decide to let the physician get some obviously needed sleep. Repairs could be done later. The salty breeze coming in from the sea was warm, and it felt wonderful to the woman. At least there would be no need of a fire this night.

His silvery hair shining like a mirror in the moonlight, Doc was slumped over a large mound of something that proved to be a snapping turtle, the creature thankfully aced. The animal was huge, over a yard wide, the hard shell covered with the scars of countless battles. The Webley was jammed into its mouth, the lethal jaws deeply embedded into the cushioned grip.

Lying on the beach nearby was Doc's ebony walking stick, but the sword it contained was thrust completely through the throat of the mutie turtle, the Spanish words etched into the steel blade almost visible from the smears of dried blood. The deadly LeMat was still holstered at his side, the black-powder charges staining the white sand where they had dribbled out of the blaster. Clearly, the man had been in a battle for his life with the aquatic monster and come out victorious.

"Well done, Theo." Krysty smiled, double-checking to make sure the snapping turtle was aced. The leathery hide was cold, but it was normally that temperature, so she withdrew the sword and slit open the throat of the animal, almost removing the head entirely.

Leaving Doc where he was, Krysty continued her recce of the beach, pausing at the sight of the LARC laying on its side, partially submerged just off the beach. The gentle waves were cresting onto the badly dented hull, and she thought there was something wrong with the craft, when she realized the redoubtable LARC was bent, the Navy transport resembling the boomerang of a barb. With a shrug, Krysty wrote off the craft as useless. Even if the diesel engine still worked, which was highly unlikely, there was no way they could steer it now. Unless they planned to only travel in circles.

A low groan sounded in the night and Krysty spun with her blaster out and ready. The groan came again, and she proceeded that way warily, until spotting Ryan lying in a tidal pool, his body surrounded by countless tiny fish.

"Lover?" Krysty asked, reaching out to shake the man.

At the sound of her voice, his good eye snapped open and he partially drew the panga before fully awake.

"Hey," Ryan growled, easing the knife back into the sheath. "Not…aced, I see."

"Not yet." She smiled at him, reaching out to pluck a strand of seaweed from his hair.

"Everybody else alive?" Ryan started, then frowned. Fireblast, when the frag had it become night? Adjusting his leather eyepatch, Ryan slowly stood and looked around, easily finding the muddy waterfall on the opposite side of the wide bay. If the giant man and his people hadn't found the companions yet, then he wasn't hunting for them. Then again, Ryan could barely believe it himself that the companions had survived going over the thundering falls. The bay had to be very deep, that was the only possible explanation. Mildred had once told him about crazy folks who deliberately went over Niagara Falls and somehow survived. He'd seen pics in old mags. That waterfall was ten times bigger than this one. The trick seemed to be a combination of missing the rocks, mixed with a large dose of dumb luck.

"Wag okay?" Ryan asked, patting his clothing to check on his weapons. Everything was intact, except for his backpack. That had been left behind on the LARC, and was probably at the bottom of the bay. Which meant no candles, bedroll or food.

"The LARC is done," Krysty answered, jerking a thumb over a shoulder to indicate the wreckage.

"We couldn't fix it if we had a year and two machine shops."

Accepting the loss, Ryan shrugged and rummaged in his pockets for anything edible. He found only a stick of chewing gum from an MRE pack, and broke it in two to share with the woman. However, the trickle of flavor didn't ease the hunger in his belly, and it made a loose tooth ache badly. Nuking hell, it looked like he was going to be on soft food for a couple of weeks.

"Doc aced a turtle," Krysty stated, starting that way. "The damn thing is big enough to feed us for a week."

"Have to eat it raw. Can't risk a campfire," Ryan told her, matching Krysty's stride. "The light would tell everybody for miles exactly where we are, and I don't want to tangle with those bastards from the cliff again."

Moving to where Doc rested in the warm sand, the two companions dragged the turtle into the bushes. Finding a clearing, they flipped the animal over and started the butchering. The flesh was pale, salty and thankfully very soft. It was also delicious and filled their exhausted bodies with new strength. Afterward, Ryan took the first watch, while Krysty caught a quick nap.

Watching the surface of the moonlit bay for any sign of incoming boats, the one-eyed man cleaned and oiled his blasters, then went hunting for coconuts. He'd noted the trees in the near distance. Opening the husk was easy work for the panga, and he found the sweet milk satisfied his raging thirst for fresh water. An hour later, Krysty awoke to relieve the man, and Ryan settled into the warm sand to sleep until dawn. He had no dreams.

At first sign of light on the horizon, Ryan and Krysty awoke the others and got them into the cover of the lush foliage. Breakfast was raw turtle steaks and bananas, washed down with coconut milk. The primitive food was eagerly consumed by the other companions, then the medical repairs began.

Bracing herself against a tree, Krysty held J.B. motionless while Ryan slapped the man's broken nose back into place. Tears filled his eyes from the explosion of pain, but J.B. never made a sound, only the trembling of his hands as the man lit the stub of a cigar showed how much it had hurt.

Next, they did Mildred, the physician sliding a strip of old leather between her teeth as a precaution. This time, Ryan held the woman, while Krysty took her wrist, rotated the arm slightly, then pulled with all of her strength. The joint popped back into place with an audible noise, and Mildred inhaled sharply, then slowly relaxed, panting hard.

"Well done. You're both apt pupils," she said hoarsely, warily testing the shoulder. "This didn't hurt anywhere near as much as last time in the monastery."

Relatively undamaged, Jak and Doc only had some cracked ribs, thankfully not broken. Mildred directed the wrapping of both men with layers of duct tape. That made it hard for them to draw a deep breath, but it minimized the pain and got them moving again. Then the physician stitched shut the hole in Doc's cheek with a curved upholstery needle and nylon fishing line. The man grunted every time the big needle penetrated his flesh, but his only words were those of thanks when she was finished.

"What I wouldn't give for a proper medical kit again," Mildred said, tucking the makeshift items back into her canvas bag.

"Now, the Trader used to say, make a wish in one hand and hold the other under the ass of a cow, and see which gets filled first," J.B. replied, smoothing out his fedora before returning the item to its accustomed position. In his opinion, no man could think straight with his brain exposed to the direct rays of the sun. Just wasn't natural.

"How…vivid," Mildred demurred, shocked and amused at the same time.

After finding some tree branches for Doc and Jak to use as crutches, the companions did a brief recce of the beach for anything useful that might have washed onto shore. They found a couple of MRE packs, the airtight envelopes bobbing in the waves like Mylar balloons, but that was it. Everything else was gone.

"I guess we rig a litter and drag the turtle along with us," Krysty said, warming her face in the rising sun. "The meat should still be good by tonight, and by then we'll be far enough away from the beach to risk a campfire."

"Just meat, no organs," Jak warned. "I see once. Man got aced bad."

"Probably vitamin A poisoning," Mildred guessed, chewing a lip. "I know that the Inuit in Alaska liked to remove their enemies by taking them hunting for polar bears, and then giving them the liver as a treat.

The poor bastards died right after the meal, and then the Inuit stole their belongings."

"Good for them," Ryan mumbled, tonguing the bad tooth. "If you can't outgun them, outthink them."

"You can load that into a blaster," J.B. agreed, pulling out his minisextant. After drying the optical instrument with a cloth, he carefully located the sun behind the clouds overhead, balanced the half-mirror on the horizon, then did some fast calculations. Finally he checked the predark map in his munitions bag.

"This is…San Clemente Island," J.B. announced. "We're just off the coast of the California archipelago."

"That would explain the big pile of warships you saw yesterday," Krysty said thoughtfully.

"Some kind of mil base located here?" Ryan asked hopefully. Those always had caches of weapons and food stashed away in case of emergencies. If a smart man knew where to look, crumbling ruins could yield the wealth of the predark world.

"Hell, yes!" Mildred replied. "This island used to be the training facility for the U.S. Navy SEALs!" There was a clear note of pride in her voice as one of her cousins had been a SEAL. "They were the toughest, smartest mothers in the history of the whole damn world!"

"So why name after seal?" Jak asked, clearly referring to the animal. "They easy chill."

"Different type of seal." Mildred laughed. "The letters stood for sea, air, land. The SEALs could fight anywhere, and did a lot of rescue missions under impossible conditions." Her face brightened. "They would have extensive medical supplies for field operations!"

"Which also means lots of weapons and wags," J.B.

said, fishing in a pocket for a cigar. But his fingers found only a sodden mess of crumbling leaves, unfit to smoke.

Facing the muddy waterfall on the other side of the bay, Ryan mentally retraced their journey to the grassy plateau, then turned toward the jungle. "The wrecked ships should be that way," he said, pointing to the south. "While the ruins should be to the north."

"Ruins," Jak said, clearly stating his preference. The teen had found one of the M-16 assault rifles undamaged. Unfortunately, the rest had all been smashed inside the LARC. He had ten full clips of brass for the rapidfire. That was three hundred rounds, more than most villes had for their entire troop of sec men.

Nobody disagreed.

"Okay, then, let's start walking," Ryan declared, slinging the Steyr.

Trudging into the forest, the companions saw that the ground remained mostly sand and never became honest dirt. Slowly a proper forest began to spread, first as low bushes, and then tall stately oak trees, whose branches interlocked overhead to blot out the searing noonday heat.

However, after a few hours, the exhausted people had to abandon the heavy carcass of the turtle, as the litter was slowing them way too much, especially since Doc and Jak were exempt from the work because of their damaged ribs.

Walking through the dabbled shadows, Ryan drew the SIG-Sauer and watched the branches for anything dangerous. Stickies liked to hunt in the ruins of predark cities, but flapjacks liked to drop on their prey from the branches of a tree. Between the two, Ryan would rather fight a dozen stickies than one flapjack any time. Their barbed pseudopods locked into your flesh and drained off your blood to replace it with poison. It was a triple-bad way to buy the farm.

There was a lot of wildlife on the island, with fuzzy cooneys constantly darting around in the bushes, and deer boldly walking into view to nibble at the leaves. It was as if they had never seen people before and didn't know they were dangerous.

"Fish in barrel." Jak chortled, triggering a short burst from the assault rifle. Several of the fat coneys dropped while the rest scampered out of sight.

"For lunch," Jak said, claiming the twitching bodies.

"Excellent shooting, my dear Jak," Doc said. "But I'm rather surprised that you didn't ace a deer, instead."

"Can't skin while walking," Jak explained pragmatically, producing a small knife and starting to slice off the fur.

By the time noon rolled around, the companions were more than ready to stop and cook the rabbits. Krysty seasoned the meat with some crushed pine nuts, and Mildred filled a small pot with water from a stream, boiling it thoroughly before adding a few drops of iodine. That would kill almost any bacteria in the water, and was good for the thyroid glands of the companions. Iodized salt was a thing of the past, so the physician kept a close watch on the others for the first sign of a suspiciously sore throat or low-grade fever that never got any better.

After the meal, the companions felt vastly refreshed

and continued their trek through the barrens. Strangely, there was an ever-increasing amount of wildlife in the forest, which was starting to make them nervous. A complete lack of people often meant there was some sort of a mutie around that had chilled everybody.

Crossing a field of Shasta daisies, the group paused as a bald eagle screamed defiantly from the sky, laying claim to the entire plateau. In a blur of motion, a stingwing launched upward from some laurel bushes like a leathery missile. The two predators collided in an explosion of feathers and blood. The furious battle was short, and soon the headless corpse of the stingwing tumbled from the sky, the eagle majestically winging away in triumph. The mutie had been vanquished, but found inedible by the eagle, and thus was simply abandoned. The interrupted hunt for clean meat continued unabated.

"'And thou, wretched boy, who did consort him here, shall with him hence,'" Doc said with a wry smile.

"Romeo and Juliet," Mildred replied, closing her collar against the encroaching chill. "You ever see the play?"

"Several times, madam. After all, I was once a teacher of literature," Doc replied, gesturing with the stick. "Once, my students even performed a truncated version of the play, and I was drafted to play the Jewish apothecary to a twelve-year-old Romeo who barely reached my waistcoat."

"I saw the vid in a redoubt once," Krysty said unexpectedly. "It was rather hard to follow the story, but I liked the parts about family honor. Funny, I didn't know they had blasters back in the, you know, the predark times before our predark times."

Blasters? Doc and Mildred looked at each in confusion.

"You must have seen the modern-day remake of the seventeenth-century classic." Mildred chuckled in realization. "Yeah, John Leguizamo was excellent! But then he always is…was."

"So, they didn't have blasters back then?"

"Nope, just swords and knives."

"Nothing wrong with that." Jak smiled.

"Speak for yourself," J.B. retorted, patting the stubby barrel of the Uzi.

"And what is this I see?" Doc asked in a conversational tone of voice, drawing both of his blasters and clicking back the hammers.

Everybody tensed at the actions. Off to the side of the field was a large stand of trees with thick brambles growing around the trunks. But upon closer examination, it was fake. The brambles were actually a cluster of sharpened poles thrusting into the ground. Pungi sticks, Mildred called them. The companions had used such things many times before around a temporary campsite, or while repairing a wag out in the wilds. Using pungi sticks to fill in the gaps between trees was a deuced clever idea. It would quickly make a crude wall to protect you from the predators of the night.

However, these pungi sticks looked old and weathered, as if the poles had been here for many winters. And there was a gate attached to a tree, a stout barrier of bolted planks, the outer surface studded with so many pungi sticks it was difficult to see the wooden beams underneath. Whatever else the place might be, this was definitely not a temporary structure.

"Odd configuration," Mildred said, walking closer. Then she saw a thick purple substance smeared onto the needle-sharp tip of every stick. "Don't touch those poles! They're poisoned!"

"Have to be, or else this wouldn't have lasted a week," Ryan stated, studying the treetops for any sniper platforms hidden among the branches. He easily found several, but they were empty and piled with loose leaves.

"This place is abandoned," Krysty said, looking over the bristling wall. "Nobody has been here for years."

"Mebbe," J.B. countered warily. "But I never did trust folks that liked to use poison as a defense."

"Perhaps poison is all they had," Mildred suggested, taking a scalpel from her med kit. Carefully, the woman sliced through the end of a pole, then used a handkerchief to slip it into one of her precious plastic zippered bags for later examination.

Starting to walk toward the right, Ryan pointed at J.B. and he started off the other way. A few minutes later the men returned from opposite directions.

"Four hundred ten feet around," Ryan stated. "This is no campsite, but a small ville."

"And this is the only gate," J.B. added accusingly, clearly not ready to trust anything about the place.

Dropping to a knee, Jak inspected the ground. To the rest of the companions it seemed smooth and featureless.

"Something big tried get in," the young hunter stated. "Didn't like wall. Tried bunch times, finally went away."

"How big, and how long ago?" Doc asked.

"Couple months. Size…" Jak merely shrugged. "Big as some dinos saw at museum."

"Indeed," Doc murmured, clicking off the safety on his assault rifle. The ancient beasts on display had been only ossified skeletons, but that had been more than enough to disturb the man for many days. The Holy Bible clearly spoke of monsters in the olden days, and who could say for certain those hadn't been dinosaurs of a sort? It was a most disturbing possibility.

Indeed, similar creatures stalked the Deathlands to this day. Nobody alive had ever seen a kraken completely out of the water, but the companions had personally witnessed one of the giant muties drag a four-masted sailing ship underwater with a hundred tentacles, each thicker than a telephone pole.

"Most dinosaurs were peaceful herbivores," Mildred said. "They only ate grass and leaves."

"But not all of them," Ryan countered. "Right?"

Sadly, Mildred admitted that the man was correct. The largest creatures to ever walk the planet had been carnivores, meat eaters. Just before she had gone into the cryogenic unit, the woman had heard about the discovery of the skeleton of a proto-alligator from the Jurassic period that was over sixty feet in length. That was longer than two city buses! The blasters and grens carried by the companions wouldn't even annoy such a primordial behemoth, much less chill it.

"We still have two implo grens," Krysty said, patting the pocket of her bearskin coat.

"Keep one handy, just in case," Ryan ordered. "How are we on pipe bombs?"

"More than enough to handle anything this side of a kraken," J.B. said confidently, one of the explosive charges already in his hand. "And I have a stick of TNT primed and ready to go."

"Smart move." Proceeding around the open gate, Ryan led the others inside the hidden ville. However, there was nothing to be seen, only a weedy field that stretched from the ring of trees and back again. There were no buildings, tents or structures of any kind.

"Now why would anybody put a wall around a fragging empty field?" J.B. demanded, tilting back his fedora.

"Corral?" Jak asked, frowning. "Mebbe prison?"

"Mayhap there once was a ville, but it burned down?" Doc suggested hesitantly.

Spreading out, the companions checked for any signs of fire damage or foundations. But there was only the weedy grasslands, exactly the same as outside the trees.

"Don't like this," Ryan muttered, tightening his grip on the Steyr. "Something wrong here."

"Pain," Krysty said in a soft voice, her eyes tightly closed. "I can still hear the screams of the dying."

"Ville jacked by nightcreep?" Jak asked with a scowl.

"They weren't attacked," Krysty whispered, swaying slightly. "It was something worse…much worse… so much pain…and there's blood everywhere…" With a shudder, the woman straightened. "We need to leave right now," Krysty said in a tight voice.

Studying the woman for a moment, Ryan nodded in

agreement. "Okay, let's roll. The main things we want are food and brass, and there is none of that here."

"I concur wholeheartedly," Doc said, then abruptly went silent.

Wondering what made the man stop talking, Ryan glanced sideways and was surprised that he couldn't see Doc anywhere. Turning, Ryan felt his combat instincts rise at the startling realization that Doc was gone, as if he had vanished into thin air.

Get FREE BOOKS and a FREE GIFT when you play the...

LAS VEGAS GAME

Just scratch off the gold box with a coin. Then check below to see the gifts you get!

YES! I have scratched off the gold box. Please send me my **2 FREE BOOKS** and **gift for which I qualify.** I understand that I am under no obligation to purchase any books as explained on the back of this card.

▼ DETACH AND MAIL CARD TODAY! ▼

366 ADL E4CE   **166 ADL E4CE**

FIRST NAME

LAST NAME

ADDRESS

APT.#   CITY

STATE/PROV.   ZIP/POSTAL CODE

7	7	7	Worth TWO FREE BOOKS plus a BONUS Mystery Gift!
🍒	🍒	🍒	Worth TWO FREE BOOKS!
🔔	🔔	☘	TRY AGAIN!

Offer limited to one per household and not valid to current subscribers of Gold Eagle® books. All orders subject to approval. Please allow 4 to 6 weeks for delivery.

The Reader Service — Here's how it works:

Chapter Nine

Quickly, Ryan scanned the trees for any suspicious movements, nets or a lasso being hauled out of view. But there was nothing in sight. Fireblast! Inhaling deeply, the man cut loose with an ear-splitting whistle that would have stopped traffic in ancient Manhattan. But there was no reaction or response. Just silence.

"Theophilus! Theo!" Krysty shouted, her hair tightening in response to her agitated state of mind.

"All right, nothing grabbed him from above, or we would have seen it flying," Mildred snarled, jerking her head in a different direction. "Which means he's underground. Maybe there was a sink hole…"

"Bullshit, gotta be trap," Jak retorted, prodding the weeds with his crutch in one hand, the Colt Python in the other.

"Stay in pairs!" Ryan barked. "We could be facing a drinker!"

The memory of the deadly subterranean mutie made the other companions grimly alert, and fingers tightened on the triggers of their blasters.

Trying to recall where he had last seen the silver-haired man, Ryan strode through the knee-high weeds looking for anything out of the ordinary. If at all possible, Doc would have left behind some trace to warn the others. Even if that was only a… As the ground shifted under his boot, Ryan tried to throw himself backward, but it was too late. He dropped down into inky blackness, barely managing to fire his longblaster into the sky before crashing into a writhing nest of insects.

A split second later, a net swung down from the darkness and pressed him flat against the crunching bugs. Red fury filled the one-eyed man, and he tried to reach the panga, but his arms were held immobile. Changing tactics, he fired the Steyr, the brief muzzle-flash clearly showing the net. It was made of knotted ropes stretched across a wooden frame, crude, but highly effective.

Pressing the barrel of the Steyr to a corner of the frame, Ryan trigger the longblaster again, and the wood exploded into splinters, easing the pressure on his arms. Releasing the Steyr, Ryan forced his arm forward in jerks to finally reach the panga sheathed at his side.

Braced for the onslaught of the crackling bugs, Ryan wiggled his hand around, sawing at the ropes holding him prisoner, then he suddenly understood he wasn't lying on a bed of bugs, but just some dry hay. The noise it made when he moved was remarkably similar to that of the army ants from Chicago. The fact that he wasn't about to be eaten alive eased his mind somewhat, but the hard reality of the net made Ryan keep cutting at the bonds until one of them parted. Jerking his arm free, Ryan hacked at the other ropes, the stiff material parting easily under the razor-sharp steel.

Fighting his way loose, the one-eyed man sheathed the blade and reclaimed the Steyr, working the bolt to chamber a fresh round. Wherever he was located inside the ground, it was pitch black, without any bastard sign of the bright sunshine only a few yards away. Straining to hear any movements in the dark, Ryan flicked his butane lighter alive. The tiny flame filled the room with a flickering nimbus of illumination, and he scowled at the heavy shackles and chains that hung off the stone-block walls. There was a door, thick and banded with iron straps, but it was wide open, showing only more darkness beyond. This was a prison of some sort. But one that wanted to capture outlanders alive? That was when cold adrenaline flooded the man at the sight of the bones on the floor. They had clearly been gnawed upon, and not by animals.

"Cannies!" Ryan snarled hatefully.

Just then, the ceiling exploded and Ryan stepped to the side to avoid being hit by the broken pieces of wood and other falling debris. A rectangle of sunlight streamed down from above, then a gloved hand holding a mirror peeked over the edge, closely followed by the taut face of J.B., his other hand clenching the Uzi.

"Hey, Adam!" J.B. shouted suspiciously, looking around in frank disgust. Even from his angle he could see the chains on the walls and guessed their purpose.

"The name's Cain!" Ryan replied, using the alphabet code to signal the area was clear.

"Glad to hear it," J.B. said, easing his grip on the machine pistol. "You hurt any?"

"Just bruised," Ryan shouted back, brushing some hay out of his hair. "We got enough rope to haul my ass out of here?"

"Not a chance, lover," Krysty said, coming into view. "You'll have to find the exit."

"Yeah, thought so."

"Any sign of Doc?"

"No, but he can't be too far away," Ryan said. "He must have fallen down another of these mantraps."

"Thankfully, they wanted folks alive!"

"This one did, at least!"

That raised a nasty possibility while Doc hadn't been heard from yet, and the man and the woman frowned.

"Make some room!" J.B. yelled, removing his glasses. "I'm coming down to join you. Two blasters are better than one."

"Aim for the middle," Ryan advised, stepping out of the light.

Easing himself over the edge, J.B. lowered his legs as far as possible before letting go. The drop wasn't very far, and he hit the pile of hay in a crouch. Instantly there came an audible click as some mechanism under the cushioning material was triggered by the impact. The wooden frame jerked up, only to slam back down again, knocking J.B. sprawling.

"Fragging cannies," the man snarled, kicking the damaged netting aside to stand. "Dark night, this reminds me of Castle Rock in West Ginnia."

"Just a lot less screaming," Ryan agreed, spotting a torch set into the wall.

It was just a bundle of green reeds soaked in tar, but there was still some residue left in evidence. Using the butane lighter, Ryan got it going, and the room was filled with the bright torchlight that showed every detail. There were a lot more bones than Ryan had originally assumed, and over in the corner were a pair of withered corpses still chained in a stone-block corner. From the clothing, they seemed to be a man and a woman, but it was impossible to say for sure anymore. Any significant features had shriveled and become indistinguishable over time. Oddly, both of the prisoners had large sections of their arms, or legs missing. Thick leather dangled from their desiccated forms to show where tourniquets had once been tightly lashed around their limbs.

"Son of a bitch, not just a trap. This was also their larder," J.B. said curling a lip. "They kept the poor bastards alive and cut off chunks!"

"That explains those feelings Krysty had about all the blood and screaming," Ryan commented, glancing at the woman in the ceiling.

"Here I come," she shouted, just as there came the muffled bang of an explosion and some dust rained from above.

"Hold it a sec," Krysty said, and wiggled back onto the grassy field. She returned in less than a minute. "Okay, Jak found the entrance! Head to your left and we'll meet you there in ten!"

"Make it five!" J.B. shouted, turning away from the bodies chained to the wall. An overactive imagination was a bad thing for anybody who worked with high explosives. Remaining calm and cool was the key to staying alive and in one piece. But even he could feel the bad vibes of this hellhole. Suddenly the Armorer longed for the honest filth of the slaughterhouse back in Hobart.

It took a few tries, but Ryan got another torch working. He and J.B. left the cell and started down a long corridor. These walls were made of logs fastened together with some kind of glue, yet the floor was made of slabs of concrete from predark sidewalks, which meant that some ruins had to be fairly close, as these things were particularly difficult to transport without breaking into pieces.

"The cannies really put a lot of effort into this," J.B. noted, impressed in spite of his feelings.

"This was their home," Ryan said simply, as if that explained the matter. "Nothing lives in their own drek but stickies."

Blasters in hand, the two companions passed several rooms along the way, but they proved to merely be sleeping quarters and such. No sign of Doc anywhere. Encountering some more torches set into the walls, the men ignited each in turn, leaving the corridor behind them brightly illuminated, the ceiling alive with thick smoke.

Reaching an intersection, Ryan held both torches while J.B. got on his hands and knees to check for traps. Sure enough, the man found another pressure plate, a board with a nail drive-through positioned on top of a live brass set into a rusty coffee can. Inside was a good five pounds of black powder, enough to collapse this entire section of the corridor.

After disarming the trigger mechanism, J.B. took the can of powder for Doc to use in his LeMat.

There came the sound of boots on concrete, and Ryan whistled like a nightingale. There came back the song of a meadowlark, and Krysty stepped into sight, followed by Mildred and Jak.

"No sign of him yet?" Mildred asked anxiously. She enjoyed arguing with Doc, but it also helped to keep his damaged mind sharp and alert. What a mat-trans jump did to a person's stomach, apparently time travel did to their mind. First and foremost, Mildred was a physician and always concerned about what was best for a patient, even if that included busting their ass on a regular basis.

"Nor anybody else," Ryan stated. "This place is deserted. The cannies are long gone."

"Wonder why?" Jak asked, hobbling forward, inspecting the support ceiling and log walls. "No signs fight. Seems okay."

"Indeed, it is, my dear Jak," Doc whispered, stepping out of a black doorway, an arm clutching his side. "This is virtually the Gibraltar of hellholes."

"Sit down, you fool!" Mildred admonished, rushing to the man. Cupping his face with both hands, she thumbed open his eyelids to check for internal bleeding, then felt along the base of his skull for any trace of posterior swelling.

"Any dizziness?" Mildred demanded, listening to him breathe.

"Not since I last ate your cooking," Doc replied, trying to pull away. "Unhand me, madam! My mettle is in fine fettle!"

"Said what, did who?" J.B. asked with a grin.

"The old coot is fine," Mildred declared, then leaned in to peck him on the undamaged cheek. "Never do that again, you hear me, Doc?"

"Absolutely, I shall endeavor to do my best to comply," Doc intoned, giving a stiff bow. "From the hay attached to your clothing, my dear Ryan, I see that you, too, received an impromptive surprise from the absent landlords of this charming little charnel house."

"Damn near broke my back," Ryan said, rubbing the seat of his pants.

The tall man smiled. "Quite so. I only escaped from that accursed slide by using my sword as a brake. The blade bent in a most alarming manner, but the steel held true, and it allowed me to roll out before descending into a pit full of spikes." He frowned. "There were quite a few others down there, thankfully deceased."

"A slide, eh?" Ryan asked, then told about the hay and rope net. "Seems they wanted some folks alive, but others aced."

"Food and fun," Jak replied simply. The plain statement was said so casually that it startled the rest of the companions. Although only in his teens, Jak was a widower and combat veteran who knew more about the brutal realities of life than many people twice his age.

"Encounter anybody alive?" Krysty asked, passing over a canteen.

Taking a drink before answering, Doc wiped the excess coconut milk off his mouth with a handkerchief. "Only ghosts, dear lady." He sighed, returning the container. "The few cannies I found had shuffled off this mortal coil a very long time ago, and at their own hands, I might add."

"Fight each other. Run out food?" Jak said as a question.

"Not quite," Doc answered, taking a torch off the wall and stepping back into the room. "But come see for yourself."

Trailing after the man, the companions proceeded along a narrow passageway, the walls coming alarmingly close together. Ryan soon recognized it as a shatter zone, a killing box where invaders could be easily disposed of with a minimum of fuss. Not for the first time, the Deathlands had to accept the hard truth that nuke-ass crazy didn't also mean stupe. The underground ville was very well built, and if the cannies had still been alive, getting out of here would have been a nightmare fight for the companions, in spite of their superior firepower.

The narrow passage ended in a circular room composed entirely of doors, each adorned with an amazingly detailed painting of a different flower. As Doc went toward a door to the right bearing a rose, Jak sniffed the air and took a step to the left toward a door decorated with a yellow daisy.

"Stop there, lad!" Doc shouted, holding up a restraining hand. "The daisy seems to mean death to the cannies. That door leads to their…well, kitchen, for want of a better word."

Scowling, Jak relented and followed the old man through the rose door. However, as Mildred passed the daisy, she had to take a quick peek inside. As her sight adjusted to the gloom, Mildred gasped and slammed the door shut. Sweet Jesus, the physician hadn't seen anything like that in her dissection classes in medical school!

Quickly rejoining the others, Mildred saw that the walls along this corridor were heavily pockmarked with bulletholes, and there were constant signs of explosions. Soon, the torchlight exposed the tattered remains of the cannies, their teeth filed to sharp points, and every inch of skin covered with tattoos of wild plants. Instantly, Mildred understood it was camouflage for hunting people in the forest. Ghastly.

Opening a door marked with sunflowers, the companions entered a cramped room, the stone-block wall only a yard wide.

"Here is where I escaped," Doc said, lifting the torch high.

Coming down from the ceiling, a wooden trough cut through the room at a very steep angle. Studying the slide, Ryan saw the inside was well greased to facilitate the passage of a prisoner. Taking a stone from the ground, he dropped it inside and watch the rock tumble away, rapidly building speed and disappearing into the blackness to the right. The echoing noise faded to end with a clatter of metal grinding against metal.

"It's a fragging garbage disposal!" J.B. muttered, the firelight reflecting off his glasses.

"The term is oubliette," Doc said, feeling pretty sure that he had just mangled the medieval word. "It was created by the English as a way of disposing of their enemies as cruelly as possible."

"Not cannie invent?" Jak asked with a scowl.

"Sadly, no," Doc said. "This one came from our own ancestors."

"Why did you want to show us this?" Krysty asked, her shoulders hunched as if warding off a blow. Her hair was tightly coiled and barely moving.

Exiting the tiny room, Doc said, "Because, dear lady, while I was searching for an exit back to the surface, I discovered something far more interesting. Come now, only a little bit farther!"

Down the corridor was a guard station, the cannies behind the sandbag nest bristling with arrows. One stout woman had an iron baling hook buried in her skull. Past that was a large room filled with tables and benches. The companions paused at the sight of more bodies scattered around the dining hall, dozens of them mutilated forms of men, women and children.

Most of the cannies had slit throats, or a knife in their back, and from their expressions they had clearly been caught by surprise. Most of the men had been aced by blasters, and axes had been used on the majority of the children, including the babes in their cribs. Several of the cannies had wrapped ropes around their throats and twisted the ends until closing off their own throats. Another appeared to have impaled himself on a spear. A skinny woman sat cross-legged on the floor, her hands still wrapped around the grip of a homemade scattergun, her head gone, and the nearby wall stained with a dark and lumpy residue.

"Happen last moon, mebbe six weeks," Jak said, looking at the dried brains.

"Can't say that I have much of a prob with cannies acing each other," Ryan stated gruffly, kicking a flint-lock blaster from the stiff fingers of a burly cannie, his lips forever drawn back into a rictus of pain. "Wouldn't mind knowing why, though."

"They're cannies," J.B. growled. "That's good enough of an explanation for me."

"No, John, the real reason is over here," Mildred

declared, going to the large table in the middle of the room.

Heavily decorated with more paintings of flowers, the table had a small hole in the middle, the edges tinged with dried blood. Looking underneath, the companions saw a small iron cage located under the hole.

"I've seen this before," Ryan said, his voice coming from the other side of hell. "These weren't cannies, but screamers."

"Dark night, we haven't run into any of those since that winter in the Dakotas with Trader," J.B. snarled.

"What are screamers?" Krysty asked, not sure if she wanted to hear the answer.

"Most cannies only eat the flesh of their victims," Ryan explained. "But for some damn reason, who the fuck knows why, other cannies prefer to eat the brains of their victims." He paused to scowl. "Their living brains."

Suddenly, Krysty understood what the hole in the table was for, and tried not to be sick. Mother Gaia, she thought. Could this be possible?

Mildred shuddered in revulsion. She'd had her own experience with cannies and eating brains.

"Eat alive?" Jak asked softly.

"See that hole?" Ryan said, pointing. "They'd chain the poor bastard in place, then close the hole around their victim's neck to keep him, or her, still. That way only the head would be above the table. Then they sawed off the top of the skull and scooped out the brains."

"Eat brains makes go mad?" Jak demanded.

"Possibly," Mildred said. "Could be a variation of the oozies."

"I heard that brain eaters go permanently insane," Ryan said. "And die screaming with laughter. And they never stopped laughing, even after our cannons blew them in two," Ryan growled in open revulsion. "The Trader hunted down a band of these things once. Chilled them all, then burned down their ville and sowed salt into the dirt."

"We didn't want anybody eating something from a plant grown near the place," J.B. explained, curling a lip. "The Trader was afraid it might spread the madness, and cause more people to become nuking screamers."

"People? These were not humans, but abominations!" Doc shouted. "Foul things, monsters from the very bowels of the abyss!"

"Was this the important find, Doc?" Ryan asked, sounding annoyed. The one-eyed man had nothing against exploring, and Mildred had taught him the wisdom of learning new things. Sometimes knowledge was power, although it never hurt to have a loaded blaster at your side. However, these were an old enemy, and screamers had nothing to teach the companions except a new way to get chilled.

"Oh no, that is down this last corridor," Doc said, striding across the dining hall to pull back a curtain.

Yet another tunnel was revealed, this one made entirely from wooden planks. More bodies littered the floor, but these corpses were all facing down the tunnel, not randomly, and there was a sandbag wall sealing off the tunnel, more dead cannies lying across the top.

Warily, the companions entered the tunnel. Somewhere along the way, the bloody slaughter had turned into a civil war, with two different sides fighting to the end. The last handful of cannies establishing a shatter zone to stop the remaining screamers from ever proceeding any farther in this direction.

"What find?" Jak asked eagerly. "Cannie arsenal?"

"Much better than that," Doc announced proudly, a smile crossing his face. "I found our salvation!"

Impatiently, Ryan began to demand a proper answer from the old man when a dirt-encrusted form rose from the pile of rotting corpses. It was a naked woman, her mouth and pointed teeth smeared with something sticky, the scalp of the cannie at her feet peeled back to show a large hole in the gleaming white skull.

Even as the startled companions reacted to the unexpected appearance, the screamer swung around an AK-47 assault rifle from behind her back and began to insanely giggle as she cut loose with a yammering stream of high-velocity death.

Chapter Ten

In tight unison, the companions opened fire on the thing, the barrage of bullets tearing her apart, making her sagging breasts flap around obscenely.

Still chuckling, the screamer eased to the floor to lie in a spreading pool of her own blood. Not trusting the bitch, Ryan walked closer and put another round in the back of her head. The body jerked and went still.

"Screamer," Jak snarled, putting a wealth of hatred into the single word.

As if that was their cue, more of the supposedly dead bodies began to rise around the dining room, softly giggling. In horror the companions could see that the screamer had gutted the other cannies, and were actually wearing their skin as a sort of camouflage! Caked with filth, insane faces peered out from the folds of rotting human hides, the front laced closed like a bodice. The sight even gave Ryan pause for a moment. In all of his travels, the one-eyed man had never encountered this bizarre tactic before. It was beyond wild, or crazy; it was genuinely insane.

In a crash, the dining table was flipped over to block the companions from reaching the wooden tunnel, then the screamers charged, laughing happily as they brandished knives, sharpened pieces of bones, or holding blasters by the barrel to wave them like hammers.

Pressing their backs to the wall, the companions met the first rush with concentrated blasterfire, the rapid-fires cutting a crimson path of destruction through the naked lunatics. The giggling screamers were torn apart by the thundering volley. But then the second wave arrived, clambering over the first even as they fell, and the fight went hand to hand.

Shooting a screamer in the throat with the last round in his longblaster, Ryan then swung the stock of the Steyr to cave in the head of another, eyes and teeth flying away. Two more fell before the makeshift club, then clawed hands raked across his clothing and face, ripping off the eyepatch and leaving behind bloody furrows.

Dropping low, J.B. emptied the Uzi into the rush of unwashed bodies, going for their knees. As the bones exploded from the arrival of the copper-jacketed 9 mm rounds, the screamers fell back, most losing their weapons. However, none had stopped laughing, and now the crippled monstrosities began to crawl forward, their slack mouths still chuckling from within the leathery masks of their last victims.

Thrusting the barrel of his Colt Python into a throat, Jak crushed the windpipe of a screamer and it abruptly stopped laughing, no longer able to draw any air into its lungs. The teen beat back two more, then holstered the blaster and jerked his hands, knives coming out of his sleeves to fall into waiting palms. Shouting a war whoop, Jak began slashing at the screamers, slicing open throats and bellies. Unfortunately, the skins they wore had been tanned into a form of crude armor, and several times his blades failed to make a chill. Crazy, but not stupe, Jak realized suddenly, adrenaline flooding his body like a graveyard wind.

As her M-16 cycled empty, Krysty threw it away as a distraction. But the screamers paid no attention to the rapidfire, the males instead focusing their attention on the living, breathing woman, their intentions abundantly clear. Several of them were already fully erect. Snarling in disgust, Krysty drew her hammerless S&W revolver, and shot the five nearest screamers directly in the mouth, the backs of their heads exploding in a horrid spray of bones, brains and blood. But as the dead fell, other screamers replaced them, eager hands grabbing her clothing to drag the struggling woman closer.

With both of his blasters empty, Doc used the selector switch on the oddball LeMat to quickly change from the miniballs to the single-shot, 12-gauge barrel. Taking aim, he triggered the minishotgun into the mob of creatures, trying for the woman. In a deafening roar, the black-powder charge sent a hellstorm of double-aught buckshot into the screamers, tearing away two of their arms and sending the rest flailing backward.

Regaining her balance, Krysty thanked the man with a brief nod, then drew a knife and started jabbing into the throng, already preparing to ask Gaia to come to her aid.

Flipping over the massive handblaster, Doc now laid into the screamers, ruthlessly pistol-whipping the monsters, his normally genial expression slowly changing into a feral mask of unbridled fury. For a moment the schoolteacher was startled at his own savagery, then he willingly embraced the visceral urge to slay those attacking his companions, and kill, kill, and kill again, until the ornate curved handle of the cavalry LeMat was dripping with gore.

Holstering the empty ZKR blaster, Mildred drew a knife and slashed away at the encrusted fingers reaching for her from the throng. As they retreated for a moment, she cut away the nylon strap holding the S&W M-4000 across J.B.'s back. As the weapon fell, she made the catch and kicked a screamer between the legs as she worked the pump-action to chamber a 12-gauge cartridge. However, the male screamer didn't fall, or even stumble from the terrible blow, and grabbed her pants in both hands in an effort to throw the woman to the floor.

Raw fear filled her belly for only a moment, then the physician snarled and discharged the scattergun directly into the face of the chuckling lunatic. His head exploded, the chunks and buckshot pelting the screamers behind, and sending several more into the great blackness.

Yanking back her boot from the decapitated corpse, Mildred put three more bone-shredding rounds into the giggling mob, clearing away the nearest screamers and giving the companions a chance to hastily reload. Only Doc was the exception, the powerful LeMat taking an inordinate amount of time to recharge the chambers, and he didn't have a speed loader for the Webley. With no choice, the man drew the slim sword from within his ebony stick. Slashing the steel around, Doc deftly removed ears, fingers, or hacked off genitalia, to keep the ravenous horde at bay for a few precious moments more.

However, the screamers now lifted their fallen comrades and held them in front as shields to advance once more, their humorless laughter sounding like a chorus of demons from hell.

Switching to the SIG-Sauer, Ryan laid down a fast barrage of 9 mm Parabellum rounds into the exposed hands and feet of the screamers. Several of them dropped the human shields, and he executed the things with a single round to the heart. The screamers reacted as if hit with an anvil, then crumpled to the floor, the giggles changing to sighs.

In a fast series of clicks and clacks, the rest of the companions finished reloading their blasters and unleashed a withering hail of hot lead, driving the screamers backward to stumble over the bodies of the fallen, then join them in the sweet silence of death.

"That all?" Jak demanded, cracking open the cylinder of the Colt again to dump out the hot brass and thumb in replacement.

"Let's make sure," Ryan growled, walking among the twitching bodies. Keeping the SIG-Sauer ready, the one-eyed man used the panga to slit open every throat, no matter the condition of the corpse. His precautions paid off as a skinless screamer jerked at the touch of the blade and reached out for the man, even as his mouth filled with blood. Half expecting some sort of ruse, Ryan fired twice into the cannie, ending the matter forever.

"All right, check them for any brass," Ryan directed, keeping the SIG-Sauer moving among the bleeding piles of putrefied bodies.

Swiftly, the unsavory task was completed with a minimum of fuss, the yield only a handful of loose rounds and a gren that proved to be empty of any explosives.

"Triple-stupe feebs," J.B. growled, slapping a fresh clip into the Uzi and working the arming bolt. "Why would they stage an ambush here instead of the entrance?"

"Because of what is at the end of the tunnel," Doc said, breaking open the top of the Webley to start reloading. The .44 LeMat was his preferred weapon, but that would have to wait until he had more time. "I found the pride of their ville. Indeed, it is the prize of the ville! A boat, or rather, a fishing trawler in fine shape and more than ready to take us back to the mainland right now."

"Let's see," Ryan said, holstering his blaster to retrieve the Steyr.

As the other companions dragged aside the feasting table, Ryan worked the bolt on his longblaster to open the breech and extract the empty rotary clip and thumb in a fresh one. The clear plastic was getting badly scratched over the long years, and he knew the clips were nearing the end of their service. They were fine for the moment. But he made a mental note to watch for any weapons that used similar clips for him to loot.

"Need brass?" Jak asked, proffering a couple of magazines to Krysty.

"Thanks, I was down to my last," she replied, accepting the spare ammunition magazines. "What kind is it, anyway?"

"Mix, hardball and tumblers."

"Excellent."

When everybody was ready, Ryan took the point and

started along the wooden tunnel, with Doc, Krysty, Jak and Mildred in the middle, and J.B. covering the rear with his Uzi.

Reaching the sandbag nest, Ryan kept guard while Jak slit the throats of the chilled cannies, just to make sure, then rifled their gunbelts. Unfortunately they all carried hatchets or homemade zip guns, the .22 cartridges streaked with rust and less reliable than the promise of a baron.

Just then, some loose dirt sprinkled down from the ceiling, and Ryan instantly fired the Steyr, the 7.62 mm rounds exploding a small furry animal into assorted bits and pieces.

"And what, pray tell, is that?" Doc asked, lowering the Webley. "Some form of mutant rat?"

"Just a common vole," Mildred identified. "It must have been attracted by all of the blood."

"Mole?" Jak asked with a scowl.

"In the same family," she explained. "Just meaner. A whole lot meaner."

"Meaner than screamer?" the teen asked with a grin.

"Brother, if Daniel Webster ever encountered those assholes, he would have to change the dictionary," she stated with heartfelt conviction. Jak merely shrugged.

Continuing onward, the companions could suddenly smell the salty breeze of the ocean long before they heard the sound of waves breaking upon the shore. A warm breeze carried away the stink of battle and cleared their minds like a healing potion.

"Wonderful! If anybody ever doubted that we come from the sea, all they have to do is smell the ocean,"

Mildred said, loosening her collar slightly to let in the fresh air.

"Or mayhap the Garden of Eden was near the shore, and God used muddy sand to form them, both he and she," Doc countered with a slightly garbled quote.

"Crazy old coot," she shot back, trying not to smile. Sometimes the man said the damnedest things.

Continuing deeper into the tunnel, the companions encountered nothing further until reaching a second sandbag nest that closed off the end of the tunnel. Bright daylight streamed in past the bodies lying still on the cloth bags, and the air was thick with buzzing flies.

This time, J.B. kept guard while Krysty did the honors. But there was little need, as these bodies were in an advanced state of decomposition. They had to have been the first folks chilled in the fight between the cannies and the screamers.

Located at the mouth of the tunnel was a concrete dockyard, the chains and cleats forged of predark steel. There was more than enough space at the dock for a dozen boats. But it was empty, without even a fishing pole dangling in the water.

Vast and empty, the deep azure Cific Ocean stretched in front of the companions all the way to the horizon. There were no other islands in sight to break the perfect monotony of the gentle rolling waves. A few miles offshore, a humpback whale erupted into view, closely followed by a dozen more of the behemoths. Rising incredibly high, the whales soared skyward as if planning on taking flight, but then they rolled over and came crashing down to throw out stupendous waves as they frolicked in innocent play before disappearing below

the surface again, leaving no trace that they had ever
breached the sublime serenity of the oceanic view.

"So, where boat?" Jak asked in a whisper.

Wordlessly, Doc jerked a thumb to the right.

An old Quonset hut stood to that side of the dock, the
curved roof festooned with green moss and white bird
droppings. The arched front was wide open, the waves
lapping onto a concrete ramp that lead inside. Masked
by the shadows inside the structure was some sort of a
boat, condition unknown. However, this was a predark
dry dock of some sort, or maybe even a repair facility,
that the cannies had found and taken over. That was
very promising.

There were clusters of halogen lights set into the side
of the hut, and a fire hose was neatly coiled behind a
glass door, ready for instant use. Nearby was a set of
fuel pumps that seagulls had been using as a toilet for
the past century, and also a full cord of split wood, the
quarters dried, seasoned and ready to burn.

Suspecting the truth of the matter, Ryan scowled at
the disappointing sight.

"Might be there for the kitchen," J.B. suggested
hopefully.

"Mebbe," Ryan answered without much conviction.

Staying low, the companions listened for any movement aboard the sturdy little craft, but there was only
the sound of the waves and the gulls, the music of the
sea.

Assuming combat formation, Ryan took the lead
once more and the companions swept into the hut
ready for battle. However, the repair shop proved to

be completely deserted and fully stocked—with useless items. The workbenches were piled high with tools of every possible description, and condition, including corkscrews, soldering guns and bathroom plungers. Clearly the cannies had simply been stockpiling anything and everything they could find in the crude repair shop.

"Dark night, this stuff is useless." J.B. declared, briefly inspecting some of the items. Lifting a Stilson wrench, he wasn't overly surprised when the head simply fell off to land on the worktable and explode into corroded bits.

"The salt air has eaten through everything," Krysty said, her hair moving against the breeze. "The damn fools didn't know to protect the metal from corrosion."

"And they had the right stuff, too," Ryan said, lifting an unopened jar of petroleum jelly. Removing the cap, he saw that the pink gelatin was in perfect condition. Just a dab smeared on anything made of metal, and rust would have been held off for years.

"No way these are the descendants of the original sailors assigned to this dock," Mildred said bluntly. "Even a green recruit would know better than to let steel tools rust in the salty air."

"Then we can have little hope for the condition of the boat," Doc rumbled, his shoulders sagging.

Sitting in the wooden cradle of the dry dock was a civilian cabin cruiser, the fiberglass hull unblemished from the passage of the years. However, there had plainly been extensive modifications. Car tires hung along the gunwale as protection from the cradle, there was now a black-powder cannon set on the foredeck, thick slabs of wood had been bolted to the exterior of the wheelhouse as crude armor and a fat smokestack rose directly from the rear deck. Painted across the bow in flowery script was the name *Moon Runner*.

"Dark night, what a tumbledown tub," J.B. said with a sigh. "At least, it still floats. Kinda."

"The engines are what matter," Ryan countered, rubbing one of the scratches on his cheek. With a start, the man realized that his eyepatch was missing, and fumbled in his pockets to find a handkerchief. Quickly, Ryan tied it across his face as a temporary replacement until he could make a new one.

The rest of the companions waited until the man was finished, then proceeded to board the craft.

The cabin cruiser was a little cramped for six people, so everybody waited on the deck while Ryan and J.B. warily entered the wheelhouse and then took the companionway that had to lead to the engine room. A few minutes later the men returned, not looking happy.

"The engine is gone?" Krysty guessed, thumbing the hump of her hammerless revolver.

"Worse. It's been replaced with a steam engine," Ryan stated. "On top of which, the screamers have been playing with the engine."

"Playing?" Jak asked.

"A lot of pipes are joined together in random patterns, nonsensical stuff, and some of the machinery is gone," J.B. added, resting the Uzi on a shoulder. "We found a safety valve that had been carefully removed, polished brightly, then beaten flat with a hammer and hung as a decoration."

"And I will assume the valve is critical?" Doc rumbled.

"We wouldn't get more than a half mile offshore before this thing exploded without it," Ryan stated, resting a boot on a coil of rope. "Replacing the part is easy. J.B. and I had lot of work on steam trucks used by the Trader in the past, but first…"

"We need a replacement part," Mildred finished with a frown, then her face brightened. "Think we might find one in the ruins of the SEAL base?"

"If they took showers, or there was a big kitchen, there was a water heater, and those always have safety valves," J.B. said. "Worst comes about, we can check the wreckage of an aircraft carrier."

"Because they used steam catapults to throw the jets overboard," Krysty said, getting the idea.

"Into the sky," J.B. corrected. "But yeah, and the carrier would carry dozens of spare parts. Most of them would still be in storage, safely packed in jelly."

"If find drek," Jak added. "What better place look boat than Navy yard?"

"True," Krysty agreed. "Gaia knows, we aren't going to swim a hundred miles to reach the mainland!"

"Not with a kraken in the area," Ryan agreed, brushing back his hair and looking at the mouth of the wooden tunnel. "Doc and Jak, go with J.B. and seal that bastard tunnel at both ends. I don't want anybody else coming through ever again."

"Done and done," J.B. stated, hefting the munitions bag.

The first explosion sounded dull and distant, loose dust and dirt bellowing across the dockyard like a hur-

ricane from Kansas. The second pipe bomb collapsed
the mouth of the access tunnel, wood splinters and
wreckage blowing out across the water for a hundred
yards.

After rigging some low-yield explosives in the dockyard around the *Moon Runner*, the companions started
off along the sandy coast toward the ruins of the U.S.
Navy base. According to the map, the trip shouldn't take
them more than a few hours. San Clemente wasn't that
big an island.

Days later, they were still walking.

Chapter Eleven

The sea water foamed across the bow of the cargo barge, the huge, flat vessel skimming along the southern coastline of Clemente with remarkable speed. Across the bow in oddly flowery script was the name *Tiger Shark*.

Although equipped with three massive diesel engines, the barge had only one in operation at the moment to conserve fuel. The flat deck was divided into compartments by sandbag walls lashed into place with strong netting, the gunwale bristled with pungi sticks and barbed wire, and there were two .50-caliber machine guns bolted to the deck, along with a brace of crossbows with a span over six feet wide. A wrinklie had once called the weapon an arbalest, which was just feeb talk as why would a thing have two different names? The captain had executed the fool for lying.

A dozen sec men stood alert on the deck, watching the land through binocs, searching for any sign of the outlanders and their strange war wag of a boat. Only the deadly *Tiger Shark* had been deemed fast enough to challenge the outlanders and their unknown vessel. The rest of the fifteen-ship fleet was moored in Black Mountain Bay, safe from any possible attack by norms or muties. Not that there was much danger of the latter.

Unlike ville sec men, the sailors wore whatever was

available. Uniforms were for lubbers, not wave-riders! Blasters were worn around the waist or across the chest. Some had swords, while others carried axes. However, each man and woman had a gold ring in their left ear, fishskin boots and a host of tattoos, which gave them an oddly similar appearance.

"Anything?" Captain Bart Carlton asked, sweeping the horizon with a set of military monoculars. The special functions of the computerized device were aced, as they required a battery pack to function, but the optics worked fine, much better than any set of civilian binoculars, or telescope.

"Not yet sir," reported First Officer Frank Godderstein, giving a crisp salute. The man was enormous, his wide chest and oversize arms giving him a definite simian appearance. An M-16 rapidfire rested in a scabbard across his back where it was protected from the salty spray, and a curved throwing ax dangled from his belt, the blade nicked from constant use, but mirror-bright from a daily polishing.

"Well, keep looking, Frank. The island isn't that large," Carlton ordered, tucking away the monocular.

Although only five feet tall, the blond man radiated an aura of command that few people could deny. His plump face burned with an intensity of purpose that frightened coldhearts, pirates and mercies alike. His clothing was stark white and painfully clean. Only his combat boots were old and scuffed. A predark watch adorned his left wrist, even though it no longer worked, and a squat 9 mm Ingram rapidfire was holstered at his side, a shoulder holster carrying five extra clips. The open display of wealth intimidated most people, and those it didn't soon discovered the error of their judgment, as Carlton was lightning fast and always hit what he aimed at.

"Tell me about their weapons again," Carlton ordered.

"They had rapidfires, longblasters and wheelguns, but there was no smoke from the muzzle when they fired," said Digger O'Malley, the insignia of Sealton ville removed from his uniform. "Only flashes of light."

"Mutie shit," a sec man drawled from the starboard bow. "T'aint possible."

"It's true, I saw it myself!" Digger insisted, a hand going to the matlock at his side. "Only one of them had a proper blaster, a tall man with silver hair. He looked like a wrinklie, but moved like a sec man."

"And you say that he had a son?" Carlton asked. He didn't know who these strangers were, or who they served, but if he wasn't their leader, then they had to be aced. Clemente Island was his personal property. End of discussion.

"A son? Sure enough," Digger said, bobbing his head. "There was this shorter young fellow, lean and hard. Looked like a real coldheart. His hair was the same color as the wrinklie, mebbe a touch more white than silver, but with hair like that they had to be kin."

"Excellent," Carlton said with a cold smile. "People are always so much more cooperative when family members are involved in negotiations."

"But the silver-hair guy wasn't in charge?" Godderstein asked. "Nor his son?"

"No, there was another man," Digger replied. "He

was clearly the leader. Big fellow, muscles like a hunter, black hair, scarred face, one eye, carried a couple of blasters and a weird long knife." The man started to tell about the redheaded woman, then decide to keep that piece of intel to himself.

"You know, I took a big chance coming to you with this," Digger said, drumming his fingers on the wooden handle of the matlock.

"Which is why you will be given Sealton. After Jones is chilled, of course," Carlton said, standing on the deck. Both hands clasped behind his back, the man swayed to the motion of the ship as if he were an integral part bolted into place. "I rule the sea, you barons have the villes. That is to be our accord."

"Fine by me!" Digger grinned.

In the distance, a pod of small whales broke the surface and Carlton rushed to the prow. Holding out his hands, the man began to softly hum. A few moments later the choppy surface of the ocean erupted into a geyser of writhing tentacles, then they arched over the gunwale to surround the captain, flexing and moving constantly, but never touching the smug man.

"By the coast gods," a young sec man whispered, making an ancient sign of protection. "The captain can talk to muties?"

"He can talk to any animal alive, lad," Digger boasted. "That's why we shifted our allegiance to him!"

"But that means he must be a…a…mutie!" the boy finally got out, his face pale with terror.

"Yes, I am," Carlton said, dismissing the kraken with

a wave of his hand, and thought. "Does that disturb you, youngster?"

"Aye, it does! I'll never work for a filthy half-breed!" the boy snarled, and clawed for his brand-new blaster—only to find the holster empty.

"And who doesn't have a touch in their blood these days?" Godderstein snorted, tucking the stolen blaster into his belt.

"My lord?" Digger asked, licking dry lips.

"Chill him," Carlton said, not even looking in that direction.

Spinning, Digger rammed the matlock into the stomach of the young sec man. With a cry, the boy went backward, soaring over the gunwale to splash into the waves.

Reaching out with his mind, Carlton summoned the kraken. Almost instantly the choppy water around the speeding barge was filled with tentacles. Still fighting to stay afloat, the boy screamed in raw terror, then disappeared under the foamy red waves.

"Such a damn waste," Godderstein rumbled. "His boots were brand-new."

Pulling out a home-rolled cigar, Carlton lit it with a match. "As you say, such a waste." The mutie puffed away, deep in thought.

THE SUN WAS HIGH in the cloudy sky, the heat oppressive and unrelenting. A cool breeze blew in from the ocean, making the shoreline tolerable. Just on the other side of the sand dunes, the companions would have believed that they were back in the Great Salt.

"John Barrymore, how big did you say this island

was again?" Doc rumbled, wiggling his bare toes in the shallow water along the sandy beach. A length of twine dangled off the end of his ebony sword stick. A shiny hook wafted in the water. But the tiny fish darting around didn't seem to be fooled, and were boldly nibbling on the bait and avoiding the hook entirely.

"According to my map, Clemente should be about twenty miles wide," J.B. answered.

"And how far have we walked, sir?"

"Thirty-five miles," J.B. muttered, thrusting away the map and paper. "Dark night, I've done this math over and over. Everything says this is San Clemente in the Channel Islands!"

"However…" Mildred prompted.

"In the middle of the bastard ocean!" J.B. replied hotly. "We should be drowning by now!"

"Map wrong," Jak said simply, wringing out his socks before laying them flat on a large rock. The salt water helped kill the smell, and seemed to be doing a small bunion he had a world of good.

"Because of the nuking, it's possible," Mildred suggested, "that San Clemente got shoved into other islands to become a single landmass. I've heard of that happening before." She paused. "Just not in this millennium."

"Makes sense," J.B. grudgingly relented.

Just then a sharp whistle sounded from the distance and the companions looked up to see Ryan and Krysty walk into view down the beach. Impatiently, they waited for the man and woman to rejoin them.

"Find a ville?" J.B. asked hopefully.

"More important, got food?" Jak asked, his empty

stomach growling loudly. The coneys were long gone, and the wildlife that was so abundant in the interior of the island was almost nonexistent along the blazing hot coastline. For the past two days the companions had been living on the clams and sea urchins recovered from the tide pools. Each were excellent, but there was never enough of them to satisfy the companions' growing hunger.

"We found everything," Ryan answered, dropping his bulging backpack onto the sand. "There's a fresh water river up ahead, and more of these bastard fruit trees than we could count."

"What kind?" Jak asked, scurrying over. Opening the backpack, he eagerly withdrew a red and yellow sphere with a shiny skin. "What is, mutie?" he said, his lip curling. The teenager had once almost starved to death, but he would never be hungry enough to eat a mutie plant. That was just suicide!

"Don't know if it's natural, or not," Krysty said honestly, lifting out one of them and polishing the skin on her sleeve. "But we saw the birds eating them, and a cougar eating a bird. That sounded good enough, so we tried it." She smiled. "They're wonderful!"

"They're called nectarines," Mildred said, taking one and biting deeply. Juice gushed from the fruit to trickle down her cheeks. "Yep, this is a nectarine, all right."

"Indeed," Doc rumbled suspiciously. "I had a neighbor in Vermont who had an apple farm, and loved to talk about different types of fruits grown from around the world. He had several books on the subject, yet I have never heard of…what was the name again?"

"Nectarine," Mildred mumbled her mouth stuffed.

"It's a sort of peach. Some people thought it was a simple crossbreed of a plum and a peach, or something like that." She paused to swallow. "Best thing in the world. I honestly never thought to see one again."

"So okay?" Jak asked, sniffing. It smelled great, and his mouth began to water.

"Hell, yes!"

"Even more importantly, there's a ville just past the orchard," Ryan said, taking out a nectarine and biting into it. He chewed twice and swallowed. The man had consumed several already, but they really were the best thing he'd ever had off a tree.

"The gate is open, so we suspected another cannie trap, or mebbe a plague ville," Ryan continued. "But there was a straight-up fight, spent brass everywhere. Coldhearts, mercies, doesn't matter, they aced the sec men and the civies are gone. But they left everything behind."

"Like food?" Jak insisted.

"Tons of it," Krysty said, reaching into a pocket and tossing something over.

The teenager made the catch and beamed with delight at the self-heat can. Spaghetti! After pulling the tab to activate the heating device, Jak waited impatiently for the wisps of steam to rise, showing the food was ready to eat.

Yanking off the lid, Jak smelled the spaghetti just to make sure, then started wolfing it down without wasting time with unnecessary chewing.

"Goof!" he mumbled, his face smeared with red as if he had just ripped open an enemy's throat with his bare teeth. "Amp bear 'eapballs!"

Trying not to smile, Mildred translated that into "And there are meatballs," and happily accepted a can herself. This one had no label, and after it grew warm, she removed the top to find the military container full of tuna casserole. She paused at the thought of yet another fish dinner, then the smell of the tangy cheddar cheese sauce wafted upward, and the woman dug in with gusto.

"Delicious!" she said after a moment, using her fingers in lieu of a spoon.

"We found twenty cans, but we each only get one for dinner," Ryan said, fishing off another nectarine. "Too much food too fast, and it only comes back up. We can't afford a waste like that."

That statement slowed everybody, and the food began to be chewed before being swallowed. More fruit was served as dessert, and everybody simply sat after the meal, allowing their bodies to absorb the repast. A U.S. Navy self-heat was designed to sustain a sailor for an entire day. However, for the companions it barely "fed the tiger" as the saying went. The fruit helped, along with the knowledge that more was available.

"Dark night, I needed that." J.B. grinned, tossing away the empty can. Then he paused to burp. "I like fish, but at the rate Doc catches them we'll be aced of old age before he gets enough to make a pot of stew."

Arching an eyebrow, Doc bristled, then shrugged as it was unfortunately true. The man had many talents and skills, but fishing in Deathlands was sadly not among them.

"When you're feeling better, we'll start walking," Ryan said, leaning back on the rock and closing his eye.

"It's only about a mile to the river, and another three to the ville."

"Ready now," Jak said, kneeling on shore to wash his hands and then rub his face clean.

In only a few minutes the companions had gathered their meager belongings and started along the upper part of the beach, past the high tide mark. Grass and some weeds grew there, which made walking a lot easier than marching through shifting sands.

Along the way, the companions passed the burned-out wrecks of U.S. Navy vessels dotting the ocean, some of them completely submerged, only the tip of the deck guns reaching the open air as if the vessels were snorkeling.

Several times Ryan checked his rad counter, but the device never reached the danger level, and soon they left behind the radioactive ruins of the predark battle. Everything they wanted and needed was probably on those ships, and in abundance. But rich in rads, the food and weapons were deadly, and so the companions simply ignored the predark bounty as if it didn't exist.

Reaching the river, Ryan turned inland, and the group marched a ways before pausing to wash the salt spray from their clothes and hair. The river ran murky for a few minutes, then slowly turned clear again, and the soaked people emerged greatly refreshed and smelling infinitely less like a bay at low tide.

Passing through the orchard, they refilled the backpack, taking only the very best of nectarines. The trees were festooned with ripe fruit, but the ground was surprisingly clear of any fallen fruit.

"Rats?" Jak asked with a scowl.

"If so, there must be a million of them," Ryan countered gruffly.

After a few more miles they saw the walls of the ville and dutifully checked their blasters before proceeding.

The outer defenses of the nameless ville were quite impressive, some of the best the companions had ever seen. A deep moat encircled the ville, then a sloped ramp of concrete covered with broken glass. The wall itself was formed of massive limestone blocks, and reached some twenty feet tall. Doc recognized the material, saying the soft stone was easy to cut, but very resistant to the weather.

"Whoever built, expect trouble," Jak stated, patting the five-foot-thick walls as they passed through the open gates.

There were two of them, one on either side of the wall, and each forged of assorted pieces of metal into a single massive slab. There were dents in the outer gate, probably from cannonball impacts, or possibly grens, but there were no actual breaks in the resilient material.

Past the double gate was a sandbag nest for the local sec men to stand behind to fight off any invaders. There was an old howitzer cannon, but the companions could see that it was a piece of drek, just something to intimidate outlanders. However, there were quivers of arrows and a rack of wooden crossbows, the arms made from the leaf-springs of a car. Those were very powerful weapons, fully capable of driving an arrow completely through a person at five hundred feet.

The rest of the ville was pretty standard, dirt streets

and a lot of small veggie farms. Ramshackle huts for
the ville people, wooden barracks for the sec men and
a big stone house on a hill for the baron. That's where
they went first, as all of the best stuff would be located
there. Rank doth have its privileges, as Doc liked to say,
while Mildred always countered with, It's good to be
king.

There was a lot of spent brass everywhere, as if the
ville sec men had been in the fight of their lives. But
no bodies, only the occasional piece of torn cloth or a
broken blaster. Curious, Ryan lifted one to inspect the
weapon. It was a classic, a Browning longblaster, one
of the best blasters ever created. Obviously this had
been the property of the sec chief or the baron. Only
now the weapon was compressed flat, as if a smithy
had laid it on an anvil and pounded the weapon with
a sledgehammer. Ryan found the idea that somebody
would ace a perfectly good blaster stupe, and tossed the
weapon away. It landed in a clatter near a water trough
that had recently been smashed into splinters.

"Something wrong here," Mildred said, looking up
at the cloudy sky. "From the bloodstains, I'd say this
fight couldn't have happened more than a few days ago,
so where are the scavengers? I'd expect the sky to be
full of vultures and eagles, flocking in to feast on the
decaying bodies."

"What bodies?" Jak asked with a scowl.

"My point exactly," Mildred replied, testing the draw
on her blaster.

In the center of the ville, situated on a small hill to
make it dominate the landscape, was a brick building,
formerly a public library, and now the castle of the

baron. Ryan noted more dents in the brickwork from cannonball impacts, as well as a couple of breakthrough points.

"Strange, but I don't see any cannonballs partially buried in the ground," J.B. observed, working the arming bolt on his Uzi. "That's either mighty good shooting, or else the winner took back their balls."

Unable to stop himself, Jak made a rude suggestion, and everybody laughed at the sage wisdom of always taking your balls along with you, just in case of trouble.

The front doors opened into the audience room, a fancy throne set at the far end to make folks have to walk over to meet the ruler.

"Intimidation through the positive use of negative space," Doc muttered. "Very clever. The ruler here was no fool."

Checking behind the throne, J.B. located the hidden escape route that most barons fashioned, and it naturally led to his private armory. However, that had already been looted to the walls. Every ammo box, wooden barrel and shelf was empty; there wasn't a single live brass left behind, only some empty gunbelts, a bundle of fishing spears and a couple of wooden shields covered with scaly leather.

"I guess the winners did take everything back home with them," J.B. noted, removing his fedora to massage his scalp before putting the hat back into place. "To the victor goes the spoils, eh, Doc?"

"Indubitably, John Barrymore," the scholar agreed pensively. "As well as everything else, it would seem.

I am surprised that Ryan and Krysty found what little in provisions that they did."

"The self-heats were on a top shelf, out of sight from below," Krysty answered, checking some boxes set into the wall. From the strips of tape left behind, it was clear this had been where the locals stored the grens. Those had also been taken, or else all used.

"Kraken hit ville?" Jak asked with a scowl.

"This far from the sea?" Mildred scoffed. "I doubt that highly. Besides, there isn't enough wanton destruction. After a kraken attack there usually isn't anything left standing."

"Kraken, or not, this is the second ville we've found destroyed," Ryan stated grimly, rubbing his unshaved chin. "And I'm starting to feel that these aren't random events. I think we landed in the middle of a bastard war. Somebody wants to take over the whole damn island, and is arranging for any troublemakers to get aced."

"Okay, we do a fast recce for any food or wags, then leave," J.B. commanded. "I don't want to be here if this warlord comes back with his army to inhabit the ville."

Everybody else agreed, and the companions quickly left the library via the kitchen. There was plenty of dried fish on the upper shelves, along with a few jars of preserves, but absolutely nothing on the dented lower shelves. The companions left with their pockets full, but feeling positive that they had just missed some vital clue to the destruction of the ville population.

In the back courtyard a dozen chickens were trapped inside a wire enclosure. The scrawny birds fluttered eagerly around the food dish, thinking they were going to be fed at last. Instead the companions snapped the necks of the chickens and stuffed them into their backpacks.

As expected, the garage was located directly alongside the baron's home. Unfortunately there were no wags, nor any signs that the locals even had any wheeled transport aside from some buckboard wags and a few wheelbarrows. However, wags meant horses and the companions located them in a corral behind the garage. There were a dozen gaunt animals standing listlessly around, too weak to move. Their feed bags were flat and as empty as the water trough. A stallion was lying aced on the ground, tongue extended and covered with maggots. Everything within reach of the animals trapped in the corral had been consumed, including the leather halters, hemp ropes and canvas bags.

"Water first," Krysty decided, going to a hand pump. Working the lever, she filled a plastic bucket and sloshed some water into the trough. By the third bucket, the horses shuffled closer to lap at the tepid fluid, their tails weakly moving in delight.

"I find feed," Jak stated, running into the barn. He soon returned with a half bag of oats and poured some of the contents into each of the feeder troughs. The oats had to be spread out, as he knew full well that the starving animals would fight one another to the death for the meager handful of food.

"Looks like we're here for the next couple of days," Ryan said, reaching out to pat one of the mares on the muscular throat as she continued to lap up some water. Pausing in her drinking, the horse nickered her thanks, then went right back to putting as much water inside her belly as possible.

"We can travel a lot farther and faster on horseback," Krysty agreed, laying aside the bucket. "They're in good shape, too. Just hungry." There were no signs of the animals ever having been beaten by their owners, or having suffered the use of spurs. A good kick in the rump with the heels of your boot got a horse moving fast, there was no excuse for the use of spurs except plain old-fashioned sadism.

"There certainly is enough green grass growing about to feed them properly without tapping into our own limited stores," Doc said, looking over the ville. "And I will wager that they would love to try some of those nectarines from the orchard."

"Just remove that huge pit first," Mildred warned, but then stopped as there came a low rumble from the ground.

"Dark night, is this an earthquake?" J.B. asked, glancing around the ville. However, there were no telltale spurts of dust rising up from the soil. Then at the far end of the street, something large stepped through the ville gate.

At first, the thing resembled an oversize African rhinoceros. But there was nothing special about those; the companions had encountered dozens of the huge, ungainly beasts, the descendants of the original animals on display in city zoos. Before the civilization completely collapsed, many of the zookeepers released their charges into the wild to fend for themselves rather than slowly starve to death in their cages. The survivors roamed parts of the Deathlands to this day: zebras, gorillas, lions, giraffes, emus and such. None of which were particularly dangerous to people armed with rapidfires.

"Wonder if taste good?" Jak asked, swinging up the M-16 and clicking the selector switch from single shot to full-auto.

"I'll gut the big bastard if somebody else digs the firepit," Ryan offered, then paused as the huge beast lumbered past the dented gates. The height of its over-size horn perfectly matched the location of the dents in the thick metal. That was when he saw the crea-ture had three-toed feet instead of the usual two. Its ears were flat against its skull, and its eyes were a dull yellow. Clearly, this wasn't a rhino heading their way, but some mutie animal that only resembled the peaceful herbivore.

"Oh, hell," Mildred whispered, looking down at the street. In a flash she could identify the flat patches in the dirt as footprints. Three-toed footprints.

"We chill," Jak said confidently.

"My dear Jak, the entire sec force of this ville failed to stop that monster before," Doc whispered, drawing his second blaster and cocking back the hammer. "Pray tell, what makes you think that we can?"

Before the teenager could answer, the rhino turned its squat head in the direction of the companions standing near the corral. Pawing the dirt like an enraged bull, the animal lowered its head and charged.

Instantly, Ryan swung up the Steyr and took aim.

"Lead won't stop the brute," J.B. snarled, pulling out a pipe bomb and lighting the fuse.

The reverberations in the ground steadily grew

stronger as the thundering beast grew ever closer, and the man swung the explosive charge overhead on the end of a short rope. When the beast was less than a hundred feet away, J.B. let go, and the sizzling bomb sailed down the street to land directly in front of the rhino and violently explode. The blast filled the street, smashing open the doors of a dozen huts and throwing out a billowing cloud of dust. Then the mutie appeared from the heart of the cloud, still moving, its smooth hide completely undamaged from the powerful detonation, or the hail of deadly shrapnel.

In stark clarity, the companions could now see that the entire hide was covered with oddly shaped scales. Her hair tightly coiling, Krysty recognized them as the scales sewn into the shields in the ville armory. Gaia, the thing was armor-plated!

"Aim for the mouth!" Ryan snarled, shooting as fast as he could work the bolt. In fast succession, he hit the beast three times, but with its head lowered for the charge, the mouth was well protected and the 7.62 mm steel-jacketed rounds merely bounced off the adamantine hide.

In a surge of motion, the companions separated, everybody going in a different direction to try to confuse the animal.

The rhino paused for a heartbeat, trying to choose, but that was enough. A second pipe bomb from J.B. exploded, showering the beast with the slimy contents of a rain barrel. Shaking off the water, the rhino glowered at the animals trapped inside the nearby corral. Instantly the horses released the contents of their bladders as a sign of submission. Sniffing the air, the rhino turned away and stomped off in search of other prey. Human prey.

We smell wrong, Doc mentally noted, running sideways toward the barn, discharging both of his mammoth blasters, the LeMat and the Webley sounding louder than pirate cannons. The big rounds slapped onto the rhinoceros and ricocheted off harmlessly.

Scrambling up a tree, Jak kept going along a thick branch until diving for the roof of a building. He landed flat, cracking several of the ceramic tiles and sending down broken pieces in a loose flurry. Heading that way, the rhino circled the house, then it slowed to a stop and bellowed in frustration, the thundering challenge sounding more like a reptile than a mammal.

Aiming the M-16 carefully, Krysty emptied an entire clip into the face of the creature, trying for the eyes. But they were protected by a sloping ridge that seemed as impervious to bullets as the rest of the armored body.

Coming out of the shadows, Ryan stepped onto the balcony of the gaudy house and fired twice more at the rhino. The slugs slammed deep into a black nostril, but instead of a gush of blood, the beast merely snorted as if stung by an annoying bee.

Pulling out a hatchet, Jak threw it from the rooftop and the blade thudded into the back of the beast, glancing off without even leaving a mark.

Popping into view from the second floor of the barracks, J.B. put a long burst of 9 mm rounds from the Uzi straight into the beast's backside. The soft lead rounds flattened upon impact and tumbled to the ground. An armored rear end. Now J.B. had seen everything.

Spinning, the rhino bellowed in rage and charged,

crashing straight into the wooden building. Windows shattered, the whole structure shook and roof tiles slipped off by the score. The chimney toppled over, and the rhino came out the other side, covered in dust and debris, but still looking for its mysterious attacker.

"Son of a bitch! How did the locals stop this thing?" Mildred demanded, snapping off rounds from the branches of another tree. But then the physician understood that they hadn't; this juggernaut had trampled every living person in the ville.

No, that was not quite right, Mildred silently corrected. The thing chilled every person in the ville. But it ignored the horses and chickens. This was a people killer, nothing more.

"Not mutie, biowep!" Jak shouted, reloading his blaster. A round slipped from his hands and tumbled along the slanted roof to hit a rock on the ground with a musical ping.

With both ears twitching, the rhino turned at the tiny noise and trotted closer to sniff suspiciously at the fallen cartridge. Then it smashed the brass into the dirt with a three-toed hoof.

"This is why that picket fence around the cannie ville was tipped with poison," Krysty snarled, working the arming bolt to clear a jam from the ejector port of the rapidfire. The bent shell spun away, glittering in the sunlight like stolen gold.

"I still have that piece of wood," Mildred offered, touching her canvas med kit.

"If you feel like diving onto that thing armed with a sharp stick, you go right ahead!"

"I'll pass!"

"An implo will take him out!" J.B. yelled, tracking the beast in the street with the barrel of his Uzi. "But we only have two left, and I hate to waste one on an overgrown armadillo!"

Especially since there could be more of these things in the area! Ryan thought, twisting his hands on the longblaster. Briefly, there came to mind the unbidden image of a herd of the unstoppable rhinos stampeding across Clemente Island, flattening everything in its path.

"Save them until we got no other choice!" Ryan yelled, firing a single round at the beast. The 7.62 mm slug smacked directly into the panting mouth and disappeared. If the slug did any damage, it wasn't readily apparent.

Lighting a fuse, J.B. threw a stick of TNT at the lumbering behemoth. The hissing cylinder landed alongside the rhino, and it galloped away, shaking the ground. A few seconds later the explosive charge detonated, throwing a wealth of dirt and grass into the air.

"Son of a bitch is smart," J.B. muttered unhappily, returning the second stick to his bag. "Got any ideas?"

"Give me a pipe bomb!" Ryan shouted, holding up a hand.

Leaning out the window, J.B. dangled the charge at the end of a rope and slowly spun it into a blur, then let go. Trailing the short rope behind, the bomb sailed over the rhino pawing at the dusty street, and Ryan made the catch.

"Now what?" Krysty yelled through cupped hands.

"Cover me!" Ryan answered, twisting off the fuse

to only a tiny nubbin before going back inside. A few moments later the one-eyed man appeared at the front door of the tavern and sharply whistled.

As the rhino turned, Ryan shot it in the face, then ran for the gate. Lurching into hot pursuit, the beast bellowed an angry challenge and galloped after the hated two-legs. However, Ryan immediately changed direction to head for the sandbag nest in front of the open gate. Reaching the nest, he climbed over the wall and dropped out of sight. Roaring in victory, the rhino plowed straight into the sandbag nest just as the dropped pipe bomb exploded.

The sandbag wall channeled the full force of the blast directly into the beast, and it staggered backward from the swirling cloud, the entire hide bristling with arrows. Then with a groan of tortured metal, the howitzer toppled over to smack the rhino across the back, the body deeply bowing as the spine audibly cracked.

Scrambling up a guard tower, Ryan reached the top of the wall just in time to see the rhino straighten and the arrows start to fall off the thing, the tiny punctures in the thick hide closing to disappear completely.

"Fireblast, the fat bastard regens!" Ryan shouted, aiming the longblaster, but withheld firing. What good would copper-jacketed lead do against a juggernaut like this?

At the cry, the rhino ran at the wall and slammed into the limestone blocks. The blunt horn cracked off a piece, leaving behind a dent that strongly resembled cannonball damage. With nothing in sight to throw at the rhino, Ryan forced himself to do nothing, while the thing rammed the wall again and again, the impacts making the gates creak as they moved.

Finally tiring of the useless assault, the rhino trotted back down the main street of the ville and returned to the horse corral. Using its curved horn to open the wooden gate, the rhino walked inside. Whinnying in terror, the panicking horses backed into the far corner, but the behemoth ignored them and went straight to the decaying carcass and began to eat. Maggots, worms, flesh and bones, the rhino chomped on everything, the bones audibly cracking under the brutal eating of the blunt jaw.

"A herbivore no more, madam!" Doc shouted from the second-floor window of the barn.

"It needs the calories to fuel that regeneration!" Mildred yelled back. "Nothing is free!"

Loading in a fresh rotary clip, Ryan almost smiled at that. So, the big beast needed to constantly eat to fix its wounds? If the companions could trap it in a pit, the thing would soon starve to death. That was potentially useful, but no method came to mind on how to lure the behemoth into a pit, even if the companions had one available.

However, there were pits, and then there were pits, Ryan noted sagely, a plan forming in the back of his mind. It was triple crazy, and more dangerous than asking a cannie for a kiss, but unless they wanted this thing chasing after them all the way to the mainland, they had to chill it, here and now. This would be the last attempt. Next they would have to use an implo gren, which would mean the companions could never go back to the redoubt full of supplies. Two implo grens and three Cerberus clouds equaled six aced companions.

Checking the clip in his blaster, Ryan started back for the gaudy house. It was time to make a move and see what happened.

Chapter Twelve

Going back inside the tavern, Ryan checked the bottles behind the counter, then the stock in the root cellar. As expected, the best shine was reserved for the baron, and Ryan took every bottle, along with a handful of rags.

Searching among the bedrooms of the gaudy sluts, Ryan found a ladder to the roof and hauled up the collection of rags and bottles.

Using hand gestures, the man explained the plan to his companions, then started tossing over the bottles of shine, rags tied firmly around the necks.

The only mishap occurred when Doc dropped a bottle. It shattered on the street, and the rhino stopped eating its ghoulish meal for a moment, looking around intently with its piggy eyes, before continuing with the horrid gorging.

When everything was ready, Jak climbed off the roof and crept along the ville wall to reach the open gates. The albino teen had to dig in his heels, and his face went purple from the exertion, but he finally got the slab of metal moving and managed to close the inner door and lock it firmly.

As Jak returned to the roof of the barracks, Doc exited the barn, crawling along the ground to reach the corral. Using his sword stick, the man cut away the bundle of ropes holding the wooden rails in place, then gently eased them down and crawled back into hiding. It took a few minutes for the terrified horses to comprehend that freedom was suddenly available, and they bolted out of the corral, racing toward the gate, only to find it closed. Then they began running around the assorted buildings in a desperate search for another avenue of escape.

"Now!" Ryan shouted, throwing an unlit bottle.

In rough unison, the companions rained the glass containers along the wooden fence of the corral, the shine soaking deep into the dry wood. Glancing up from feasting, the rhino grunted at the odd noise, but didn't stop stuffing the rotting flesh into its mouth. The hunger urge couldn't be denied until thoroughly sated. The genetically designed military weapon was a slave to the iron demands of its own body.

Making a bundle of his last four sticks of TNT with some duct tape, J.B. twisted the fuses together and lit them with his butane lighter. As the twine began to sizzle, he swung the charge overhead, slowly building speed, then released the bundle as the fuses separated and started toward the separate sticks.

Sailing across the street, the bomb landed alongside the grunting rhino, and it turned at the noise exactly as the explosives detonated.

The thundering fireball lifted the creature off the ground for a dozen yards, sending it tumbling and turning to land with a resounding crash. Stunned for a moment, the rhino struggled to rise on its shattered legs, yellow blood trickling from its mouth and rear.

Now the rest of the companions lit the rags around their bottles and threw down the makeshift Molotovs, setting the entire corral on fire and forming a wall of flame between the rhino and the half-eaten carcass.

Bellowing in rage and pain, the regenerating beast lumbered weakly forward, but the heat of the blaze forced it back, only to have the organic programming embedded into its artificial brain command it forward once more. Pain meant nothing, it could and would regenerate, once it got that carcass!

But as it neared the flames again, the companions appeared from the smoke, shooting from every direction. Roaring in unbridled fury, the rhino started to attack, but then turned back toward the burning food. Fuel came first. That was a primary order.

Getting ready to throw his last pipe bomb, J.B. proffered it to Mildred, who rammed it up the gullet of a dead chicken, then tossed it into the corral to land smack in the middle of the rotting corpse.

Everybody took cover and a few seconds later a blast rocked the corral, chunks of decaying horse smacking wetly into the barracks and the huts.

Struggling through the firewall, the smoldering rhino stiffened at the sight of nothing on the other side but a smoking crater. Tricked!

On the far side of the corral, Ryan whistled sharply and the beast turned to limp in that direction. Stepping dangerously close to the flames, Doc triggered both of his handblasters, the heavy rounds slamming into the blackening hide of the cooking rhino, leaving gaping holes. A steady flow of yellow blood ran from a dozen wounds, the movements of the rhino noticeably slowing. As it staggered closer to Ryan, he raced away, and Krysty whistled shrilly from the opposite side.

Lumbering awkwardly, the rhino threw itself after the female two-legs, but it only got halfway there before Mildred and Jak returned from the baron's home, their arms full of shine and bottles of fish oil lanterns.

The crude fire bombs pelted the beast, its screams taking on a pronounced tone of anguish, but still it fought on against its tormentors. Bullets hammered its face, until both eyes shattered, releasing a thick vicious fluid from inside the head that oddly resembled boiling rice pudding. More bottles of shine and fish oil crashed onto the ground underneath the creature, and soon it was engulfed in flames, top and bottom, hot lead smacking it from every side, the pain reaching intolerable levels.

Switching to an unexpected tactic, the rhino crawled to the feeding trough and thrust its fiery head in after the grain.

Muttering something in Latin, Doc stepped in quickly and thrust his sword deep into an empty eye socket, then savagely twisted the blade. The entire five-ton body of the rhino shook violently, then the jaw limply dropped and a torrent of yellow blood gushed out, on and on, as if there was an unlimited supply.

Jerking his sword free, Doc distastefully backed away from the tidal wave of inhuman gore, then drew the LeMat and triggered a single round, the .44 miniball bursting open the charred head, the bubbling brains spilling onto the dirty ground like congealed vomit.

Rising on stiff legs, the rhino shook all over, then dropped, assuming a splayed position that no living creature could ever duplicate.

"Keep the fire going," Ryan commanded, tossing an

armload of wood onto the body. "I don't want any part of this thing left intact to come after us again!"

Holstering their weapons, the rest of the companions went in search of anything that could burn, and soon they had a bonfire blazing in the corral, the flames licking high into the sky. In only a few hours the rhino was reduced to piles of charred flesh and smoking bones. The smell was beyond description.

Finally satisfied that the mutie was aced for good, the companions wearily started rounding up the horses, then went to search the gaudy house and upper floor of the barracks for anything edible that the beast might have missed the last time it was here.

However, the companions found very little intact that was of any possible use. In the cellar of the barracks, Doc unearthed a clay pot full of salted vegetables, while Ryan discovered a hidden cache of live brass under the bed of the madam of the gaudy house. None of the shells fit the blasters of the companions, but brass could save your ass in more ways than one. There was nothing better as payment.

Searching among the huts, Mildred located the home of the ville healer. But going inside she was severely disappointed. There were plenty of knives for surgery, but also lots of rope for tying down a patient and leather straps to keep them from screaming. If the healer had any knowledge whatsoever of antiseptics, or even basic cleanliness, there was no visible evidence. A shelf of jars in the back room looked promising, but they contained only sulfur, salt and dirt. The first two were for dusting wounds, and she could guess that the third was

for packing into shallow cuts to turn them into mildly
pleasing scars.

"Anything useful?" Krysty asked, tucking a bar of
homemade soap into her pocket. The stuff was very
soft and smelled like a rose.

"Nothing, unless I was looking for a nifty new recipe
for dysentery," Mildred replied in annoyance. "Is that
soap any good?"

"Yes. Want some?"

"Always!"

Gathering at the home of the baron, the companions
made sure the windows and doors were locked tightly
against any intruders, then settled in for the night and
some much needed dinner. Dinner was southern fried
chicken, one of Mildred's specialties, the coating made
from stale bread crushed into crumbs, then mixed with
salt and pepper from the MRE food packs.

Sitting around a table, the companions had the unique
experience of eating off plates, using knives and forks.
The room was lit by candlelight, and there was a roaring blaze in the fireplace to help cut the smell of the
cremated mutie outside. The stink seemed to stick to
their clothing and hair, and everybody had been forced
to wash several times to finally cut the reek down to
a tolerable level. Now the women smelled like roses,
while the men had taken this opportunity to shave. It
was the most civilized meal the companions had enjoyed in several years.

"Excellent meal, Millie." J.B. sighed, laying aside
his empty plate. There was nothing left of the chickens
but gravy and bones.

"Good, but needed garlic," Jak added, removing the napkin from around his neck.

"You think everything could use garlic." Mildred laughed, leaning forward to rest her elbows on the table.

"Can," the albino teen stated with a wink, strolling off to start his shift of guard duty.

The ville walls were tall and strong, with both of the metal gates closed and locked, but unless they were inside a thoroughly recced redoubt, the companions always prepared to be attacked in the night. The predark concept of paranoia simply didn't exist in a world where every hand was turned against you.

"I shall go check on the horses," Doc said, pushing back his chair. "The throne room downstairs is secure and warm, but it is a new environment for them, and the horses will need a soothing voice to help them sleep." Tucking the ebony sword stick into his gunbelt, the man smiled. "Besides which, it has been a long time since I last enjoyed an equine encounter that did not end quite badly for them and me using a toothpick."

"Horses are okay, but I prefer wags," Ryan said, extending his arms in a long stretch. His boots were off and his gunbelt hung from the back of his chair, which was just about as relaxed as the man ever got.

"But my dear Ryan, unlike horses, I have yet to meet the gasoline engine that could make another," Doc declared. "Indeed, sir, horses are the hallmark of true civilization! Furthermore—"

"At ease, Doc!" Ryan said, giving a rare half smile. "Go tend the bastard horses."

"By your command, my baron," Doc rumbled in a mock apology, bowing slightly.

Scowling at the hated term, Ryan threw a chicken bone at the man, but it missed the hastily retreating Doc and he made it into the kitchen unscathed.

"Was his time really that different from this?" J.B. asked, watching the scholar snag a basket of nectarines before starting down the back stairs.

"John, even their wars had rules of decorum," Mildred stated truthfully, unfolding a stick of sugarless gum from an MRE pack. "A different time? Hell, it was a different world—as was mine."

Just then, Krysty returned from her stint of standing guard on the roof, and the group settled in for the night, doing some routine maintenance on their assorted weaponry, and mending a few rips in their clothing, before trundling off to bed. Tomorrow promised to be a long day.

Banking the fire to keep the room warm, the companions went to their separate rooms and bolted themselves inside, sliding tables under the handles in case of a nightcreep.

Thumping a clenched fist on the door to make sure it was good and secure, Ryan turned to get hit in the face with a piece of cloth. It was a sports bra, and the man looked up in time to see Krysty step out of her pants.

"Coming to bed soon, lover?" she asked softly, folding her garments neatly over the back of a chair.

In the flickering candlelight, her skin seemed to glow like molten gold, her long red hair moving down her back to sway tantalizing across the tops of her shapely buttocks. Then Krysty turned slightly to smile invitingly in a form of communication created by men and women long before words were invented.

Starting to remove his own clothing, Ryan drank in her amazing beauty, his heart quickening at the sight of her dulcet form silhouetted by the tallow candles. This room carried no trace of the outside world, the air was clean and smelled of roses. Suddenly the man was very glad he had washed thoroughly after the fight in the corral.

Sitting on the bed, Krysty stretched out a leg, running her toes across a wolfskin rug on the brick floor. It tickled a little, and she tried not to laugh.

"Something funny?" Ryan asked, laying aside his shirt. The naked man walked toward her, the hard muscles moving beneath his tanned skin like oiled machinery.

"Tell you later," Krysty purred deep in her throat, running a hand along his hairy chest. Ryan carried the story of his life burned into his flesh, his skin covered with countless scars, bullet holes, laser burns and knife cuts.

Krysty knew he was a ruthless killer when it was needed, and yet Ryan only wanted to find someplace where they could live in peace. His calloused hands had taken hundreds of lives, but Ryan looked at her with surprising gentleness, demanding nothing, only asking, giving her the power to decide. That filled her with emotions for which there were no words. She took his powerful hands and kissed them, her hair reaching down to caress his fingers.

His heart beating fast, Ryan leaned in to kiss the woman, their lips touching gently at first, savoring the

sweet moment, trying to maintain the intimacy. But then
their passions grew and their mouths opened, tongues
intertwining, tasting, probing, exploring. Gently raking
her nails down his sides, Krysty moved in from his
thighs and cupped his manhood, thrilling at the pulsating sensation of him growing larger and harder.

Still deeply kissing the woman, Ryan stroked his
fingertips along her cheek and down her throat to finally
cup a shapely breast. The nipple instantly hardened at
his touch. Krysty was more than beautiful, she was
beauty itself, as vital to the man as the air in his lungs
or the blood in his veins. She was his life, and he told
her that silently, in every way he knew how.

Low murmurs of love and devotion came from the
locked room, then the sounds of lovemaking and hurried breathing. And for a brief span of time, the couple
found comfort and peace, deep in the heart of the savage
Deathlands.

WHAT REMAINED of U.S. Navy radar station #4 stood
on the far end of a small peninsula attached to the main
island of Clemente. The concrete structure was old and
potted with countless small holes created by the acidic
droppings of the seagulls. But the thick walls had been
breached, and the wind howled around the reinforced
building. Inside, the banks of electronic equipment, still
in perfect condition behind the electromagnetic protection of their antinuke Faraday Cages, waited for the flip
of a switch to become live once more. Unfortunately,
after so many decades, there was nobody alive who
had any idea how to operate the complex machinery,

and so it stayed in perpetual readiness, a technology fly trapped forever in the amber of ignorance.

Surrounding the radar station was a sprawling ville of over a hundred homes, every one with a plastic roof as protection from the acid rains that came every spring. Many of the younger people called their home Radar ville, but always in secret. The baron and his sec men adhered to the old ways, and would only refer to the place as Radar Station #4, and nothing else.

A great bank of rusting machines formed the main wall, sealing off the peninsula from the mainland, the corroded hulks joined into a single, homogenous mass by the liberal application of quicken, a sort of home-made concrete made from burned clay, crushed sea-shells and sand. Reaching over twenty feet tall with no gate of any kind, the wall kept out all of the muties on the island, including the triple-cursed thunder kings.

There was a sheer cliff separating the ville from the turbulent sea, with only one small pathway leading down to a sandy cove that had been hewn from the wild rocks by sheer strength of will and black-powder charges. Access to the ville was achieved by a fleet of catamarans, sleek double-boats that streaked effortlessly over the choppy waves to a sandy beach a good mile from the buildings. Any invaders would have to cross that distance just to reach the first structure, and that was a fortified pillbox armed with blasters, crossbows and a catapult of amazing accuracy for something copied from a book.

Why some former baron had sealed the ville off from the rest of the island nobody knew for sure, but the stories were many and varied, each more inventive than the next. He was the last survivor of the predark government and carried a secret so big it could shatter the world. Another version was that the baron had actually been a machine, immortal and indestructible. A more popular version was that the old baron had created the thunder kings and been exiled here as his punishment. But what kind of punishment was that? Radar ville was paradise on Earth compared to a lot of places, especially some of the rad holes on the mainland. The only person who might have known the truth was Beltrane, but the kid was triple crazy, even more so than most doomies, and extracting a grain of truth from his mad ramblings was becoming harder every year.

In a loud crash the double doors were slammed aside and Baron Eileen Halverson strode into the dark room surrounded by a cadre of armed sec men. In spite of the warm breezes, a huge blaze crackled in the fireplace. Sitting in a chair, a wizened youth huddled under a thick blanket, staring into the flames. A demijohn of shine sat on the floor nearby, the cork dangling from a short string tied to the handle.

"Well?" the woman demanded. "Is this it?"

"Yes, they are coming for me," Beltrane whispered, his voice raspy. His face was heavily lined, as if Beltrane was a wrinklie, yet the youth had been alive for less than eighteen years. The terrible gift of his ability to see things that had not yet happened was draining away his life, aging him rapidly, and soon the boy would be on the last train west. Nobody in the ville wanted the young doomie to get chilled. He was far too useful predicting storms and attacks by coldhearts. But Beltrane eagerly looked forward to the end of his pain and the sweet tranquility of nothingness.

"Who comes for you?" Baron Eileen said, kneeling to keep her face on an even level with the doomie.

Beltrane smiled at the courtesy, and briefly recalled how they had been lovers almost all of last summer, before his accursed gift stole away even that pleasure, leaving him nothing but pain, and his visions of the future, swirling and mixing, endlessly being reborn as each decision yielded a thousand new possibilities. The future wasn't carved into stone, it was alive and forever changing with every action taken by the living in the present. Even the past could be changed, something whispered in the deepest recesses of his mind, just ask the time-walker! But he forcibly banished those thoughts as too painful to endure.

"They have no names in my mind, and I can't see their faces," the doomie said, the words almost too low for the others to hear. "They will smile and speak of peace, but there is chilling in their hearts, and death spreads around them like an invisible plague." Weakly, the youth reached out a withered hand for the demijohn, but it was much too heavy for him to lift.

Taking the ceramic container away from the doomie, Baron Eileen poured a few inches of the home brew into a plastic tumbler and passed it over. She knew the shine had been dosed with jolt, the powerful mixture of drugs helping him to stay sane and to ease some of his pain, but also shortening his life even more. It was the only thing the woman could do to help the young doomie without endangering the ville. She had a touch of the talent, and would sometimes have a dream of things yet to come, but she was only a flickering candle in comparison to his erupting volcano of abilities.

Eagerly, Beltrane grasped the tumbler in shaking hands and drank, only stopping when he needed to drag in air.

"Thank you," he wheezed, letting the tumbler drop to the floor.

"Who are they? Spies from the coastal barons or mercies from the mainland?" the baron demanded, recovering the tumbler to pour another dose.

"Something blocks me from seeing their faces," Beltrane said, a touch of strength returning to his voice as the drugs took effect. "Events are still in motion, and they have not yet made the final decision to chill. But I know that they will, and I'll be forced to feed the cloud."

That caught the baron by surprise. Feed the cloud? What the nuking hell did that mean?

"Is that the same thing as buying the farm?" a sec man asked in confusion, shifting the heavy blaster on his shoulder.

"Yes…no…" The doomie exhaled and his head dropped forward as sleep claimed him from the tremendous effort of staying awake for a few minutes.

Standing, Baron Eileen tucked the heavy blankets around the emaciated figure, then filled the tumbler once more and laid a small glass vial alongside it. The vial contained the last of the dust, a silvery powder made from the dried guts of the blowfish. If handled correctly, it was a painkiller better than anything found in the military stores of the old predark bases. If done wrongly, it aced faster than a dagger in the throat. This batch had been tested on some wild cats before being administered to the invaluable doomie.

"Is that wise, Baron?" a sec woman growled.

"He has suffered enough," the baron said, slowly standing to dust off her pants. "If he wishes to leave this world a little early, then he has my permission. Ten times his warnings have saved this ville from disaster. The very least we can do is spare him some pain."

"And what about the outlanders?" a fat sec man asked, a longblaster resting on his shoulder, a bandolier of refilled brass draped across his chest like a badge of honor.

"Arrest everybody who lands on our beach," the woman stated, hitching her gunbelt. "If they resist, ace them on the spot."

Softly mumbling something, the doomie began to snore, and the baron brushed a hand over his uncombed hair. She had also never told him about the child growing in her belly from last summer on the beach. The birth would be in a few months, and Beltrane would never last that long. With luck, the babe would be a norm, but if not, well, the ville could always use another doomie, sad to say.

Chapter Thirteen

In the morning, the companions awoke to the sound of rain.

Rushing to the window, Ryan started to throw open the shutters when there came the telltale reek of sulfur. Fireblast, that was acid rain! Getting a plastic shower curtain from his backpack, the one-eyed man draped it over his head for protection before risking the shutters. However, the ville was completely dry, not the slightest sign of rain damage. But in the distance, Ryan could see a wild storm raging at sea, the gentle breeze carrying to the land the reek of the deadly acid rain. Softly there came the noise of the hard rain pelting the choppy waves, which oddly sounded exactly like a steak sizzling on a grille.

"Thank God the wind is blowing in the right direction, or else we might have been stuck here for days." Mildred yawned, rubbing the sleep from her face as she joined them.

"It could shift anytime," J.B. stated, pushing back his fedora, as he stood behind her. "We better wait a bit before riding out. Don't want to get caught in the open."

Starting to reply, Ryan paused at the sight of something moving along a thin peninsula that extended from the main island. Racing for its life, a fat walrus was flopping along, desperately trying to reach what appeared to be a small cave. But it was too slow, and the deluge struck while it was scrambling over a low rill.

As the first drops hit, the walrus screamed, dark fumes rising from the searing contact. Then the animal began to dissolve under the deadly chemical assault, the blubbery hide sluicing off in horrid streams. Redoubling the frantic effort to escape, the walrus bawed in unimaginable agony as the nightmarish process continued, and it left behind a ghastly contrail of blood and internal organs.

Suddenly, Krysty was standing alongside Ryan and handed him the Steyr.

Without saying a word, the Deathlands warrior worked the arming bolt to chamber a round, then centered the crosshairs of the telescopic sight on the poor beast, adjusted for the wind sheer and squeezed the trigger. A second later the walrus jerked and flopped over sideways, the pain gone forever. The rain finished the job until there was nothing left of the animal, except for a reddish puddle of fatty sludge among the irregular rocks.

"Thank you," Krysty said, resting a hand on the man's shoulder.

Working the bolt on the Steyr, Ryan merely shrugged.

Just then there came a rush of damp air from the direction of the kitchen, and Doc appeared wearing a plastic sheet like a poncho.

"Well done, sir," the man rumbled in his deep stentorian bass. "An exemplary shot."

"Hard to miss a target that big," Ryan said, shouldering the longblaster. It had been a waste of brass, and if his son Dean had been present, he never would have done it to demonstrate to the boy that ammo was to be used only for survival, never casually. However, the soulful wails of the animal had sounded far too human, and having seen people die the same way, the ruthless killer felt true sympathy for anything caught in the awful grip of the all-destroying rain.

After a quick breakfast of fried bread and cold chicken, the companions gathered their meager belongings and went down to the throne room. Walking around nervously, the horses were nickering in fright at the smell of the distant storm, but the companions easily calmed the animals with gentle words and a generous supply of nectarines.

Using a pocketknife, Doc cut a nectarine in two, then stabbed the pit with the point of the blade and flipped it away. Putting the fruit on a flat palm, to make sure the animal didn't accidentally bite his fingers, Doc fed the treat to his roan mare and scratched her behind the ears.

The mare whinnied in unabashed pleasure at the sweet fruit, then nuzzled the old man and licked his cheek to the sound of sandpaper on rock.

"Good girl," Doc said, feeding her another.

"Be sure to use an extra blanket," Krysty advised, throwing a second one across the back of her dappled mare. "They're still pretty skinny, and may develop saddle sores if we don't."

"Easy fix," Jak added, draping the reins over his horse. "Cover with raw steak to protect."

"Most excellent, sir!" Doc boomed, lashing down a saddlebag. "Exactly as Attila the Hun did to keep his mighty army constantly in motion."

"Of course, afterward, the Mongol horde ate the steak," Mildred reminded, tightening the belly strap.

"They eat?" Jak asked in shock, then grinned. "Shit, no need weapons after that, just breathe on enemy."

"Speaking of riding, we should walk the animals for the first day or two," Krysty suggested, hanging a canteen over the pommel of her saddle. "Let them grow a bit stronger and get used to us more."

"Fair enough," Ryan said, sliding the Steyr into a leather boot attached to the saddle. "Or, at least, until we encounter another rhino. Then we ride 'em until the horses drop or we get away."

"Ah yes, the cold logic of pragmatism," Doc sighed, cleaning his damp cheek with a handkerchief. "Then let the storm hide our scent, distance blur our shapes, and good fortune cloak us in anonymity."

"Luck be a lady tonight," Mildred said, almost singing.

Puzzled, Doc shot her a look, then dismissed the matter. The lady physician knew as many obscure literary references from the twentieth century as he did from his own. In a contest of jocular effluvia, they were equally matched.

Leading the horses out of the throne room, the companions proceeded warily down the hill and through the ville, checking for any sign that somebody had sneaked inside during the night. The ville seemed unchanged, but just in case, J.B. climbed a guard tower to check outside the ville to make sure nobody was waiting for them to open the gate, especially another rhino.

"All clear," J.B. announced, waving his hat in the air.

Standing guard, Ryan kept the Steyr ready as Krysty and Jak got the two gates unlocked and pushed aside. The deep dents in the metal now carried new meaning to the companions, and everybody tightened the grip on their blaster.

As the companions moved away from the ville, Jak briefly glanced backward over a shoulder. "Not feel natural leave gate open," the albino teen said uneasily.

"Agreed, but there's no way to lock the bastard things from this side, so what's the point of merely closing them?" Ryan stated, chucking the reins slightly to make his horse walk a little faster. Snorting, the animal promptly did as requested. That pleased the man greatly. This had to have been the mount of a sec man, as it was very well trained and clearly bridle-wise.

"And so shall the next visitors reap the harvest we leave behind," Doc said, gesturing with a free hand. "The treasures of Xanadu are there for the taking."

"What leave?" Jak scoffed. "Burned rhino in corral, chicken bones in kitchen, horse drek in throne room."

"There are also pots and pans in the pantry, boots in the barracks and bedsheets in the gaudy house," J.B. countered, tucking the nubbin of a cigar into his mouth. "Not to mention the whole damn ville itself."

"The difference between garbage and treasure depends entirely upon how fragging poor you are,"

Krysty stated, the words carrying the ring of bitter experience.

Leaving the dirt road, the companions started across a field to try to hide their passage. However, they kept a close watch on the rain storm over the ocean. If it made the slightest shift in their direction, they would gallop hell-bent-for-leather for the forest of pine trees. The dense greenery would offer some small degree of protection from the acid rain. Not much, but it was better than nothing.

After a few miles, twisted chunks of metal began to dot the landscape, the chunks becoming larger and closer together until the companions came across a huge crater in the ground. It was filled with water, and even had a few fish darting in the weeds, but the bottom was a congealed slab of steel.

"This must have been a major space station. It's way too big to merely be a satellite," Mildred guessed, using a hand to shield her face from the morning sun with the other. "Eventually, it ran out of fuel for the retro rockets, couldn't correct the flight path and plummeted back to Earth like a meteor."

"Or got shot Seven Sisters," Jak noted with enthusiasm.

"Nonsense. Those are just a damn myth," J.B. scoffed. "Seven huge battle stations still orbiting the Earth and fighting the Last War? Utter crap."

"Oh, but they exist, John Barrymore!" Doc exclaimed excitedly. "I actually saw them once when I…" His voice trailed away, and the time traveler began to whistle a happy tune.

Surreptitiously, the rest of the companions exchanged glances with one another, but said nothing. Doc had been places and seen things they would never truly know about, as his journeys through time had scrambled a lot of his memory.

Privately, Ryan hoped that the man never made it back to his family. They might not recognize Doc anymore, and that would probably do what barons, cannies and muties had never been able to achieve—break his spirit and kill the man. There were still elements of the peaceful schoolteacher buried deep inside Doc, and Ryan knew that was how the man saw himself, as a teacher and a scholar, a man of books. But the truth was a lot more ugly. Doc Tanner was a true product of the Deathlands: born in pain, abandoned to fate, forged in betrayal and honed in combat. He would be as out of place in the predark civilized world as a rampaging kraken.

Coming to an abrupt halt, Jak raised an arm high and closed his hand into a fist. Instantly everybody stopped walking and drew their blasters, glancing around to try to see what the albino teen had spotted.

Going to a ragged clump of laurel bushes, Jak took a stick from the ground and used it to gently push the leaves apart. Hidden on the other side of the bushes was the basement of a predark house, the upper stories completely gone. The splintery remains of wooden stairs led down to the concrete floor, the rusting remains of a furnace sitting in the corner. A crazy array of water pipes went nowhere. The floor was littered with piles of windblown trash, dried feces and a large pile of gleaming white bones. Some of them were animals—dogs, bears and such—ßbut there was no mistaking the smashed human skulls, and off to the side was a heap of torn clothing. Jak scowled at the sight.

"Stickies." The teenager spit hatefully, strangely holstering the Colt Python. "Safe. Gone long time."

"Indeed, lad, but are they deceased or simply departed?" Doc inquired, not relinquishing his grip on the LeMat and Webley.

"No fresh bones," Jak stated, as if that settled the matter. "Drek on floor month old, mebbe more."

"Fair enough, but no talking for the next few miles," Ryan whispered, patting the neck of his horse. The animals didn't seem frightened by the smell of the old nest. More proof that they had belonged to sec men. Stickies were the terror of the Deathlands, and most animals blindly ran at the first whiff of a mutie. Or worse, that terrible hooting they made just before attacking.

Easing away from the old nest, the companions watched every group of trees or clump of bushes with renewed intensity, fully expecting a mob of stickies to come charging out of the shadows, waving their bizarre hands and hooting their inhuman battle cry. Each of the companions had the oddest feeling that they were being watched, but nothing dangerous was in sight for miles in every direction, all the way from the fiery volcano in the far east and the snowcapped mountains to the west.

Keeping a safe distance from any predark ruins, the group marched deeper inland, leaving the sounds and the smells of the sea far behind. Skirting around the cracked black ribbon of a paved airfield, the companions moved farther into the foothills, until the ground became too steep for there to be any more settlements.

Slowly the sun rose higher behind the dark clouds that perpetually blanketed the scorched sky. Noon came and went, the companions eating the last of the self-heats while walking, and then stuffing the litter into their saddlebags to try to hide their trail. Jak even cut some branches from a pine tree and tied them to the saddles for the horses to drag along behind to erase their footprints. He claimed it was an old swamp trick, while Doc and Mildred both remained tactfully silent on the fact that ploy had been invented by the Native Americans long before the Europeans arrived.

Eventually the hills eased into a rolling glen. A small waterfall gushed from the side of a ragged escarpment splashing into a pool that flowed away to become a babbling creek. Sweet grass and juniper bushes grew along the banks in abundance, and the companions had to be stern with the horses to keep the hungry animals from stuffing their bellies. It was cruel, but necessary. Although several times larger than a person, a horse only had a brain the size of an orange. If given the chance, the animals would eat themselves sick, and then spend the rest of the day moaning with a bellyache. Ripping choice handfuls of grass from the sloping bank, the companions fed the horses while walking, only stopping for them to drink some water before continuing the long trek.

"This right direction?" Jak asked, squinting at the ragged mountains in the murky distance.

"Dark night, no," J.B. replied honestly. "But we're heading for where the SEAL base used to be located, and that's the best place to start the search for the part we need to fix that engine."

"If not there?"

"Then we carve oars from planks and row off this bastard rock," Ryan growled, swatting at a mosquito on his neck. For some damn reason, his new eyepatch seemed to be attracting the damn bugs, and he alone was bearing the full fury of their bloodthirsty attacks.

"Here, smear this on your skin," Krysty said, passing over a small bottle.

"Shine?" Ryan asked, removing the top. He caught a familiar smell. "Diesel fuel?"

"It works fine. Just don't trigger a blaster too close to your face."

Hesitantly, the itchy man applied the oily fluid and was surprised that it did work. Then Ryan spent the next hour wiping his gun hand clean on leaves in case there was any trouble.

Following the creek, the companions were pleased when it joined another at a muddy delta to form a shallow river. Soon more tributaries fed into the waterway and it became a proper river. The water was only about a yard deep, just enough to swim in, but there were a lot of colorful fish darting through the reeds and the small stands of bamboo growing alongside a small sandbar located only a few yards off the muddy shore.

"This is a good place to break for the day," Ryan

announced, looking over a small clearing. "We push the horses any farther, and they'll get sick."

"No damn flapjacks in the area," J.B. said, noting the presence of bird nests in the trees. "And no ruins for stickies to hide in."

"We are avoiding the small predark ruins to head for much larger predark ruins of an entire city," Doc said, brushing back his silvery hair. "Good Lord, how the universe does love its irony."

"But none here, which fine by me," Jak stated, dropping his backpack, then hanging the reins of his horse over a thorny bush. The animal shuffled its hooves until the pine tree branch was removed from the saddle, then it shook all over and visibly relaxed.

"I will gather firewood, if somebody else will rustle up some lunch," Doc offered, lashing his reins to a splintery tree stump. Immediately the horse began chomping on the thick growth of green grass nearby.

"Done and done," Krysty announced, going to the stand of bamboo.

Cutting a length, the woman trimmed a point onto the end, then carved a small notch just above that. Stepping into the reeds, Krysty squinted, then stabbed down with the spear. As she pulled up the bamboo, there was a wiggling trout impaled on the notch. With a flick of the wrist, she sent the fish sailing into the clearing, then turned to stab into the water again. In only a few minutes Krysty had a small pile of flopping fish on the ground. One of them had crude wings and another possessed a third eye on a flexible stalk. Those were thrown back into the river, but the rest seemed normal.

"I clean." Pulling a thin knife from his belt, Jak started cleaning the fish, deftly removing the guts and scales, but leaving on the heads.

"Would you please remove those?" Mildred asked hopefully.

"Best flavor," the teen replied, his hands busy.

"My dear Jak," Doc gasped, dropping an armload of dry wood. "Do you really plan on eating those heads after what we saw in the cannie ville?"

"Fish not screamer," Jak stated, then looked questioningly at Mildred.

"Eat all you want." Mildred sighed. "Fish don't have enough brain tissue to matter. Besides, they would have needed to be eating their own kind for years. Trout only eating trout, bass only bass, and so on. I doubt very highly that could happen in an aquatic environment."

"Most animals have a natural reluctance to eating their own kind," Ryan said, pitting another nectarine to feed to his horse. "Sort of a built-in safety factor."

"Quite true!" Doc grinned, dusting off his hands. "Besides which…" His voice trailed off just then, and the man stood tall, delicately sniffing the air. "Is…is that cornbread?"

"And bacon," Jak growled, wiping the blade clean before shoving it back into the sheath. "We got company."

Immediately everybody pulled out weapons and clicked off the safeties.

With blaster in hand, Ryan nodded at Krysty, then the horses. She gave a nod in reply, and went to stand guard while the rest of the companions assumed a combat formation and swept forward into the forest, using the rocks and trees as cover.

Less than a thousand feet away, the forest ended at another clearing. There was a bubbling spring situated near a crackling campfire, a battered iron frying pan sizzling softly above the flames and giving off the most wonderful aromas. Several logs had been dragged from the forest to form a crude square around the blaze to reflect back the heat at night to keep the campers warm. There were some patched canvas duffel bags hanging from a tree branch where the bugs couldn't reach them, but aside from that, there were no other signs of people. No wags, horses, cigs, drek or brass.

"Don't like this," Ryan whispered, checking for snipers in the treetops.

"Agreed," J.B. muttered, slipping a hand into his munitions bags. Effortlessly he found a pipe bomb wrapped with duct tape holding a row of nails in place. This was what he called a junk bomb. Toss the stick into a campfire and half a heartbeat later everybody not safely behind a rock was going to be picking rusty steel out of their guts and generally bleeding to death in nine different ways.

"Shitfire, ground swept," Jak said in a terse warning.

With a snarl, Ryan spun and raced back toward their own campsite. The only reason for anybody to sweep the clearing would be to hide their numbers. Which meant the cooking food had to be the bait in a trap to lure the companions away from the river so that...

Suddenly a horse loudly whinnied and there came

the bellowing roar of a black-powder blaster closely followed by the yammering rattle of an M-16 rapidfire.

Sprinting back to the river, Ryan and the others burst
out of the greenery, their blasters sweeping for targets.
Black smoke was rising from the campfire where the
fish had fallen into the flames. The horses were whinnying in fright, their great eyes showing white all around.
Hunkered down behind the tree stump, Krysty was
sending off short bursts from the M-16. Dotting the
clearing, five people in tan clothing were moving low
through the weeds, firing their blasters in return, but
clearly more interested in reaching the tethered horses
than in acing the woman.

In unison, the companions cut loose with their blasters, Jak and Mildred moving to the trees on the left,
with J.B. and Doc going to the right, so as to not offer a
group target. Ryan stayed where he was in the bushes as
the anchor man for the flanking maneuver. The barrage
cut the tops off some weeds and blew apart a shaft of
bamboo, but that was it. The angle of attack was bad,
so Ryan and the others shot high to try to drive the
strangers out of hiding and not risk hitting Krysty.

Startled curses answered the blasterfire, and the attackers circling the horses stopped moving and hugged
the ground to send back a flurry of hot lead from an
assortment of blasters.

"Everybody freeze or I'll ace the horses!" Ryan
boomed in his loudest voice. J.B. put a burst from
the Uzi into the air, while Doc triggered both of his
handblasters.

There was no reply, and for a long minute the only

sounds were of the frightened horses, the campfire and the gentle murmur of the rushing river.

"Ace the horses, and we'll chill the slut!" a fat woman bellowed in return, shifting her position amid the bushes.

"Do that, and gut slow!" Jak snarled. "Take days chill!"

"She'll still be chilled!" a skinny man replied from the trees across the river.

"And so will you!" Doc added, a tinge of madness creeping into his normally cultured tones.

"Leave and live, or stay and die!" Ryan yelled, then lowered his voice to conversational level. "Your choice."

The confident change in tone clearly bothered the strangers, as the Deathlands warrior had expected it to, and another minute passed in tense silence.

"How about we cut a deal?" the fat woman said, slowly rising from concealment. The blaster in her grip was pointed at the ground, but with a finger still on the trigger.

The woman was wide and heavily muscled, the knuckles of both hands covered with a lot of small scars. Her hair was cut short in a mil buzz, and there was a coiled bullwhip at her hip, the tip glittering with a steel hook. The burly woman wore a tan uniform with a single red stripe on the sleeve. That marked her as a corporal in a ville sec force. Not very surprisingly, the companions recognized her uniform as the same worn by the chilled sec men in the abandoned ville.

"A deal? We got nothing to talk about, except where

to bury you," Ryan answered from the bushes, needlessly working the arming bolt on the Steyr. The metallic noise seemed supernaturally loud.

Nervously, the sec woman shifted her stance, as if unsure whether to dive for cover or to keep talking.

"Look, all we want is our horses back!" a man shouted from the weeds. His face was covered by the waving plants, but his greasy hair was visible. It stuck out in every direction as if he had recently been struck by lightning.

"Your horses? How do you figure that?" Mildred asked scornfully from behind a thick oak tree. The bark was rough against her back, the shade deliciously cool.

"We're from Nimitz ville, and those animals bear the brand of our baron!" the fat woman answered defiantly. "I don't know how you managed to jack them, but—"

"Deserted!" Ryan interrupted.

"Eh? What the frag does that mean?" she demanded suspiciously.

"The ville is deserted, everybody's aced and the gate is wide open," Ryan continued. "That makes anything inside fair game to scav."

"They belong to us!" the man across the river retorted hotly.

"Not anymore," J.B. answered from the shadows.

"Hold on now, let's try to be reasonable about this," the corporal said, using her left hand to put a homemade cigar into her mouth and lighting it with a match. Her other hand still held the .22-caliber blaster, cocked and ready to fire.

As she exhaled, Ryan recognized the smell as zoom, a mix of tobacco, marijuana and wolfweed. It was potent stuff, and he guessed she was calming her nerves to get ready for a suicide charge. In the back of his mind, the man wondered why the armed sec men were so desperate to get hold of the horses. Then he shoved that question aside for later. Gotta stay on target. Protect Krysty, save the horses, ace these sons of bitches, and in that order, he thought.

"Who the frag are you, anyway?" Ryan demanded, a plan already forming.

"Corporal Moore, Janet Moore. You got a name?"

"Cawdor," Ryan replied. "What are you offering?"

The woman took a long drag on the cigar, filling her lungs with the dark smoke, then letting it trickle out of her nose in twin streams. "Okay, Cawdor, how about we—"

"Sniper!" Doc snarled, firing both of his blasters into the trees.

From amid the leafy greenery there came a cry of pain, and a norm tumbled out to hit the ground in a hard thump, a longblaster slipping from his twitching hands. Startled by his appearance, the skittish horses reared in terror, then jerked their tethers free and started to run away.

Instantly wild blasterfire filled the clearing, lead flying in every direction.

"Nuking hell, I told ya to wait for my signal!" Corporal Moore yelled, shooting into the bushes.

Even as he heard the twang of the .22-caliber round ricochet off a rock several yards away, Ryan triggered the Steyr and shot the sec woman in the throat, the slug exploding out the back of her neck in a bloody geyser.

Caught in a fair fight, the ville sec men were mercilessly slaughtered by the companions, the furious battle over almost as soon as it had begun.

"We…was…still talking…" Moore wheezed, red fluids dribbling from her slack mouth to dribble down her double chins.

"No, you were trying to get us into the open so the sniper could chill us easier," Ryan said, bending to take the tiny revolver and tuck it into his gunbelt. "We just didn't fall for the same trick twice."

"T-twice?"

Callously, the Deathlands warrior started checking the dying woman for any spare brass. "The bacon and cornbread. That was triple smart. Damn near worked, too."

"Always did…before," Moore whispered, a hand clutching her ruined throat to hold in the escaping life.

Tucking the loose rounds into a pocket, Ryan spotted the dropped cigar and crushed it under a boot. "Mebbe against ville people, and pilgrims, but not us."

"You…s-sec…men?"

"We used to run with the Trader," Ryan stated coldly.

Her eyes went wide at the startling pronouncement, then they began to fog over as death approached. "N-never…stood chance…then.."

"Not really, no."

"S-shoulda known…not t-trust…Carlton," she

gurgled, then coughed hard, a wellspring of blood gushing between her fingers. "He…s-said I'd be new baron…"

"Yeah, and who is Carlton?" Ryan asked with a scowl.

"Why…sh-should I tell a-anything t-to…a dead man?" Moore groaned with a guttural laugh. Releasing her throat, the fat sec woman grabbed something from her shirt pocket and jammed it into her mouth to blow so hard that both cheeks puffed out.

Jerking aside, Ryan half expected to be hit by a dart from the miniature blowpipe. But nothing seemed to happen, and after a few seconds the obese woman slumped into death, a strange smile playing on her stained lips as if she had just won the battle.

Chapter Fourteen

Streaming contrails of oily blue smoke, the gang of motorcycle riders plowed through the jungle vines, the iron cages around them crushing aside the lush greenery. Monkeys in the treetops screeched their disapproval of the machines, and fat snakes slithered quickly away from their rumbling approach.

The cage of metal bars welded to the frame of each bike completely surrounded the rider, offering safety from rollovers and some small degree of security from the dreaded jumpers. At the front of the gang, the cage of the point rider was thickly festooned with bits of leafy vines and the occasional spiderflower. Violently torn from its web, the thing was still horribly twitching, and even as it died, the mutie plant hissed softly at the sec man. However, he turned away just in time, and the cloud of hallucinogenic pollen dissipated harmlessly on the wind. When he was sure that it was safe, the sec man ripped the flower off the bars and crushed it into pulp before throwing it away. Then he wiped his hands clean on a rag tied to his gunbelt for just such a purpose.

"Better a spider than a jumper, eh, Corporal?" Baron Jones shouted over the combined roar of the engines.

"If you say so, Baron," the sec man growled in reply,

revving the flathead engine of his bike to force a path through the giant ferns and hanging moss.

As the riders crested a low hillock, Baron Carson Jones called a halt and throttled down the ancient two-wheelers to checked the gauges before turning off the knucklehead engine. Reaching into a saddlebag draped over the rear fender, the baron extracted a pair of binocs and looked down into the valley at the base of the hill. Slowly, the baron gave a cold smile.

"Find something, dear?" Lady Veronica asked, stopping her bike alongside. Her long black hair was tied off her face with a silk scarf, and the checkered grips of her blasters jutted up from a wide gunbelt like samurai swords. The Plexiglas windshield was covered with a juicy splattering of winged bugs, and a longblaster was tucked into a leather scabbard alongside the hot engine. As she forced down the kickstand, the spurs on her half-boots jingled softly.

"Look down there," the baron commanded, passing over a pair of bincos.

Accepting the device, Lady Veronica did as requested. "That's Nimitz ville, sure enough," she said hesitantly. "But it seems to be deserted." The woman dialed for greater clarity. "No, by the coast gods, there's spent brass all over the place! There was some sort of an invasion, or rebellion!"

"Has to be Carlton," the baron said with absolute conviction. Taking a canteen off the handlebars, the man took a long swig, sloshing the brew in his mouth before swallowing. Jungle Tea tasted nothing like pre-dark coffee, but it had just as powerful a kick and helped keep his mind sharp.

"And by that, you mean the dirty traitor Digger," Lady Veronica replied with an expression of pure hatred, her hands tightening on the binocs.

"Pardon my asking, Baron," a sec man said respectfully, "but if Digger now works for Carlton, why is he heading inland and not to sea?"

"What better place to have a secret harbor for your oceangoing war ships than a mountain lake connected to the Cific by a river?" Lady Veronica answered, her hair stirring angrily.

The idea startled the sec man. Captain Carlton hid his fleet in the foothills? Damn, that was triple clever!

"Wonder where he got the cannon to knock open the front gate?" Baron Jones asked nobody in particular, capping the canteen.

"That's not cannon damage," Lady Veronica replied curtly. "Look at those depressions in the ground. The ville was attacked by a thunder king."

The baron frowned. "So the little bastard can summon a king, eh?"

"So it would appear, my love," Lady Veronica growled, her pretty face distorting into a feral grimace. When she was only a child, a herd of the muties had taken both of her parents, leaving her an orphan of the street. Her detest of the things was only equaled by her raw hatred for the mutie master, Captain Carlton.

Taking back the binocs, the baron checked for any signs of life in the ville. But it was completely abandoned, even the front gate was open. A couple of stickies wandered around the huts and buildings searching for anything edible. With delighted hoots, the things converged upon the smoldering corpse in the corral and started to rip off chunks of the burned flesh with their suckered-covered hands.

"Musta been a nukestorm of a fight," another sec man commented, wiping his dirty face and neck with a soiled handkerchief. The trickles of sweat were replaced by smears of engine grease.

"We going after them, Baron?" a fat sec man asked, checking the load in his new longblaster. The wooden stock of the BAR was wrapped in canvas strips to prevent any slippage from sweaty hands, as was the trigger and arming bolt.

Once the weapon had had a telescopic sight, but the sec man had traded that to a pretty young gaudy slut for a month of her favors. It was a good deal, since he hadn't used the scope in years. The man was a natural gunner, and lead always seemed to hit whatever he wanted it to.

"Not across those open fields," the baron scoffed, tucking away the bincos. "There's nothing out there but stickies, screamers and thunder kings." He frowned in thought. "Mebbe Carlton can summon a king, but there's no nuking way to control one, or to make it stop once it gets the smell of blood."

"I'd rather face a live nuke than a king," a burly sec man said with feeling, cracking his knuckles. His arms were covered with a zoo of crude tattoos depicting everything he had chilled: norm, animal or mutie.

"Agreed! We'll stay in the jungle, where it's safe," Lady Veronica added blandly.

The troops chuckled at that. The only place safe on Clemente Island was in the grave.

"If Carlton and his sailors manage to reach high

ground alive, we'll ambush them in PacCom," the baron declared, starting the big knucklehead engine again. It rattled and belched, then settled into a steady purr of power.

"Everybody good on juice?" Lady Veronica asked. "Got enough oil? Air pressure?" There came an answering chorus. "Good. Now, stay in formation!"

"And watch for jumpers!" the baron shouted, revving the knucklehead bike to the red line, then twisting the handlebar controls.

The gang of caged hogs surged back into the thick jungle, smashing through the thick foliage, leaving a path of destruction in their wake. Gradually the crushed plants began to rise again, ever so slowly returning to their former positions. In less than an hour there was no sign that people and bikes had ever passed this way. The dense jungle fully returned to its original pristine condition.

REACHING OUT, Ryan snatched the item and gave it a cursory glance before tossing it to Mildred. "Is that what I think it is?" he demanded.

Making the catch, Mildred looked at the tiny metal pipe and was startled to see it was a predark item. She had owned one for a while as an intern just to annoy her neighbors when they played rap music too loud for her to study. Then the implications hit her, and the physician cast away the thing as if it were white-hot.

"Horses!" she bellowed, turning to sprint for the trees. "We have to find the horses right fucking now!"

Without hesitation, the rest of the companions took flight after the woman.

"Millie, what is that thing?" J.B. demanded, hugging his munitions bag close to his chest.

"A dog whistle!" she shouted, pelting along. "An ultrasonic dog whistle!"

"We can handle a pack of dogs, madam," Doc retorted, starting to slow down, then his pace quickened. "By the Three Kennedys, you mean an ultrasonic rhino whistle!"

"Exactly!"

As if on cue, there came a thunderous roar in the distance, closely followed by a soft pounding in the ground that grew louder every second.

Unfortunately it was soon painfully obvious to the companions that the horses hadn't stopped, and were still running for the horizon.

"Fireblast! We're not going to catch them until hunger brings them back," Ryan panted, slowing to a halt.

"If ever," Krysty agreed, looking around quickly. If there had been a cliff for them to climb, or even some boulders, the companions might have stood a chance at making a stand. But the gentle rolling hills offered no natural protection. Just a lot of wide-open fields, a shallow river and pine trees that a rhino could knock over as easily as stomping on a dandelion.

"Dark night, we're well and truly nuked!" J.B. muttered, reaching into the bag to haul out a stick of TNT. The long cylinder was wrapped in duct tape to hold a double row of predark roofing nails in place. He had cobbled the junk bomb together the previous night in anticipation of fighting another of the armored giants. There were two more of the junk bombs in his bag, the last reserved for him to shove down the throat of the biowep as it trampled him flat. If this was his day to board the last train west, then the man would go down fighting!

"Still got stick?" Jak asked, jerking out the ammo clip of the M-16 rapidfire.

"Sure," Mildred said in confusion, then dug out the bag to carefully smear the sticky poison along the top bullet.

The vibrations in the earth were coming closer together now, and there was a hard pounding sound like an advancing machine.

With a grim expression, Jak slammed the clip back into place and wrapped the carrying strap around his forearm to help steady his aim. He would have only one chance at this, and couldn't afford a miss.

"Okay, we don't have a choice this time," Ryan growled. "J.B., Krysty, use your implo grens. Everybody else, start running back toward the ruins! Mebbe you can trick the thing to fall into a basement. That won't hold the bastard for long, but it'll give you a chance to reach the ville again."

"Never stop firing!" Krysty added, yanking the tape off the gren. "That at least slows down the mutie!"

Suddenly a flock of birds erupted from the forest and a pine tree toppled over to the sound of splintering wood as the ugly head of a rhino appeared from the laurel bushes. Its piggy eyes glanced around to lock upon the companions, and the biowep lumbered forward, each step coming a little faster.

Instantly the companions cut loose with their blasters, but the barrage of soft lead rounds ricocheted off the armored mutie as if they were throwing autumn leaves. Only Jak didn't fire. Kneeling, he was tracking the advance of the beast, trying to get a clear shot of the mouth.

"I'll make it whimper!" J.B. snarled, lighting the fuse of a pipe bomb.

"No, wait, I've got an idea!" Mildred cried, but it was too late.

The cylinder went tumbling forward to land directly in front of the beast. Incredibly the mutie swerved and the charge detonated loudly a yard away, the hail of nails hissing through the air, smacking into the rocks and trees and peppering the side of the rhino. It grunted from the impacts, and Jak fired, the poisoned bullet glancing off the creature's jaw to spin away crazily.

Incredibly, Ryan's stallion charged out of the woods, the horse throating a challenge at the racing mutie. Turning fast, the rhino headed straight toward the new danger. Rearing onto both hind legs, the horse pawed the air, an iron-clad hoof scoring a furrow across the forehead of the rhino, narrowly missing an eye.

Ducking low, the mutie used its main horn to protect its face from another strike, and the two combatants circled each other, the rhino thrusting the horn for the vulnerable throat of the horse, while the stallion snapped at the brutish enemy with his large teeth, nipping at one ear, then the other.

The rhino unexpectedly reared up, its broad toes digging into the soil, and the mutie rammed the horse with a stout leg. Knocked dizzy, the horse stumbled, and the rhino gored the stunned animal with its main horn, the curved length going in all the way. Mortally wounded, the horse screamed in pain, then the rhino jerked its brute head aside, ripping open the belly, the ropy intestines slithering out to fall onto the ground.

Collapsing into the dirt, the stallion weakly pawed its legs at the enemy, but the rhino climbed onto the other animal and began stomping it flat. The horse briefly screamed, then went silent, and there was only the juicy crushing of warm flesh and the splintering of bones.

Quickly, J.B. threw a second pipe bomb at the dead horse. As the sizzling charge landed, the rhino snapped at the bomb and started chewing it when both animals vanished in a thunderclap of flame and smoke.

As the fumes cleared, the horse was gone, blown into pieces. But the accursed rhino was still standing, although with both horns removed. Its face was a mottled array of bleeding wounds and nail holes, strips of torn flesh dangling loosely.

Thrusting its head down, the rhino started chomping on random bits of the horse, feeding the voracious engine of its body as the damage started to be repaired.

"Okay, everybody start running," Ryan commanded.

"No, don't!" Mildred stated, placing a hand on his fist. "Head for the river!"

Annoyed, Ryan stared at the woman as if she had been smoking wolfweed.

"Trust me on this," Mildred said, looking him in the face.

After a moment Ryan nodded his acceptance and

turned to race for the nearby river, with the others close behind.

"Now what, madam?" Doc asked, stopping at the edge of the water.

"Get on the island, you fool!" she shouted, sloshing forward.

"Island, what island?" J.B. shouted. "That is a fragging sandbar, Millie!"

"Just get into the fucking river!" she yelled over a shoulder, the rushing water rising only to her waist before it started dropping once more.

Following her lead, the rest of the companions crossed the shallow river and rejoined on the tiny strip of damp sand. They needed to stand very close together, and the grim companions could feel the body heat of the person next to them.

"What next?" Jak demanded.

But just then, the rhino appeared from the trees, its gore-streaked face still reforming as it charged once more toward the companions.

Stepping knee-deep into the river, Ryan lifted a pipe bomb high.

"Don't bother, we're safe now," Mildred panted, a sly smile crossing her face. "Watch this."

Lumbering on like an express train, the rhino crossed the forest clearing in only a few seconds, running directly over the campfire as if not even noticing the flames. But as it approached the muddy bank, the mutie abruptly slammed to a halt. Hesitantly, the rhino took a step forward, a squat leg touching the water. But it immediately withdrew and loudly roared in frustration, its double horns slashing the air wildly.

"See this, not believe," Jak said, trying to figure out if the rhino was playing some sort of trick.

Once more, the rhino dipped a foot into the river and hastily withdrew. Radiating fury the way a furnace did heat, the mutie once more bellowed in unbridle rage and began to march along the shoreline, only yards from the cluster of people.

"Good Lord, the beast will not enter the water," Doc whispered in amazement, lowering his two blasters. "Madam, how did you know?"

"Basic science," Mildred said, massaging the back of her neck. "The creature is armor-plated, built like a tank. But it's too small to have any real buoyancy, way too dense, which means it can't possibly swim. Deep water would chill that thing faster than shoving it off a cliff."

"But the water isn't deep," Krysty said hesitantly, securing the tape on the implo gren.

The physician smiled. "Yeah, but it doesn't know that."

"The mutie can smash through granite, but it fears water?" Ryan said slowly, almost lowering his fist.

"Of course! It was the pounding of the legs that reminded me of a documentary I once saw about elephants. It explained how they can swim, but just barely. Any heavier, and it would be impossible." Mildred gestured with a palm. "And behold, there is your proof. Anything that could survive a pipe bomb in its mouth would have to be denser than concrete."

Waddling over to one of the chilled sec men, the rhino started to noisily eat the body—boots, blaster and all going into the chomping jaws.

"Hold breath?" Jak asked, covering his mouth with a palm for no sane reason.

"No, the metabolism is too fast," Mildred answered confidently, finally holstering her blaster. "See how fast it breathes? The mutie would suffocate under water in only a few seconds trying to supply oxygen to its heart. Too big, too muscled, too bad."

Finished with the first corpse, the rhino glared at the companions huddled on the sandbar and stomped the ground a few times defiantly before going to the next body.

"What should we do now, my dear Ryan?" Doc asked, rummaging in his pockets. The man found two replacement brass and slipped them into the cylinder of the Webley, closing the blaster with fingertip pressure.

"Get to the other side of the river," Ryan said, walking into the rushing water, "and start looking for those bastard horses!"

Chapter Fifteen

Sloshing to the opposite bank, the companions went to check the bodies of the chilled, while Ryan stood guard. Steadily munching, the rhino hatefully watched them from the other side of the shallow river, its piggy eyes never leaving the big man.

Untouched by the rhino, the blasters were in fine condition, just old and dirty. The sec men had been heavily armed and carrying a wide assortment of blasters, several of them crude affairs built from old lavatory plumbing and iron bailing wire. Since they already had better weapons than these, the companions concentrated on recovering any live brass.

"Keep the very best, dump the rest," Krysty commanded. "We're carrying enough deadweight as it is."

"Never enough brass, though." J.B. chuckled, pouring a handful of loose 9 mm rounds into his munitions bag. The jingling was music to his ears.

"Pity there was no black powder," Doc rumbled, rotating the cylinder of the LeMat. Then he dry fired the gun a few times to check the action.

Along with the blasters and brass, there was an abundance of whips, knives and boomerangs, all of which was left behind. However, the companions discovered a host of other useful items: a small compass, a couple of wax candles, beef jerky, beans and five more self-heats.

"Must have been saving these for something special," J.B. said, tucking the cans into his munitions bag.

"What better celebration than their own demise, eh, John Barrymore?" Doc asked, carefully adding a copper percussion nipple to the LeMat before holstering the weapon. Now he was fully armed, with almost more ammunition for the two blasters than he could carry. It was a delightful feeling, and one that he wished to experience more often.

"No sign of the horses yet," Ryan announced, resting a combat boot on a fallen log. "All right, make camp and let's have some chow."

"Right here, Ryan?" Doc asked askance, glancing at the bloody corpses strewed around. Flies were starting to arrive in droves, along with new swarms of mosquitoes.

"Don't know about you, but I was hungry before this fight started," Ryan replied, never taking his gaze off the rhino. "Now, I'm bastard famished. Besides which, it is getting dark and a campfire might attract the horses."

"We'll just move upwind," Mildred added, "and build an extra fire between us and the dearly departed."

Soon enough, the two fires were crackling away, and the air was filled with the smell of frying fish, coffee sub, bacon and beans from the self-heats.

"Ah, pure ambrosia!" Doc exclaimed, inhaling deeply. "A meal fit for a baron."

"Just beans." Jak grinned, adding a dash of shine to the bubbling legumes.

"My dear Jak, you seriously underestimate your skills as a culinary expert," Doc said, smiling as he squatted down on his heels. "You could make even the best French chef jealous."

"Prefer MRE," Jak said honestly, taking a taste with a wooden spoon. Then he frowned.

"Needs some garlic?" Mildred asked with a grin.

"No, filia powder," the teenager replied. "But good enough for now."

Accepting the M-16 from Krysty, Doc took his turn as guard, and Ryan came back to wash and have dinner with the others. In the middle of the meal, Mildred replaced Doc, who dived into the meal with obvious gusto.

Across the river, the rhino snorted at the smells of the cooking food and pounded the ground to show its displeasure. The companions ignored the beast as much as possible.

As true night arrived, the companions could see a soft glow on the western horizon and the vague outline of a predark city, hundreds of lights twinkling among the crumbling buildings.

As expected, the horses individually started coming back during the night, and soon all five had returned, hungry, dirty, their manes full of burrs.

Tending to the animals, the companions gave them food, combed out the burrs and treated some deep scratches with witch hazel. The horses nickered at the sting of the antiseptic fluid, but clearly had been treated this way before, and none of them bolted.

"We were lucky and didn't lose much," Krysty stated, checking the contents of a saddlebag. "But now that we are down a horse, somebody is going to have to pair up in the morning."

"Millie can ride with me," J.B. said, looking up from thumbing fresh rounds into an exhausted clip for the Uzi. "Plenty of room on my saddle."

"I'll say!" Mildred replied in a lusty voice that made the man blush and the rest of the companions roar with laughter.

Across the river, the rhino snorted in frank disapproval at the sound of merriment and went back to eating the dead.

Taking the first shift, Jak settled in with a rapidfire and a cup of hot coffee sub, while the others banked the two fires with extra wood. Crawling into their patched bedrolls, the companions were warm enough, and made sure that their weapons were close at hand. Just in case of trouble. At first, it was difficult for them to get to sleep over the steady munching from the other side of the river, but eventually their tired bodies yielded to the demands of nature, and soon a chorus of gentle snoring mixed with the nearby rush of the water and the breaking of bones.

In the morning the companions were pleased to discover that the rhino had departed. However, they felt sure he was still in the area, watching and waiting for them to make a mistake and cross the river into his part of the world. Suspiciously, the corpse of the fat sec woman was untouched, the blaster still lying in her outstretched hand.

Well-fed, curried and rested, the horses now accepted the companions as their new masters, and made no complaints as they climbed into the saddles. With the loss of his stallion, Ryan took the next-largest animal, a barrel-chested mare with a reddish-brown coat and a thick black mane.

"Okay, let's ride. But close to the river," Ryan directed, sliding the Steyr into a gunboot set alongside his saddle. The leather sleeve hadn't been made for this particular weapon, and the telescopic sight made it a snug fit. That meant Ryan wouldn't have to worry about the longblaster bouncing free if they were chased over rough terrain.

"No argument there!" Mildred replied, wrapping her arms around the waist of J.B. while the man shook the reins and got his gelding into motion.

Staying at an easy pace, the companions rode on through the next few days, stopping only to cook meals, sleep and regularly check for any saddle sores. But the horses were in fine shape, and actually seemed to relish the relaxed pace of the ride, along with the steady supply of food. Each of them was starting to noticeably fill out a little, the gaunt look easing in their long faces, muscles swelling, a healthy shine returning to their coats.

There was no further sign of the rhino, but the companions wisely stayed close to the river anyway, until it snaked away to the south, with the predark ruins just to the north. With no choice in the matter, Ryan led the group away from the waterway, feeling steadily more vulnerable as it receded.

"What weapons got left?" Jak asked, his body moving to the motion of the horses as if he had been born in a saddle.

"Two pipe bombs, the two implo grens, a jar full of firecrackers and a dozen road flares," J.B. answered.

"If that damn thing charges us again, you can fragging guess which I'm using first!"

Hearing the worried tone in his voice, Mildred gave the man a squeeze around the waist, and he replied by patting her hand.

At dawn the next day the companions reached the outskirts of the city. Traces of a paved road appeared sporadically under the thick grass, and occasionally the rusted remains of a mailbox would appear inside a clump of weeds. There was a large irregular hole in the ground alongside a tall sign announcing a gas station, and a U.S. Navy Hummer sat in the middle of a field of clover, the interior now, ironically, a humming beehive.

By noon, the ruins were coming closer together, the scattered remains of the suburbs giving way to office buildings and stores. There were a lot of cars scattered on the streets, and an APC rested amid the rubble of a smashed fountain.

None of the buildings rose more than ten stories. Palm trees grew randomly, often out of the wrecks of cars or store windows. A large building seemed to have a small rain forest thriving on the roof.

"Must have once had a rooftop garden," Mildred guessed, using a hand to shade her face from the sun. "They made good insulation, and even better PR."

"Better what, madam?" Doc asked, titling his head.

"Public relations," Mildred replied, feeling sheepish for some reason. "A lot of business executives didn't care how they made money, as long as they were liked by the public."

"Scalawags." Doc snorted in contempt.

She nodded. "At the very least."

"Folks revolt and hang?" Jak asked, checking over the passing ruins.

"Sadly, no," Mildred said with a sigh. "But sometimes, it sure would have been nice if they had."

"Bastard odd place," Ryan muttered, the Steyr lying across his lap for quick access. "The city looks like it was nuked before skydark."

"It was," Mildred answered. "Well, sort of, anyway. This isn't a real city, but the training grounds for the SEALs to practice fighting in an urban environment. This was built to resemble the ruins of a bombed-out city."

"They make like this?" Jak asked. The teen wasn't sure if he was more shocked or offended.

"Deuced clever, I must admit," Doc rumbled, riding past the marquee of a crumbling movie theater. "Albeit, a tad Draconian."

"The only way to practice putting out a fire is to set something ablaze," Krysty said pragmatically, her hair steadily flexing and coiling to show her unease. Ever since the companions landed on this island, she had the feeling of being watched, but never so intently as now. It was as if a thousand eyes were studying her every move.

"Something like that," Mildred agreed. "Although the SEALs mostly practiced rescue operations, saving hostages, recovering stolen nukes and such."

"Mostly," Ryan said. "But not always."

"Sometimes they did nightcreeps on terrorists," Mildred admitted honestly. "Or at least, I think so. All of their work was very hush-hush, burn-before-reading, that sort of thing."

"Midnight soldiers," Doc muttered, using his ebony sword stick to flick aside a rusty soda can from the top of a crashed jetfighter, the fuselage oddly marked with what appeared to be Cyrillic lettering. The can skittered along the cracked sidewalk and rattled around inside a pothole, the noise echoing slightly along the rows of artificially destroyed buildings.

Suddenly a fuzzy little monkey appeared in a window. Scarily larger than a sewer rat, its fur was a deep brown with a distinctive white belly and matching bib just under the jaw. It chattered nosily at the riders, clearly annoyed over the invasion, then hissed with surpassing volume, exposing dagger-like teeth, the front two dripping a greenish fluid.

Instantly, Ryan fired from the hip, the slug slamming the animal off the ledge and sending the corpse tumbling away.

"Acid," Mildred cursed, thumbing back the hammer on her Czech-made ZKR target pistol. "The little bastard had acid-based venom!" The wood was rapidly dissolving where the venom splattered on the windowsill, tendrils of black smoke rising from the sizzling splotch.

"Hopefully, he was alone," Krysty said, hefting the M-16 rapidfire. She was down to her last clip, the same as Jak. In short order, they would be back to their handblasters.

Just then there came a scrambling, scratching noise from the sewer and a second monkey appeared, closely followed by another, then a dozen or so more.

"Ace them!" Ryan yelled, cutting loose with SIG-Sauer. The first few rounds blew away the nearest monkey, then two more behind. But the rest kept coming, as unstoppable as the morning tide.

However, the rest of the companions opened fire, the hail of lead from the rapidfires chewing a crimson swatch through the howling monkeys. Immediately the rest of the tiny creatures changed direction, wildly jumping back into the sewers and drains. Some of them fled under the rusted wrecks of predark cars, or hurtled themselves through the smashed windows of stores in a frantic effort to escape. In only moments the street was clear of any live animals. A score of furry bodies were sprawled on the weedy asphalt, twitching into death.

"Little bastards afraid blasters," Jak growled, pleasantly surprised at the reaction.

"Indeed, my young friend," Doc muttered, easing down the hammer of his LeMat. "They must have encountered firearms before and the survivors of that experience informed the others to beware."

"Well, they certainly have now," J.B. snarled, glancing around. Scampering along the ruins on the corner, a dozen monkeys ducked out of sight.

"Stay razor, people," Ryan added, turning his head to check his blindside. Sure enough, a monkey was crawling through the leafy vines growing over the hood of a burned-out ambulance. The man stroked the trigger and the 9 mm round plowed into the creature, throwing it backward to smack into a brick wall, leaving a ghastly stain of green venom and red blood.

"These little bastards like to jump at you from behind," Mildred added, holstering the ZKR to haul the scattergun from the boot. As she worked the pump-action, a monkey leaped toward her from the stained-glass window of a church. Instinctively the physician triggered the weapon. The blast shredded the tiny simian, and finished the destruction of the century-old window.

"We better find that part, then get out triple fast," Krysty said, then she heard something scramble overhead.

Looking up, the woman cursed at the sight of a monkey scampering along a telephone cable stretched across the street. She fired twice, the first round blowing off the head of the animal and the second cutting the line. As the cable dropped to the ground, more monkeys rushed around on the roof of the apartment building directly alongside the telephone pole. Damn little muties were smart. Too damn smart for her liking!

"Make haste, Ryan. Where do we try for the part we need?" Doc asked, tucking the LeMat into his belt to crack open the Webley and quickly reload.

Brushing back his long hair, Ryan scowled over the pretend city, dourly noting the incredible number of monkeys that were jumping around the companions, always trying to stay behind the group.

"Mildred, you sure this place was fully operational," Ryan demanded, "and not just a mock-up, like one of those displays in a museum?"

"Everything worked," she stated with conviction. "That was the only way for the SEALs to rehearse an operation."

"Okay, then, a plumbing store would be the best, I reckon," Ryan decided, looking down each of the streets of the intersection. If there had been any signs, they were long gone, consumed by the acid rains or ripped away by tropical storms. "After that a hotel or laundry would do fine."

"A laundry?" Doc asked quizzically, then nodded. "Because of the industrial water heaters needed, of course."

"How about an air plant?" Krysty said out of the blue, riding around a blast crater in the street. At the bottom of the depression was a gigantic diesel engine, a small bush starting to grow around the smashed slab of technology.

"That'll do fine," J.B. said with a growing smile.

As the companions rode toward the building, the monkeys followed along, jumping from roof to roof, scampering between the parked cars, always in motion, always trying to get closer.

Guiding their horses into the empty parking lot, the companions managed to leave the monkeys behind, the vast expanse of cracked asphalt offering the creatures nowhere to safely hide. There were a couple of big rigs at the other end of the lot, a Mack truck and a flatbed Fleetwood, parked near a fuel pump. But they were too far away to be used as cover.

Sliding off his horse, Ryan passed the reins to Krysty and pulled out his Navy telescope to check inside the building.

"Clear," he announced, compacting the device once more. "Krysty and Doc, stay with the horses, everybody else with me. Watch your six. These little rad suckers mean business."

"Me, too," Jak growled, hefting the M-16 rapidfire.

Taking the point position, Ryan eased up a short flight of concrete steps to the loading dock and then inside the cavernous building.

The interior was thickly coated with dust, which the companions took as a good thing, since it showed there hadn't been any recent monkey activity in here. Filling the cavernous room were row after row of compressed air cylinders, each standing six feet tall and topped with a brass valve. Hundreds of the cylinders were still connected to the overhead feeder lines, flexible hoses snaking down from a rigid main line. Every few yards there was a safety valve, or a pressure meter, to check for leaks. Fire extinguishers were everywhere. A lot of other equipment stood around, hulking machines covered with dials and gauges.

Dimly, Mildred remembered seeing a news report about a fire at a compressed-air plant. The company not only sold compressed air, but also medical tanks full of pure hydrogen, pure oxygen and nitrogen. The blaze exploded the hydrogen tanks, and the oxygen fed the flames until the nitrogen tanks popped their valves on top. Weighing no more than a hundred pounds, but charged with two thousand pounds of compressed gas, the cylinders took off like rockets, zooming randomly in every direction, smashing through brick walls and people with equal ease. The death toll had been staggering, and several of the flying bottles had finally come to rest almost a full mile away, usually in the wreckage of a house.

"Careful of what you shoot," Mildred warned. "One bullet in the wrong place and we could all be blown to kingdom come."

Pushing aside a set of double doors, Ryan paused as they swung out of the way, then broke off from the corroded hinges and slammed to the concrete floor with a deafening crash. That brought a chorus of screaming from the dozens of monkeys hidden behind the bottles, and they scampered away, one brave soul pausing to spit venom at the two-legs before joining the others.

As the globule of deadly saliva smacked into the cinder-block wall nearby, J.B. swung up the Uzi, but withheld firing. If any of those bottle was still charged, the 9 mm Parabellum rounds could start a chain reaction of gaseous explosion that would level the building, as well as the companions.

Squinting into the gloom, Jak flicked a butane lighter alive, then walked to a sign and blew off the dust to read that it was the hydrogen charging line. Quickly he released the lighter and backed away.

"Need light or they ace," the teenager warned.

"That's the plan!" J.B. muttered, and opened fire with the Uzi. The small windows set along the top of the walls exploded under the assault of the chattering machine pistol, the rain of glass heralding an infusion of sunlight. As the falling shards shattered among the rows of cylinders stacked in the corners, the companions heard monkey screams, and a host of bloody forms darted out of the shadows to race away, clutching their ghastly wounds.

As the reverberations faded away, there came a sharp whistle, and Ryan waved the others closer. Located behind a locked iron grille was the repair shop for the air plant, the shelves stacked full of spare parts for the compressors, meters, gauges, feeder lines and pressure regulators.

"Jackpot!" J.B. grinned and got out his tool to trick open the lock.

While the rest of the companions stood guard, Ryan and J.B. moved along the shelves, taking what they needed, as well as some additional items.

"Teflon tape, plumber's dope, liquid weld. Nuking hell, what a find!" J.B. chortled in delight, packing his munitions bag full. "I haven't seen a find like this since that salt dome city in New Mex."

"Here's the real prize," Ryan said, lifting a tapering valve into view. "Adapters. With these we can connect anything to damn near anything. The boat is as good as fixed."

"Thank God." Mildred exhaled. "I was starting to think that we might never get off this accursed rock."

"Once we're back on the mainland, we can trade these for a month of bed and food at any ville," J.B. added, tucking away a Stilton wrench. Dimly, he recalled that his father used to call the huge tool a monkey wrench. There was some sort of irony at work there, but the details of it escaped him at the moment.

In the distance, a monkey popped up on top of a cylinder. A few flecks of red paint still adhering to the sides marked it as containing pressurized hydrogen. Bringing up the rapidfire, Jak withheld firing. The tiny animal chattered angrily and ducked back out of sight. The fragging muties were starting to understand that the norms wouldn't shoot at the gas tanks.

"Time to go," Jak stated, flexing his hand. A knife dropped into his palm and he flipped it forward.

With a meaty thud, the blade slammed deep into the chest of a monkey, driving the animal off the bottle and out a window.

Knocked off balance, the cylinder toppled to hit another cylinder, which fell into a group of them, the clanging and banging sounding louder than a thousand church bells.

As the companions started for the exit, the cylinders continued to topple over like dominoes, the chaos spreading like wildfire. A dozen valves were snapped off cylinders to no result, then one shattered. A long hissing rush of a pale yellow gas spread out in a roiling cloud. A scampering monkey darted into the cloud and stopped dead as if hitting a brick wall. Shuddering, it collapsed to the floor, bloody foam bubbling from the slack mouth.

"That's sulfur dioxide!" Mildred cursed, slapping a hand over her mouth. "Hold your breath. Don't breathe until we're safely outside."

Doing as they were told, the companions backed away, trying to skirt the billowing cloud. But rolling around on the floor, propelled by the hissing exhaust, the canister collided with a score of other cylinders, sending them falling. More valves snapped off, one canister hissing loudly for only a few seconds before becoming exhausted. But another twirled madly in ever-increasing speed, the stream of compressed oxygen roaring upward like a geyser. Then it tilted over and streaked across the floor to crash through the cinder-block wall, leaving a gaping hole a yard wide.

Another six-foot bottle scraped along the floor, throwing off bright sparks as it headed straight for the companions. But before they could move, it ran out of compressed argon and stopped in the middle of the room, gently rocking back and forth.

In the overhead rafters, the monkeys were howling and screaming, throwing down light bulbs and the occasional wad of feces. The companions answered with a long barrage of blaster fire, and a score of riddled bodies fell to the charging floor, knocking over more bottles and releasing even more clouds of compressed gas. Then the ancient feeder line broke, and all of the charging hoses came free, the insulated lengths slashing wildly.

Screeching, a monkey dived out of the shadows to land on J.B.'s shoulder. Instantly the man angled his head, putting the fedora between him and the little animal. Preparing to spit, it paused in confusion for a moment, and Mildred stepped in close to discharge the ZKR into its face. The tiny head exploded, and the decapitated monkey tumbled away, gushing a torrent of red life.

Unexpectedly, several large squat canisters in the corner of the room violently erupted. The bluish contents sprayed upward, washing across a score of gibbering monkeys. The animals went motionless, then toppled to the floor and shattered into pieces like glass figurines.

"Liquid nitrogen," Mildred identified as a bitter wave of arctic cold swept through the building. Frost started to rapidly spread across items in the plant, slickly coating everything.

"Time to leave!" Ryan yelled, spinning fast. But he

paused at the sight of the deadly sulfur dioxide cloud cutting off the only avenue of escape.

Just then, the support beams for the ceiling gave a hideous groan and broke apart. The ceiling sagged, then cracked, the divide yawning wide and knocking several monkeys off the rafters and into the subzero cloud. They screamed for only a microsecond, then went horribly silent and came apart, the last beat of their freezing hearts breaking them into ghastly chunks.

Loudly snapping, the steel-reinforced girders splintered, great chunks of icy steel, hoses, conduits and light fixtures crashing onto the cracking floor, sending even more pressurized cylinders tumbling in wild abandon.

Shivering with the cold, the companions quickly retreated into the storage room, as the entire manufacturing plant began to crumble, the two lethal gas clouds relentlessly headed their way.

Chapter Sixteen

An unseen hand jerked away the canvas bag covering his head, and Beltrane blinked a few times to adjust his sight, and try to see who had jacked him in the middle of the night. However, the small room was filled with impossibly bright lights that formed a sort of haze, making it impossible for him to see where he was, or who else was in the room.

"Please," Beltrane whispered, tears running down his cheeks. "I can't see…"

"That's the whole idea," a gruff voice said, a vague figure standing behind the ring of alcohol lanterns. "If you can't see us now, then you couldn't in the past, and take steps to prevent this from happening. Savvy?"

Nodding, the doomie weakly struggled against the ropes lashing him to the wooden chair. But there were too many, and they were too strong. The brief exertion made Beltrane feel dizzy and he almost became sick, but somebody forced open his mouth and poured down some shine, the soothing brew easing his discomfort.

But the odd dizziness continued, and slowly the doomie began to comprehend that he wasn't ill. The room actually was moving. Straining to hear past the hiss of the ring of lanterns, Beltrane could dimly discern a thumping sound and guessed that he was on a boat of some kind. That sent a shiver down his spine.

Coldhearts in the night, plus a boat, could mean only one thing.

Carrying a chair, a figure stepped past the haze of light and sat only a few feet away. "So you're the doomie of Radar ville," the newcomer said, crossing his arms.

"Yes, I am, Captain Carlton," Beltrane answered.

The figure leaned in closer. "You know who I am?"

"Of course," Beltrane sighed, sagging against his bounds. "I have known for years that you would come for me someday. I also knew that resisting would only get my friends aced, so I told them nothing and accepted my fate."

"Mutie shit," Carlton said, snorting in disbelief. "If you're that good, then—"

"We are on a tiger," Beltrane stated. "Correct?"

There was a pause. "The *Tiger Shark*," Carlton corrected, impressed in spite of his natural reticence. "All right, doomie, I'm finally convinced that you're the real thing and not some faker merely trying to escape a work detail."

Beltrane shrugged in response. Sometimes there were no right words to say.

"So, answer me this," Carlton said, lighting a cig and deeply inhaling the dark smoke.

"The outlanders are surrounded by ringing bells," the little doomie said without prompting. "I do not know if they will escape the death clouds or the teeth that jump."

"Teeth that jump...they're in Delta!" Digger snarled,

stepping into the light. "Nuking hell, I know those ruins. They're infested with jumpers, millions of them!"

Flicking the ash off his cig, Carlton said nothing, but highly doubted the accuracy of such a number. But the absolute fervor of the man said that there had to be a lot of the little monkeys there. Hundreds, possibly thousands. This news changed everything, and the captain quickly amended his plans for a nightcreep, into one for an ambush.

"So tell me, what are they doing in the ruins?" Carlton asked, puffing steadily. "Food, brass, or something else?"

In spite of the blinding light, Beltrane looked directly at the captain. "They seek the heart of the running moon."

The running moon…what the frag did that mean? Snapping his fingers, Carlton put out an open hand, and a sec man slapped a roll of heavy paper into his palm. "And where is the moon running?" Carlton said, spreading out the map of the island.

With a trembling hand, Beltrane placed a finger squarely on the hidden lagoon outside the ville of the screamers.

"Are you sure?" Carlton pressed. "Absolutely?"

Solemnly, Beltrane nodded, then knowing what was to come next, added, "Nothing will chill you, Captain."

Already in the act of drawing his blaster, the captain stopped for a moment. "Come again," Carlton demanded.

"Nothing will chill you!" Beltrane shouted, breaking into wild laughter.

The sound was unnerving, and after a few minutes Carlton decided there would be no more intel coming from the mutie, and pulled the trigger to blow out his brains.

As the limp body slumped to the deck of the cargo barge, the captain holstered his piece and stood to leave. But the disquieting words of the doomie kept echoing inside his mind. *Nothing will chill you.* What exactly did that mean, anyway?

CLANGING, BANGING, crashing and colliding, the chaotic pressurized containers started zooming around the building smashing into everything as the wave of ice swept steadily closer to the companions huddled in the supply room. Overhead, screaming monkeys raced along the rafters seeking an avenue of escape, a steady rain of the bodies plummeting down to smack into the cracking floor with horrid results.

"Fireblast, we've got no choice," J.B. cursed, glancing at the thinning cloud of poison gas blocking the only possible exit. Yanking out his implo gren, the man yanked the pin and released the arming lever. "Get ready to run!"

With all of his strength, J.B. threw the gren across the building, slamming it into a splintering support beam to angle away and land just past the swirling cloud of sulfur dioxide. There came a musical ting, a bright flash of light and the companion held on for dear life as a tremendous reverse hurricane suddenly filled the plant as the implosion sucked everything toward the rear of the building.

Hundreds of monkeys, aced and alive, went flying

by, the pressurized bottles tumbled away, shards of frozen steel lancing through the air like a barrage of jagged spears. Broken pieces of the floor, crumbling sections of the ceiling, tools, hoses and spent brass, all vanished into the microsecond singularity of the reverse quantum event. Only the deadly wave of liquid nitrogen ice on the floor proved unstoppable.

In a heartbeat, the sulfur dioxide cloud was gone, sucked away completely, and the desperate companions exploded out of the room to insanely charge through the maelstrom, impelled by the ferocious wind. But halfway there, the winds died and the companions abruptly changed course to dive out the exit and painfully land in the parking lot.

"Gaia, what happened in there?" Krysty demanded, one hand holding the M-16, the other holding the reins of two terrified horses.

With the Webley out and ready, Doc was holding the reins for the other three animals. All of the horses were whimpering and trying to pull away, but the man and woman held on tight, the tendons standing out in their arms from the effort.

"We…survived…" Ryan croaked, his words misty in the cold air.

Turning to glance over a shoulder, Mildred wasn't surprised to see the entire air plant crumbling apart, sections collapsing upon itself, cylinders dully exploding, the painful shrieks of the trapped monkeys rising in pitch and timbre, then stopping completely.

"As Doc likes to say," Mildred panted, holding a stitch in her side. "I have had fun before—"

"And this fragging ain't it," J.B. finished grimly,

yanking his hat out of the sleeve of his leather jacket and starting to beat it back into shape.

"Never doing again," Jak declared, mentally carving the words into stone. "Saw farm, just barely not buy."

"Amen to that, brother," Ryan said in an unaccustomed rush of feeling.

"This cost us a damn implo gren," J.B. growled, setting the battered fedora back into place. "But at least we got the parts!"

"Enough to fix the *Moon Runner?*" Doc asked hopefully.

"Enough to fix anything." The man grinned back.

"Superlative, John Barrymore!" Doc boomed, slapping the man on the back. "Then let us make haste, Hermes, and leave this modern-day Gahanna before once more the gates of Hell yawn open for our immortal souls!"

"It's a rad pit, sure enough," Ryan agreed, taking the reins of his mare and stiffly climbing into the saddle. As the horse shifted her stance to accommodate his weight, the one-eyed man quickly reloaded his weapons.

Kicking their mounts into action, the companions trotted along the old street. Monkeys were still racing away from the building, many of them minus arms or tails. As the frozen limbs warmed, the stumps began to profusely bleed, and the animals sagged to the ground, whimpering into death.

"Heard people come from monkeys. True?" Jak asked with a scowl.

"Good Lord, no." Mildred chuckled. "Humans came from primates. Those are entirely different from monkeys."

"How?" the teenager asked curiously.

Biting a lip, Mildred tried to boil down the genetic differences. "We're smarter," she said lamely, too tired to explain fully.

"Plus, we have a divine soul," Doc added unexpectedly. "I never could fully understand why creationists and evolutionists didn't get along. Why not go with the theory that primates evolved naturally, and then the Lord gave them souls, creating us into His own image?"

"Her own image," Krysty corrected politely.

Arching an eyebrow, Doc started to speak, then changed his mind. The three things you should never discuss with a friend were how to worship, how to break up with a lover and how to go to hell.

Behind the companions, the building continued to crumble back into its components parts, the rumbling destruction spreading to the structures on either side, glass shattering and wood splintering louder than cannons. Slowly a dust cloud formed from the destruction, rising above the city as if it had just been hit with a baby nuke.

"Shit," Jak drawled, giving the word several syllables. "Gotta admit, not think ever seen…" Suddenly he pointed to the right. "Nuking hell, a rhino!"

Everybody turned sideways at that and bitterly cursed.

Standing in the middle of the road was one of the armored muties. Its boxy head was bent low, and it seemed to be feasting on the pile of monkeys that the companions had aced earlier. However, at the man's cry, the beast looked up from the food, a fuzzy arm dangling from its massive jaws. It's piggy eyes narrowed in recognition, and the beast lurched forward, lowering the armored horns for a chilling strike.

"Fireblast, where's the nearest river?" Ryan started when Krysty interrupted him.

"Head for the garage!" she yelled, wheeling the horse around and taking off in a new direction.

With pause, the rest of the companions immediately followed while trying to ignore the heavy thumping of the approaching rhino.

Galloping around a corner, the riders headed for a predark car garage. Five stories tall, it was made of concrete, with open sides for ventilation from the exhaust fumes. Ryan scowled at the building. They often used such places as a refuge from the acid-rain storms, but what possible use could it be against the living tank in hot pursuit he had no bastard idea whatsoever.

"John, the gate!" Mildred cried out, leveling a finger.

Nodding in understanding, J.B. swung up the scattergun and cut loose a blast. The wooden barrier blocking the entrance exploded into splinters, and the companions charged into the dark interior.

"Left ramp!" Krysty commanded, ducking her head under a sign whose lettering had faded over the years. Dimly, she thought it had to have warned about the height of the ramps, no conversion vans allowed, over eight feet, that sort of thing. Briefly, she wondered if the rhino would be too big to get up the sloped concrete, then banished that feeble dream. The mutie was big, a lot larger than a normal rhino, but not so fragging large that it couldn't follow them anywhere that the horses could ride. If the companions were riding motorcycles it might be a different story, but for the moment, their best hope was to reach the roof as fast as possible. Then it would just be a matter of timing.

As they took the curve around onto the second floor, the companions found it full of windblown trash, with full bushes growing out of piles of dirt that had accumulated over the years. What few wags remained were sagging piles of rust, or sleek, shiny fiberglass bodies sitting on top of rotting tires. One limousine was still airtight, the desiccated driver with both hands on the wheel, a jaunty cap on his head and earphones dangling from the holes where his shriveled ears had once been located. In the backseat was another mummified corpse wearing the white uniform of an admiral, the dried figure of a woman with shockingly blonde hair resting in his lap. The details of the situation were plainly obvious, and the companions briefly smiled, then there came a stentorian roar from below, and the whole building seemed to shake as the rhino started up the ramp, the slamming of its feet sounding like the pistons of a powerful engine.

Hitting the third floor at a full gallop, the companions found a row of motorcycles parked in a neat line along the wall. As they raced by, the first bike fell over, slamming into the second, mirrors smashing, windshields loudly cracking. Then the third bike flipped over, starting a chain reaction that almost reached the next ramp before the racing horses did.

Unfortunately there was a wreck blocking the ramp. The companions managed to squeeze by along the side, but the delay cost them precious seconds. The savage pounding from below was dangerously closer now.

"How many pipe bombs do we have left?" Krysty demanded, bent low over the neck of her horse, her red hair sailing out behind exactly like the mane of the animal.

"Not enough to chill this bastard!" J.B. replied.

"Prep a couple of pipe bombs!" Ryan ordered, suddenly understanding why the woman had directed them into the garage.

"Only got two!"

"Use them both!" Fireblast, it was a daring plan, and not one he would have suggested, but there was no other choice at this point.

From the level below, the rhino bellowed in rage, its snorts as loud as a huffing steam engine. Each powerful step shook the old garage more, the light fixtures swinging freely, dust raining down in a gritty cloud.

As the companions erupted onto the roof, Krysty promptly wheeled her horse around and started back down the opposite ramp. She wanted speed, but was forced to slow her mount to prevent the animal from breaking a leg on the sloped concrete. A spill now would mean death. It was as simple as that.

"It's up to you now, John!" Mildred shouted, tightening the reins.

"Both of them!" Ryan bellowed. "Both, or we're aced!"

Nodding in understanding, J.B. slowed his mount to drop to the rear of the pack, then lit the first fuse and tossed a pipe bomb over the guard rails to land on the up ramp. With a whoop, J.B. started along the down ramp, urging his horse on to greater speed as he lit the second bomb, simply dropping it in his wake. Dark night, he thought, this was going to be close.

Just as the companions rode onto the fourth floor, the rhino appeared, heading for the roof. They passed each other on the turn, and the beast ran right past the sizzling explosive charge to surge onto the roof, its head snapping around to try to find the elusive prey.

A split second later a double blast shook the entire garage, knocking down the ceiling lights, signs, rubber cones and releasing a hundred years of accumulated grime. Swirling dust clouds billowed from the fourth floor, and the rhino roared in wild rage, stomping its foot so hard, it seemed like the building might collapse.

Moments later the companions charged back into the city streets and slowed their mounts to look back. Standing on the roof of the parking garage, the rhino was running around in a circle, constantly bellowing. From this angle, the companions could easily see that both of the ramps leading to the top floor were gone, blown to pieces.

"Think survive fall?" Jak asked with a frown. "Pretty tough, only ten-foot drop."

"Impossible," Krysty said, patting the sweaty neck of her horse, then scratching it behind the ears. "Mildred said it yesterday. Biowep or not, the damn thing is still just an animal made of flesh and bones. Mebbe elephants can swim, but they can't nuking jump. If the rhino even tries to reach the fourth level—"

"No…It's not going to…No way!" Doc whispered, going pale.

Wiggling and jerking, the rhino forced its imposing

bulk over the concrete safety barrier of the roof, and then jumped. The beast dropped like a lead safe, and the companions held their breath as the colossal thing slammed into the pavement, sinking out of sight into the asphalt to the telltale sound of breaking bones.

"You don't think…" Mildred started, when the bloody head of the beast reappeared from the impact crater. The rhino was covered in gore, with yellow blood pumping from horrible wounds. Hundreds of the armored scales were gone, the gray flesh underneath hanging in tatters with the sharp ends of white ribs clearly showing. Its jaw hung off kilter, an eye was missing, and the main horn had snapped off completely.

However, the biowep was still very much alive, and started butting the asphalt with its remaining horn, ripping out chunks of pavement to clear a path to freedom. However, its legs were pulped, and the monster could only shimmy forward on its belly, all the while hatefully staring at the companions less than a block away.

"Any more bombs?" Jak asked, aiming the M-16 at the struggling creature. He put a burst into the face, taking out the other eye. The rhino grunted at the loss, but never stopped digging for freedom.

"Just the implo," J.B. replied, almost unable to believe what he was seeing. Just how tough was this thing?

With a colossal grunt, the rhino flopped its head onto the street and lay there panting from the exertion. But even as they watched, the countless wounds were starting to heal, the blood ceased to squirt and new armored scales began to grow in place.

"Enough of this crap! This time, we blow open the head and remove the fragging brain," Ryan growled, working the arming bolt of the Steyr. "Let's see if the fragging biowep can regen that!"

"Hold, my dear Ryan. There is no need for us to partake of further action," Doc said, lowering both of his handblasters. "Behold, the Army of the Potomac!"

Charging out of every building in the city appeared hundreds, thousands, of the tiny monkeys, chattering in delight at the bounty of fresh meat lying helpless on the street.

Like ants, they converged upon the beast, ripping it apart with their bare hands and stuffing the raw flesh into their mouths with horrible gobbling noises.

"Bioweps edible?" Jak asked, lowering the rapid-fire.

"Damned if I know," Mildred admitted honestly. "I can't imagine that even the paranoids at the Pentagon ever imagined an enemy trying to eat one of the things."

Mournfully calling in pain and rage, the rhino snapped at the monkeys, catching several in its busted jaw and trying to swallow them whole. But the others yanked the corpses free and began plunging their hands deeper into the beast, yanking off the growing scales to rip away gobbets of yellow-tinged meat, causing new geysers of yellow fluids until the gibbering horde was soaked with the blood of the biological construct.

As the rhino ceased to struggle, the monkeys began to burrow into the twitching body, throwing out pulsating organs to the others dancing around the dying beast. But instead of consuming the organs, the monkeys reverently set them aside and stepped back as the females arrived, most of them with newborn infants tucked tightly in the crooks of their fuzzy arms.

"The enemy of my enemy," Doc mumbled in gallows humor, holstering his weapons.

"Is still my fragging enemy!" Ryan finished, kicking his heels into the rump of the mare to break into a full gallop. "Let's ride, and don't stop until we reach the river!" Dying didn't mean aced in his mind, and the man had no plan to relax his guard until the companions were safely locked inside a redoubt again.

As the companions raced away, the dying rhino plaintively bellowed a call for help, which unconsciously triggered a brief burst of radioactivity from a cybernetic transponder implanted inside the brain. Incredibly, as the biowep sagged into unconsciousness, it felt the tingle of a response.

Chapter Seventeen

Parking their motorcycles on the crest of a hill, Baron Jones and Lady Veronica looked down upon the smoking ruins of PacCom ville. The rest of the sec men parked their bikes in a protective circle around the baron and his lady, their hands already full of blasters. This was jumper territory, and the only thing the little monkeys feared was flying lead.

Oddly, this part of Clemente had never been nuked, yet it seemed to have more muties than anywhere else. Nobody alive could explain the mystery, although there were a lot of theories, most of them involving Captain Carlton and his highly questionable sexual appetites.

"What in the name of Atom happened here?" the baron muttered, turning off his engine and kicking down the stand.

The predark city had always been in poor condition, mostly from the acid rain and those accursed jumpers. Only now an entire building was gone, crumbling into pieces in front of his very sight. There was a fire in another, the sea breeze helping to spread the blaze as if the entire ville had been hit by lightning. Even more bizarre, there was a huge mound of jumpers feasting on the bloody yellow carcass of something that resembled an aced thunder king. Impossible!

"It was the one-eyed man," Lady Veronica whispered,

reaching out a hesitant hand, her fingers caressing the air. "I can almost see him, and the witch with the strange red hair…"

"That's because they're still here!" cried Zane Southerland, pointing with a BAR longblaster.

The new sec chief was a grizzled old veteran whose first official act had been to declare the staggering bounty of a year of leisure to the person who aced the traitor, Digger. Needless to say, this put him in good stead with the crew, even the folks who had once been friends with the former sec chief. The ville first! That was the unbreakable creed of a sec man. Before blood kin, or bed partners, the ville was always more important. Digger's act of betrayal offended the sec men deeply, and everybody knew if the bastard was ever captured alive, he would never reach the ville in the same condition.

"Where? Where are they?" another sec man demanded, using a hand to shield his face from the orange light streaming down from the clouds overhead.

Yanking out a pair of binocs, the baron quickly swept the smoky ruins, but couldn't find any trace of the outlanders. Then he spotted movement near the iron bridge on the opposite side of the ville. Adjusting the focus, he growled at the sight of the one-eyed man and his crew riding fast horses across the bridge.

"Get razor, boys, we're going after them!" the baron declared, tucking away the binocs. "Our hogs can easily catch those old nags once they hit the swamps!"

"No, it's already too late," Lady Veronica snarled, lowering her hand, her hair visibly flexing.

Just as the outlanders galloped off the bridge, the

middle span violently exploded, the struts bending and twisting from the force of the blast. In spite of the distance, they could actually hear the groan of the tortured metal as the bridge sagged, trembled, then broke apart, the sections plummeting into the Red Rock River.

"Frag it, we can catch them by using the ocean road," Southerland declared, ramming his longblaster back into the leather boot set alongside the engine.

"Which would bring us into range of those crossbows of Carlton's, if he just happens to be sailing by," the baron replied curtly, thoughtfully massaging his jagged scar.

A dutiful wife for many years, Lady Veronica knew what the unconscious gesture meant. "You suspect a trick of some kind, my love?" the woman asked, leaning on the protective cage of bars surrounding the bike.

"Ever since these outlanders showed up at the sulfur mine, the war for this island has rapidly escalated," the baron said slowly, testing each word. "First, they escape from Lava Falls, and now seemed to have aced a thunder king. I'm beginning to wonder if they're the bait and there's some sort of elaborate trap to capture us alive. Carlton wants me splayed under his knives, as much as he wants you tied to a bed to breed him an heir."

"Be assured, my love, that will never happen," Veronica declared, her voice thick with hate. A hand went to the small leather bag hanging between her breasts, and something trapped stirred at the touch, hissing and rattling, demanding freedom.

"Even if he mounts my corpse, my little friend here will make sure it is the last thing Carlton ever does, aside from beg to be chilled by his own sec men," the woman stated, releasing the bag once more. Instantly the thing inside went still.

"Ah, Chief?" a sec woman said. "Something is going on down there."

Lowering his canteen, Southerland looked down at the ruins and started to ask a question, then his blood went cold. What was in the world was *that?*

Rising from the roof of a school was a mechanical figure, a domed machine in the shape of a large spider. Standing about fifteen feet high, it had large crystal eyes, a small rotating radar dish and a sleek weapon of some kind hanging from its belly.

"Droid," the baron whispered in disbelief, letting go of the gold ring and grabbing a blaster.

Scampering along the edge of the roof, a jumper paused to chatter at the machine. Instantly the weapon swiveled toward the monkey. There was a flash of light and the creature was gone, only a pair of tiny feet left behind to show where the mutie had just been standing.

"Gaia protect us, that's a laser gun!" Lady Veronica cried out in shock.

"The rads have hit the Geiger now!" Southerland agreed.

As if able to hear the distant words, the droid raised its head to look in his direction, then started forward. But at the first step, the entire machine began to oddly shake, loose pieces tumbling free, an eye cracked and bright sparks erupted from the laser. Then the entire machine shuddered and simply fell apart, the heavily corroded metal crumbling into loose pieces of parts and reddish dust. The laser fired once more, randomly into the sky, then burst into flames.

Across the ville a weathered billboard swung aside as a supposedly solid concrete wall slid apart and out walked another spider droid. Swiftly, it strode across the roof and over the edge to plummet ten stories to the paved street. Because of the angle, the people on the hill couldn't see the results, but they dimly heard an explosion and saw a rising puff of greasy smoke.

Unexpectedly, there came the rattle of heavy-caliber blasterfire and a bank building exploded, thousands of dollar bills soaring skyward, along with the smoldering remains of a predark tank, the treads and cannon arching away in different directions.

"The ville is trying to defend itself," the baron said out loud, pleased at the concept. But he was even happier that the ancient military weapons were tearing themselves apart at the first rally.

Far out to sea, a partially sunken battleship seemed to expand under the lolling waves, then violently detonated, chunks of the armored hull, machinery, cannons and hundreds of rag-covered skeletons spreading out in a hellish umbrella.

"Mebbe the legends are correct," Lady Veronica muttered, stroking a lock of her hair. "And this really was the home of the predark SEALs."

"Sec men made out of living iron?" The baron scoffed. "That's a fragging droid, not a norm."

"Mebbe, mebbe not," she replied softly.

Down on the littered streets, a garage door swung open to reveal another spider droid. But it was already leaking smoke, and slowly it began to melt from an internal short circuit. Seconds later the garage was aflame, the blaze quickly spreading to the house and then the house next door.

"Just a bunch of drek now," Southerland stated, returning his longblaster to the boot. "No danger from these fragging things anymore."

In a parking lot, the rear doors of a truck lying on its side slammed open and out stepped a spider droid. The domed body and tubular legs were streaked with rust, but it walked along the pavement without a shinny, the belly-mounted weapon spitting tiny flashes of light. Dashing around in terror, the jumpers tried to escape, but kept exploding into puffs of crimson steam.

Scowling at the sight, the baron studied the burning ville more closely and discovered several more fully operational droids stalking the ruins, moving in a deliberate hunting pattern.

Converging at the corpse of the thunder king, the six droids ruthlessly annihilated every jumper in sight, then tracked along a side street to an intersection. Snaking probes moved across the cracked asphalt and lifted several tiny objects that glistened golden in the reflected light.

"Spent brass?" a sec man asked in a whisper, his face deathly pale.

"Gotta be," another man answered, both hands clutching the iron bars of his cage, his knuckles white. Just how smart were these metal bastards?

Moving to the head of the pack, one spider droid took the lead and began sweeping a bright light back and forth along the street. The baron felt his heartbeat quicken as the predark machines moved along the exact path of the outlanders to the destroyed bridge. Without hesitation, the spiders climbed over the side and out of sight.

Only minutes later, five of the droids appeared on the other side and assumed a combat formation before scuttling across a grassy field. Almost immediately, one of the machines unexpectedly paused as smoke began pouring out the rear. Turning in a circle, it fell over sideways and exploded, the blast discernable even to the people on the distant hill. The other four droids paid no attention to their fallen comrade and kept going until disappearing into the forest.

"Is there anything between PacCom and that destroyed ville?" Lady Veronica asked, stroking her temple.

"Nothing but a lot of empty coastline," the baron replied, then added, "Although there are rumors of a cannie ville hidden in the forest, but it's just a stretch to tell the littles."

"Or is that the location of Carlton's fleet?" she replied. "The best place to hide something is where nobody would dare go looking."

Jones scowled. That was an interesting possibility. "Think you could find the ville, the harbor, cave, whatever it is, my love?" he asked bluntly.

"I can try," Lady Veronica answered hesitantly, then grew more resolute. "Yes, I'm sure that I can."

"Then we ambush them just outside the place," the baron declared, starting the bike. "Where they will least expect trouble."

"We better move triple fast," Lady Veronica advised. "They have a witch, and she could easily detect us coming from miles away."

"Is she really that good, my lady?" a sec man asked, frowning.

"Near enough," Lady Veronica lied. In truth, she had seen the animated hair of the other woman move against the wind, exactly like the red curls of her own father, Kyrl. Veronica's black hair stirred a little now and then, but never anything like his did, or the outlander's. Clearly her norm mother had thinned the blood and robbed the lady of some special abilities. But not all. She still healed faster than a norm, could please her husband in ways no norm woman could, and was able to call upon the Earth Mother Gaia to give her fantastic strength in an emergency. Well, for a few minutes, anyway, she amended.

"Shitfire, if the fragging witch is that good, then we play it safe, go back to the ville and drive the stickies ahead of us like cattle," the baron declared, revving his engine. "That way, she'll only sense the muties."

"But not us," Southerland added, twisting the controls on the handlebars. "Then we'll force the location of the fleet out of the outlanders, and send the fat little bastard Carlton straight to Davey!"

"All right, move out!" Baron Jones commanded, lurching his two-wheeler off the crest in a spray of exhaust fumes and loose dirt.

Following the baron, his wife and the troops shouted the name of Sealton ville as a battle cry as the bikes jounced along the uneven ground and disappeared over the horizon.

Moments later something impossibly large moved

through the sea, causing a ripple effect on the surface that overwhelmed the tide. Writhing tentacles extended from the water to move along the shore, probing the rocks and debris until finding the remains of the dockyard.

Wrapping their length around some concrete pylons, the tentacles tightened and a kraken rose from the sea, its single great eye moving around for the source of the earlier cry for help. Hauling its colossal form from the water, the kraken moved along the smoky streets, crushing cars flat and knocking down several burning buildings until finding the corpse of the thunder king.

Tenderly reaching out a tentacle, it stroked the partially consumed body to make sure there was no chance of a regeneration, then the kraken lifted its body to expose a parrot-like beak. Gulping in air, the sensitive tongue of the enormous beast easily detected traces of norms and horses, but also the smell of gasoline engines from the direction of a nearby hill. Faced with a choice, the mutie laboriously turned and started hauling itself over the dry land toward the hated machines.

RETRACING THEIR ROUTE from the ruins, the companions rode the horses at a gallop for several miles before finally easing their tired mounts to a gentle canter. Slowly the miles passed and the landscape changed from sand barrens with only a few trees scattered around, to a wooden glen with numerous waterfalls, creeks and countless small ponds. The terrain was almost that of a swamp, but not quite.

"Stay sharp," Jak warned. "Stickies like weeds almost as much as ruins."

"Diggers, too," Mildred added grimly, glancing at the moist soil for any indication of the underground mutant.

"Stickies, stingwings, rhinos, jumpers, clouds…in all of their bizarre experiments with biological weaponry," Doc said, his hands folded over the pommel of his saddle, "I wonder if the whitecoats ever tried to actually make a supersoldier, a superior human, stronger, faster, smarter."

Glancing sideways at Krysty, Ryan said nothing, his thoughts deeply private. Then the man flinched as a searing wave of heat washed over his left side and the head of his horse fell off its body.

Decapitated, the beast gushed a torrent of blood, and Ryan threw himself out of the saddle to prevent being trapped under the chilled animal. He hit the ground hard, just as the horse collapsed, its legs twitching as if it was still horribly alive.

The rest of the companions cut loose with their weapons, and the laser cut a hole through the belly of Krysty's horse. It reared with a scream, throwing the woman to the ground. There came the tense hum of a microwave beamer and Jak's animal literally exploded, sending the youth flying backward to land with a splash in a shallow pond.

As the Steyr was now pinned under the animal, Ryan drew the SIG-Sauer and looked around for the enemy. He found them in an instant. Three big spider droids were moving through the field of weeds, the tufted top of the waving plants just brushing the belly-mounted weapons of the machines.

Firing a fast six times, Ryan hammered the weapon

of the lead droid. He knew that it was a laser from bitter experience. He hit it every time, but the 9 mm rounds couldn't penetrate the armored housing of the weapon. Locking onto him, the droid fired again, the energy beam slamming into the headless horse, setting its body on fire.

Incredibly the third droid hissed as its belly-mounted needler swung into operation. The tops of the weeds jumped into the air from the supersonic passage of the 1 mm steel slivers. But then the ancient weapon jammed and the needler broke free from its anchor. Pivoting randomly, the weapon cut off two of the legs of its own droid. The machine staggered from the loss, and the needler stitched a line of holes across the droid with the beamer. Smoke began pouring from the riddled spider, and the beamer pulsed in return.

"Droid!" Jak shouted unnecessarily, triggering a long burst from the M-16 rapidfire. The stream of perfectly imbalanced 5.56 mm rounds smacked into the side of the lead spider, denting the dome and cracking an eye. Then the clip ran empty. With no more reloads, Jak cast away the useless blaster to draw his .357 Magnum Colt Python.

Caught in the middle of an open field, with only some weeds and their dead horses as cover, Krysty saw the dire state of the situation, in spite of the decrepit nature of the droids. They were all streaked with rust, and two of them had cobwebs dangling off their armored hulls.

Making a fast decision, the woman primed her implo gren and threw. The deadly sphere landed in the middle of the droids, and they instantly lurched away just before it detonated. The bright flash masked what happened at first, but as the glare faded there was a reverse hurricane of tufts speeding into the implosion. Plants were uprooted, frogs, newts, beetles and a coney were sucked into the reverse quantum event, then it stopped and fresh pollen filled the air, dancing in the sunlight like a summer snowstorm.

Then, rising from their prone position on the soggy ground, the three droids advanced once more. However, their belly weapons were now thickly coated with sticky mud. The laser on one pulsed, the energy ray burning the filthy lens sparkling clean. The microwave beamer hummed, boiling the front aperture clear, but the needler jammed, then exploded, the blast ripping open the bottom of the droid. Trailing loose wiring and optical cables like intestines, the machine marched onward, seemingly unaware that it was now unarmed.

Sloshing out of the puddle, a furious Doc cursed at the sight of the black powder trickling out of the LeMat, and drew the Webley to fire twice at the droids. However, that was when the man realized that he was sinking into the sticky mud a lot faster than expected. By the Three Kennedys, this wasn't mud, Doc realized, but quicksand!

Yanking out his ebony sword stick, Doc jammed it into the muddy grass, trying to find some solid ground. As the stick encountered resistance, Doc rammed it in deeper and held on tight with both hands so that he wouldn't sink any deeper. However, for the rest of this fight he was neutralized, and a sitting duck for any of the droids.

Just then a sputtering nicker caught his attention and

Doc beamed in delight as his horse walked over to the edge of the pool and lowered her head, the reins sliding off the pommel to dangle only inches away. Risking everything, Doc released the stick and strained to reach the leather straps, his fingertips just brushing them. Then the horse shifted position and the reins were tight in his grip.

Wrapping the straps several times around his forearms, Doc did what was necessary to loosen the sucking sludge around himself, and emptied his bladder. Immediately the grip of the muddy quicksand eased.

"Now, girl, giddy up," Doc whispered, shaking the reins while watching the droids continue the attack on his friends.

The horse started to back away and the reins tightened around his arms, the leather straps cutting into his skin. Bracing himself for what was coming, Doc flexed his muscles and hoped his arms wouldn't come out of their sockets as the horse began to haul him out of the sticky muck. The pain grew as his circulation was cut off, and his hands turned purple, but the man rode through the agony, concentrating on trying to slide out of the quicksand. Don't swim, that only makes you sink, Doc cautioned himself silently. Nice and easy, there's the ticket…

Grimly holding on for dear life, Doc felt his hands going numb and the leather straps began to slide through his swollen fingers. Then a pale hand came out of the grass and Krysty grabbed his hands, holding the reins in place.

"Come on, Doc, take a piss!" she softly commanded. "Give it all you got!"

"I…already…did, madam!" he panted, the world taking on a reddish haze and a strange buzzing filling his ears. The strength in his arms was failing and breathing was becoming difficult.

Out in the field, the blasters were firing nonstop, the laser humming steadily in reply. A horse screamed, something exploded, then a droid erupted, broken machinery forming a geyser into the air. But the last droid was still in motion, the laser stabbing out constantly, burning the green plants brown, starting small fires and boiling the puddles.

With no choice, Krysty let go of the man with one hand and dragged around her canteen. Unable to unscrew the cap with just her left hand, she shoved it into the mud, then drew her knife and stabbed holes in the lightweight aluminum. There wasn't much water inside, but it did help, and Doc advanced a few more inches. Then the man gasped as his boot found purchase under the cloying mud. Root, rock or human skull, Doc didn't care. It was solid, and that was all that mattered.

In a rude sucking sound, Doc came loose from the quagmire and stumbled onto weeds. His boots and pants were caked with filth, but he was alive and free.

"Thank you…dear lady," Doc wheezed, dropping to his knees to stay out of sight. His swollen hands were badly bruised, and stiff. Using his blaster at the moment was completely out of the question.

Nodding at the panting man, Krysty rolled aside and came up firing, the .38 rounds of her blaster loudly ricocheting off the rear end of the belly laser, but achieving nothing. There was a ventilation grid there to help dissipate the tremendous heat generated by the weapon, but her copper-jacketed rounds simply didn't have the power to achieve penetration.

Just then something came hurtling her way to land in the cool green grass. Krysty blinked at the sight of Doc's Webley, then scooped it up in both hands, took a stance and fired off all six rounds. By the third time, the grid was smashed into the laser, allowing the remaining big-bore .44 manstoppers of the handblaster full access.

Although built to be bulletproof a hundred years earlier, the military weapon now succumbed to the hammering fury of the booming Webley. Fat blue sparks crackled from within the smashing electronics and smoke poured from the sides. The droid quickly spun, and Ryan stood to empty the SIG-Sauer into the laser, finishing the job. Suddenly the entire droid was covered in crackling electricity, and the companions felt a tingle in the mud through their combat boots. The last two horses reared at the sensation, nickering loudly. Then Jak shoved his .357 Magnum blaster into a red crystal eye and fired twice. The lens shattered and the rounds plowed deep into the electronic brain of the machine, scrambling the primary circuits.

Sagging into the mud, the droid went still, its head tilting sideways before it went completely motionless.

"Frag that drek," J.B. growled, and fired a burst from the Uzi into the smashed eye, the 9 mm rounds noisily ricocheting inside the machine, smashing more delicate circuit boards, relays and control elements. In only a few seconds dark smoke began to trickle from the dome, and then a fire started inside the smashed droid.

"It's dead now for sure," Mildred stated, rising into view from behind a mossy tree stump.

"Damn well hope so," Ryan said, pulling out his Navy telescope to check the horizon for any more of the machines. But the forest, glen and grasslands were clear. There was nothing in sight but lush greenery, chilled droids and the aced horses.

Cleaning off her hands with a dry cloth, Mildred went over to examine Ryan, then extracted a plastic straw from her med kit. "Good thing the laser attacked from your left," she said, gently removing his eyepatch to smear a salve over the blistered skin. "Or else you might have been permanently blind on this side."

"Losing an eye saved me from going blind?" Ryan said, and in spite of the situation, the Deathlands warrior snorted a laugh. Anybody who claimed that the universe had no bastard sense of humor was clearly out of their mind.

When Mildred was done with the salve, she wrapped his head in strips of clean cloth, and Ryan tucked the leather patch into a pocket.

"You should be fine in a few days," she said, tucking away her meager supplies. "Just try not to smile for a while." Just for a moment, the physician remembered giving almost the exact same advice to Doc a week ago. It would seem that smiles were forbidden on Clemente Island.

"Not a problem," Ryan replied out of the right side of his mouth. "By then, we should be back on the mainland. Hopefully inside a redoubt."

Gathering their saddlebags from the corpses of the three chilled horses, the companions removed the heavy saddles from the last two horses, then draped the bags across the animals. Tethered to a tree stump, the horses snorted, seemingly at the demotion to a lowly pack mule.

"Slow, but not far till boat," Jak stated, as if the matter was of little concern. His jacket was caked with mud, the feathers bedraggled to the point where several had fallen off, exposing the razor blades sewn into the collar.

Going to the splayed ruin of a droid, J.B. studied the interior for a moment, before moving onward. There was no way to scav the needler from the wreckage. The weapon had been blown asunder. Unfortunately, so was the microwave beamer. However, the laser was merely smashed, not completely destroyed, and J.B. eagerly knelt on the damp grass to pull out his tools and start disassembling the interior workings of the droid.

"Hot damn!" J.B. cried, swinging aside a service panel. Inside was a bed of gray military foam, the kind used to pack grens, and nestled into the material were rows of spare parts, enough for the droid to repair any conceivable damage to the laser.

"Give me an hour and we'll have a working laser," J.B. chuckled, lifting a prism into view, then the smile faded. "Dark night, the bastard focusing lens is cracked."

"Can't use?" Jak asked with a frown.

"Yeah, I can make it work," J.B. answered slowly, turning the optical assembly around. "But it'll never cycle through the spectrum again, that's for nuking sure.

We're down to a single color, and just the basic three—red, blue, yellow."

"What possible difference could the color of a laser beam make to the target?" Doc asked, using a stick to clean the quicksand off his boots. At the moment the man looked as though he had escaped from a grave, which was frighteningly close to the truth.

"Lasers operate on the absorption of light," Mildred replied. "An apple absorbs all of the colors in visible light, except for red. It reflects that and thus we see it as red."

"So a red laser could not harm a red apple?" Doc asked, clearly surprised.

Mildred shrugged. "Well, eventually enough heat would be transferred to wither the fruit, then it would start to brown, allowing more of the beam to be absorbed and finally the apple would be destroyed."

"That's why mil lasers look like rainbows," Krysty said in startled comprehension. "So that whatever they hit will be aced!"

"Exactly!"

"Blue," Ryan decided. "Rhino blood is yellow, norm blood is red, but I've never aced anything that gushed blue."

While J.B. got to work, Ryan stood guard over the man as the rest of the companions reloaded their weapons, affected some minor repairs and washed their clothing in one of the larger ponds.

It took longer than a hour, but soon J.B. had the bulky nuke battery removed from the droid armed with the needler, and attached to the rebuilt laser with coaxial

cables recovered from the droid with the microwave
beamer. It was a mare's nest of stolen tech, a hodgepodge held together with duct tape and baling wire.
But when J.B. flipped the switch, a deep azure beam of
condensed light fiercely lanced from the aperture at the
end. The startling beautiful power ray hit a pine tree on
the outskirts of the glen, slicing the trunk neatly in two.
To the sound of snapping branches, the tree toppled over
with a loud crash, disturbing a large flock of sparrows
that voiced their outrage at the unprovoked attack as
they took wing to the cloudy sky. Softly in the distance,
thunder rumbled and lighting flashed.

"Next rhino comes our way is dead meat," J.B. stated
grimly, resting the cumbersome device on a shoulder.

"Then let's hope that is the worst thing this island
has to offer," Mildred added, slinging the scattergun
across her back.

"Always stickies about," Jak stated, looking around.
"They here. Just not find us yet."

"And let's hope it stays that way," Krysty said,
thoughtfully biting a lip. "We're going to need a litter
for that nuke battery. Should be easy enough to make
out of some rope and branches."

"Then let's head for the trees," Ryan growled, brushing back his wild crop of hair. "We still have a fair
distance to cover before reaching the coast."

"For the woods are dark, quiet and deep," Doc said
in a singsong voice. "But there are promises to keep,
and miles to go before we can sleep."

Nobody disagreed with the man, having heard him

paraphrase the ancient poem before. It was one of his favorites.

Building a litter from tree branches, rope and a horse blanket proved to be no problem. Even dragging the rig along behind, the horses still made good time on the dry land.

Chapter Eighteen

Two days later the companions began to recognize some of the landmarks and headed to the south toward the shore. Soon, they caught the refreshing smell of a salty breeze coming off the ocean—along with crackle of multiple blasters, closely followed by the dull thud of a gren.

Quickly taking cover behind a stand of trees, Ryan climbed into the branches and used the Navy telescope to try to find the fighting.

As expected, there were people fighting all over the lagoon—the docks, the Quonset hut, even inside the mouth of the tunnel, even though J.B. had closed it off and the passageway was only about fifty feet deep. Some of the people were bare-chested and covered with tattoos, while the others were dressed in the dark blue uniform of the giant from the volcano.

"It's the baron and his sec men from the volcano," Ryan called down, adjusting the focus on the antique longeyes. "They're fighting a bunch of pirates."

"Who winning?" Jak asked, brushing the snowy-white hair off his face with the barrel of his Magnum blaster.

"Nobody," Ryan answered truthfully. Crumpled bodies from both sides were strewed everywhere, oddly mixed with the corpses of dogs, horses, a couple of stickies, a lot of stingwings, even some eagles and one blubbery sea lion. Weird. It was almost as if the animals had also attacked the people, but if they were trying to ace somebody specific, or to help one side over the other it was impossible to say.

In the center of the battle was the *Moon Runner,* or what remained of the bedraggled ship. The wheelhouse was missing, there was a splintery hole in the stern hull, a dozen bodies festooned the sagging gunwales, and deep inside, the engines seemed to be on fire. Thick black smoke poured from every porthole and hatchway to spread a murky haze over the screaming combatants.

Out at sea, just this side of the breakers, was a ship, or boat of some kind, although Ryan would have called it a canal barge. On the bow was the name *Tiger Shark.* The craft was big and flat, with sandbags lashed to the deck with netting to serve as a crude gunwale. The barge was covered with pungi sticks and barbed wire, and looked about as maneuverable as a lead safe. On the other hand, the sailors were firing at the sec men with a couple of .50-caliber machine guns and a pair of huge arbalests. As the one-eyed man watched, a sailor launched an arrow almost a yard long. It lanced through the masking smoke of the *Moon Runner* to slam into a sec man frantically reloading his flintlock pistol. The giant arrow pierced him completely, slamming the norm against the rock face of the cliff. Still horribly alive, he began to shriek, pinned in place like a trophy to the wall.

"I can hear the names of Captain Carlton and Jones,"

Krysty said, her face scrunched tight in concentration. "Along with baron."

Grunting in reply, Ryan eased down from the leafy branches to drop the last few feet and land in a crouch. Slowly he stood. At least they now knew the names of the people who wanted them chilled. That might come in useful if there was a chance at negotiations. Ryan doubted that highly. However, it was smart to prepare for what the enemy could do, instead of merely guessing what they might.

Suddenly a raven-haired woman stood into view and aimed an M-16 combination assault rifle at the *Tiger Shark*, first triggering a short burst from the M-16 rapidfire, then launching a gren. The 40 mm round smacked into the sandbags, blowing open a three-foot breech, and sending everybody on the deck flat on their backs.

"An M-203? My, my, it's good to be the king, or in this case, the queen," Mildred remarked dryly, peeking out from behind a pine tree. "With a weapon like that, she has got to be the baron's wife."

"Good thing she has it," Ryan countered gruffly. "Nobody out there is a very good shot."

"Don't really need to be, the way they're throwing around lead," J.B. added in frank disapproval.

"The damn fools don't seem to be fighting over the *Moon Runner*, control of the dock, or any damn thing else," Krysty stated with a scowl. "They're just fighting."

"Civil blood doth make civil hands unclean," Doc muttered.

"You really think that anybody out there is biting his thumb?" Mildred snorted.

"Each in their own way, of course, madam," Doc espoused, with a hand to his heart.

"So, pray tell, what is the plan, my dear Ryan? Shall we steal their bikes to drive inland, far away from the tumultuous sea?"

Touching the bandage on his face, the man scowled. "Back to where, the volcano? We'd have to abandon the bikes, swim across the bay, climb a waterfall, and even if we find the right tunnel leading to the redoubt, we haven't a single implo gren to use against three Cerberus clouds," Ryan said, rubbing his jaw. "No, we need that boat."

"Any chance repair *Moon Runner?*" Jak asked hopefully.

"Double zero on that," Krysty answered brusquely. "So we're going to do the only other thing we can."

"Steal the *Tiger Shark*," J.B. stated.

"Nightcreep," Jak said, a pair of knives dropping into his waiting palms. "Fast and low."

"Everybody else start moving down the coastline," Ryan said, sliding off his backpack, then dropping his gunbelt. "Jak and I will handle this. We'll meet you past the tumbledown."

"We'll be there, lover," Krysty replied, glancing at the laser strapped to the litter behind the nervous horses. The animals clearly didn't like being this close to violent death, and kept trying to shy away, only to be drawn back by loyalty to their new masters.

Stripping down to their underwear and boots, Ryan and Jak gave the clothing to Mildred for safekeeping. As

the rest of the companions headed for the horses, each
man carefully wrapped a handkerchief around a knife
before tucking the blade between his teeth. It reduced
the shine and gave a much better hold than wet steel.

Going to their bellies, the men crawled along the
ground until reaching the beach, trying to keep behind
a low rill of black lava. The sounds of battle got much
louder.

Skirting past a nesting brood of crabs, the two companions eased into the shallows, then dived into the
waves and ducked underwater. Several minutes later
they resurfaced behind the *Tiger Shark*. The incoming
tide was pushing the cumbersome barge steadily toward the shore, so the anchor chains were taut, rising
from the watery depths to the main deck. Using their
fingers and toes, the men crept along the slippery steel
links to reach the vessel, pausing at the deadly array
of pungi sticks and barbed wire before hopping over.
They landed on the wooden deck with soft thuds, the
noise going completely unnoticed by the sailors over
the yammering fury of the big-bore rapidfires.

"How do ya like them flying fish, Jonsey-boy!" the
sailor laughed, burping the weapon again, the powerful
muzzle-blast slapping against his face and flapping his
vest open wide like leather batwings.

Fast and low, Ryan went to the left, Jak to the
right.

"Just don't shoot his bitch, I want to moor my tug
in her harbor first!" The other sailor guffawed, working the arming bolt to clear the breech before lifting
the firing block. But as the sailor laid in a fresh belt of

ammo, Jak stepped around the sandbag wall and neatly slit his throat from ear to ear.

Gurgling into death, the man grabbed his throat and Jak stabbed him again between the ribs, twisting the narrow blade to enlarge the hole in his lungs. Unable to draw a breath, the man slid to the deck, his mouth moving in a desperate attempt to warn his fellow guards.

As the second gunner hauled out a sawed-off shotgun, Ryan ghosted up behind the sailor, slapping a hand across his mouth, the other burying the panga in his stomach. As the curved blade went in deep, it arched around the protective rib cage and entered the heart. Going stiff, the sailor began to tremble all over, and Ryan mercifully removed the blade to slash his throat. Still shaking, the bleeding man dropped to the deck and went still.

Checking the feed on the massive rapidfire, Ryan and Jak racked the dockyard freely, trying for the troops on both sides. Two of the caged motorcycles violently exploded, and a dozen of the sailors were ruthlessly executed, shot from behind by their own blasters. As the big rapidfires cycled empty, Ryan and Jak buckled on the gunbelts of the chilled sailors, then separated again to do a fast recce of the main deck for any more crew members.

Running low and fast, Jak found a sailor sitting on a coil of rope, lazily smoking a cig. The man barely had a chance to register the presence of the nearly naked albino teenager when Jak introduced him to a pair of his leaf-bladed throwing knives and the sailor stopped smoking forever.

At the stern Ryan found a row of canoes, most of them homemade, but a couple were made of predark aluminum—dented, but still in very serviceable condition. Several of the canoes were missing, and Ryan sincerely hoped they had merely been used by the landing party. If not, this fight was a long way from over.

At the bow of the rectangular vessel, a burly sailor stood from behind a sandbag, working the bolt on a BAR longblaster. The tattoo of a single red strip adorned his bare arm, clearly displaying his rank.

"Cornelius, Mel, why'd you boys stop shooting?" the boson demanded suspiciously, starting through the maze with the surety of experience. There was nobody standing at the pair of Fifties, and he couldn't believe that a bunch of ville boys could snipe a pair of seasoned sailors this far out at sea.

As the boson turned into the gunnery station, Jak rose behind him and swung a barge pole oar as hard as he could. The stout pine cracked across the back of the boson's head, and the sailor dropped to the deck. Whipping out a knife, Jak began cutting the man's clothing into strips, then using them to securely bind and gag the sailor. The youth had decided that an officer might know important details about the strange craft that could come in useful later. If not, well, there was always the ever-patient sea just a few feet away.

Discovering a companionway leading to the lower level, Ryan paused to remove the cartridges from the sawed-off blaster, then toss it onto the next level. Hushed voices gasped at the sight, and a hand darted out to grab the weapon. Ryan fired twice, blowing off some fingers, then the SIG-Sauer jammed.

"He's out! Get 'im!" a sailor bellowed, and five big men brandishing machetes and clubs boiled out of the shadows.

Kicking the first man in the teeth with his combat boot, Ryan sent the man flying backward into the others, and they went tumbling back down the stairs in a wild tangle of limbs and curses.

Struggling to stand, a plump female sailor hauled a zip gun from a pocket and pulled back the rubber band to fire. Instantly, Ryan threw the panga. The weapon spun sideways through the air like a buzzsaw and buried itself into her left breast.

Shrieking in pain, the sailor still fired at Ryan, and he felt his wet shorts jerk at the passage of a tiny .22-caliber bullet. Fireblast, the bitch was good! Too bastard good! he thought. Flinging himself down the stairs, Ryan scraped his belly along the wooden steps to grab her ankles and jerk hard. With a cry, she went over, and Ryan grabbed the empty sawed-off from the deck to swat her hard across the face. Blood and teeth hit the wall, and the zip gun skittered away, loose brass cascading from a pocket.

Ignoring the weapon, Ryan laid into the pile of cursing sailors like a Viking berserker, breaking arms and smashing in heads with the sawed-off until the double-barrel was dripping with gore.

An alabaster hand grabbed his arm in a grip of steel and Ryan furiously turned to see Jak standing close.

"They aced," the teen said simply. "Which way engine room?"

It took a few moments for the red haze of battle to clear from his mind, then Ryan stiffly wiped the sawed-off clean on the shirt of a corpse and thumbed in some cartridges. Then he recovered the SIG-Sauer and worked the slide to eject the dud brass.

"This way," Ryan growled, his throat tight from the rush of adrenaline. Since the onslaught of adulthood, a young Ryan Cawdor had come to accept the fact that someday his wild temper would put him in the dirt. Thankfully, it wasn't this day. There was still a lot to do before the *Tiger Shark* was under their control.

Heading down the corridor the sailors had come from, the two companions noted this level was made of riveted steel. Genuine predark stuff, and lovingly scraped to a surgical cleanliness by the crew. But then, this was their home, and only stickies used their nest as a lavatory and a nursery.

Reaching a wooden door, Ryan kicked it open and ducked. Wearing a greasy apron, a sailor waiting inside fired a crossbow, the arrow shattering against the iron wall. Stroking the trigger of the SIG-Sauer, Ryan shot the cook in the forehead, then moved on, having no time to waste watching the man expire.

Jak took the next room, finding only an interrupted meal of fish stew, and Ryan the one after that, which proved to be the barracks, or whatever it was called on a ship—row upon row of empty beds, each with a footlocker at the bottom and a gunrack at the top.

"Nice digs," Jak admitted grudgingly, noting the prevalence of good boots, soap and canned goods. Whatever else could be said about the captain of the vessel, he treated his crew like kin. Unfortunately that made the bastard even more dangerous, as the crew would willingly fight to the death for the man.

"I think this is their flagship," Ryan answered, then paused as a closet door started to slowly open. Firing twice, Ryan saw the copper-jacketed rounds punch clean through the thin wood. There came a muffled cry of pain, and then a sailor fell out, his sawed-off discharging into a bed. The mattress exploded and a geyser of fluff and feathers filled the air, the blizzard swirling madly.

Snatching a feather on the fly, Jak tucked it behind his ear as they grimly continued their hurried sweep of the vessel.

Passing a porthole, Ryan briefly looked outside. He could see that the fight was still raging on the dock, and nobody seemed to be coming their way yet. But it was only a matter of time before the sailors figured out what was happening and came boiling back to regain their ship. Sec men polished their blasters in the night, cavalry riders curried their horses daily, and Mildred claimed that predark pilots actually named their jet-fighters, but sailors were just plain insane about their damn boats. The feeling was more than simple dedication to the craft that was their home, hearth and harbor. It was something else, something deeper, a sort of primordial bond that couldn't be explained to anybody but another sailor.

Past the barracks was an elaborately carved wooden door, with the word "Captain" correctly spelled. Checking the latch, Ryan was surprised to find it unlocked. Moving to the side, he fired the SIG-Sauer and blew the latch apart. As the door swung open, there came a deafening roar as a sawed-off scattergun fired. The blast of lead pellets hammered into the opposite wall and ricocheted off the iron to painfully pepper the two men from behind.

"Prick!" Jak snarled, touching his throat, his finger coming away streaked with blood.

"Don't go in!" Ryan ordered, looking over the sumptuous furniture, colorful tapestries and well-stocked liquor cabinet. The bedchamber resembled something from a gaudy house, not a fighting ship, and the one-eyed man was suddenly convinced that the entire room was a trap for invaders.

Hauling out his own sawed-off, Ryan put a pair of 12-gauge cartridges into the place, and sure enough a dozen assorted traps sprang into operation, blades slashing out, another hidden blaster firing in return, and a section of the ceiling slamming down to reveal it was a foot-thick of solid steel. The impact made the entire passageway shake.

"Shit, not trust Carlton if he tell water wet," Jak stated. He hawked to spit, then swallowed instead, not sure of even that minor an affront would set off another trap. Possibly an explosion powerful enough to breach the iron walls.

The passageway ended at a set of double doors, each marked with a carved wooden plaque, one displaying a vagina and the other a puckered asshole. Ryan and Jak almost smiled at that. Obviously these were here for any newbies unable to read. But anybody smarter than a mutie could figure out what these signs meant.

Going to the Out door, Ryan wiggled in the panga and pried it aside. The room beyond was full of machinery, diesel engines, pumps, generators, fuel tanks and a scrawny sailor standing in a pool of darkness, holding an ax. Startled by the unexpected infusion of light, she almost dropped the deadly weapon, then snarled and swung the blade.

Quickly stepping back, Ryan shoved the exit door forward and the blade slammed deep into the wood. Hauling the door open, he yanked the ax handle out of the grip of the sailor and she retreated into the shadows, muttering and cursing.

Kicking open the entrance, Jak started to shoot into the gloom, but then paused. A single ricochet in here could blow the whole damn barge out of the water, with them inside.

Unexpectedly the sailor lurched into view, swinging a wrench like a club. Jak hesitated shooting her for a split second and she knocked away the Colt Python, the blaster hitting the deck and sliding underneath a loudly thumping bilge pump.

"Come here, mutie-boy," she snarled, swinging the wrench with expert ease. "I'm going do you proper!"

Yanking open the exit, Ryan extended the sawed-off, but withheld firing for the same reason the teenager had. However, the sailor flinched at the sight of the blaster, and Jak used the distraction to bury a pair of knives into her throat.

Drowning in her own blood, the sailor staggered, managing to yank out one of the blades. Now the blood spurted away in high arches even faster than before. Sagging to the deck, she clumsily threw the knife back. Expecting that, Jak sidestepped the crude attack and recovered the Colt to put a round into her temple. The sailor jerked at the arrival of the .357 Magnum round, then never moved again.

While Jak dragged the corpse out of the way, Ryan hurried straight to diesel engines. They seemed in perfect working condition, everything clean and polished to a dull sheen. The deck was corkboard in some areas, obviously protection from slipping on grease spills. Buckets of sand hung near every fuel pump, and several pegboards were situated around the room, each tool hanging neatly inside a painted silhouette.

Rapping a knuckle against the fuel tanks, Jak was pleasantly surprised to find them nearly full. There was enough juice here for the companions to ride the barge all the way to the Alaskan redoubt, if they cared to.

Going to a set of predark controls, Ryan saw the old labels had been replaced with simple wood carvings to explain the function of each switch. Mentally thanking Carlton, the man turned on one of the diesel engines, then activated an electric winch and started hauling up the anchor.

As the wet chains started rattling through a hole in the metal ceiling, Ryan turned on the other two diesels, while Jak opened the fuel valves all the way.

"All right, let's go topside," Ryan commanded, striding for the exit. "I'll take the wheel, and you get one of those bastard Fifties working!"

The albino teen nodded. The easy part of jacking the ship was over. Now things were going to get bloody.

Chapter Nineteen

"Sir! Captain!" a sailor cried, safely hidden on the lee side of the burning *Moon Runner*.

Crouching behind a concrete pylon, Carlton turned to stare in annoyance at the man. "What is it?" he replied gruffly, fumbling to reload his blaster. So far, everything had gone according to plan. That bastard Jones and his witch had taken refuge in the tunnel and had barricaded themselves inside behind a wall of the dead. It was a triple-clever tactic that was going to backfire on them if they escaped. Win or lose, Jones and his witch got chilled this day. It was all arranged.

"Sir, the *Tiger* has broken free of her anchor!" the sailor yelled, pointing with a tattoo-covered arm.

"Impossible!" Carlton bellowed, spinning. But it was true, the barge was rapidly heading up the coastline. Then the captain noticed the churning wake behind the vessel and realized that all three of the diesel engines had to be running at full power.

"You feeb! It hasn't broken free," First Officer Godderstein roared. "Our nuking ship is being jacked!"

"But we left twenty crew on board," a boson snarled, angrily standing to try to see through the haze. The instant he broke cover, a blaster sounded from inside the tunnel and the boson staggered, his shoulder gushing blood. Dropping his blaster on the dock, the sailor

foolishly tried to reclaim the weapon. An arrow lanced
from the tunnel to slam into his ear. Flipping sideways,
the boson splashed into the lagoon, a billowing stain
rapidly spreading around the sinking body.

"You three, behind the hut!" Captain Carlton
snapped, looking at the men directly. "Take a couple
of those bikes and race to the west. Try to reach the
waterfall and sneak back on board the *Tiger!*"

"You two, Smith and Mackewitz," Godderstein
added, sliding a fresh clip into his rapidfire and working the arming bolt. "Head east, in case they try for
Sealton ville!"

"Handel, take a canoe and head back to port," Carlton added. "Break out the rockets and bring back the
whole damn fleet!"

"What, all fifteen, Skipper?" the man asked, lowering a massive crossbow.

"Every fragging thing we've got that floats!" Godderstein roared, standing and firing his M-16 rapidfire
in a long burst. The rounds hit something inside the
dark tunnel with meaty smacks, but there weren't any
answering cries of pain.

Holstering their blasters, the sailors grimly nodded,
then took off at a run. Immediately a flurry of arrows
streaked from the mouth of the tunnel, chilling one of
the men. The others got out of range and separated to
their assigned tasks.

Not willing to depend entirely upon his crew, as loyal
as the members were, the captain closed his eyes and
reached out with his mind to sweep the vicinity for any
remaining animals that might help in the pitched battle.
Almost everything in the area was either useless, like

the hutch of coneys in a stand of trees over the hill, or already chilled. But then the captain sensed something else, infinitely larger and more dangerous, and he slowly smiled in grim satisfaction. Oh yes, those would do just fine.

STILL RAGING, the fight at the lagoon was starting to slow a little, mostly because everybody was beginning to run low on ammunition. Knives and arrows were replacing lead, and each side was looting the dead for any spare rounds. Smack in the middle of everything, the *Moon Runner* was gradually sinking into the lagoon, a fire still raging inside the engine room, the dark smoke covering the dockyard like a ghostly pall.

With the help of the big rapidfires on the *Tiger Shark,* Captain Carlton and his sailors had used their canoes to gain control of the dockyard and hut. Cut off from their bikes, the baron, his wife and their sec men had fallen back into the tunnel, only to discover it was blocked solid just fifty yards inside the cliff. Effectively trapped, Jones had his people build a protective wall across the mouth of the tunnel from their own dead, which Lady Veronica had the sec men reinforce with a mound of rocks and dirt scooped up by hand from the floor or scraped off the walls. The first corpse used had been that of the newly promoted sec chief Zane Southerland.

The chattering sounds of fighting never ceased outside the tunnel as the frantic sec men used their bare hands to dig into the rocky earth of the collapsed ceiling. They had dug a crawl space into the loose material, using boards taken from the roof of the tunnel to support the cramped opening. It only went in a few yards, but was getting deeper with every passing minute.

Staying bent low, wounded sec men hauled the material away in slings made from their shirts to pack it behind the wall of corpses. Incredibly, the crude barrier was holding, and the incoming lead from the sailors only made the bodies jerk about in a horrid mockery of life.

"How's the brass holding out?" the baron asked, pulling the last spare rounds out of the loops of his gunbelt to thumb into the empty clip of the Ruger. There was a single gren on his belt, but that was the key to their escape. Hopefully.

"Don't ask, my love," Lady Veronica replied, releasing an arrow from the stolen crossbow. The MP-5 rapid-fire still hung at her side, the last full clip reserved for the next rush of the sailors. The last time Carlton had ordered them to use a desk from the hut as protective cover. But the 9 mm Parabellum rounds from the MP-5 had easily cut through the flimsy pressboard, and the lady ruthlessly sent five more sailors into the arms of Davey.

Just then, a boomerang spun out of the smoke and streaked into the tunnel. It missed the baron by the thickness of a prayer and slammed into one of the wooden beams supporting the roof. Grabbing the weapon with both hands, a corporal jerked it loose and raced to the wall to fling it back outside. It spun away and clattered noisily against the tilted hull of the *Moon Runner*.

Instantly a flurry of arrows sailed forth, one of them catching the corporal in the armpit. Dumbfounded, the sec man stared at the ghastly wound, knowing in cold certainty that the location made a tourniquet impossible. As the warm red blood flowed down the side of his chest, the corporal passed his gunbelt and blaster to a new recruit, and walked over to sit with his back to the wall.

"Four rounds," he whispered hoarsely. "Make them count, brother."

Crisply, the new corporal saluted in reply and buckled on the gunbelt to check the load in the revolver.

With no way to help the dying man, the baron lit a cig and passed it over. The pale corporal eagerly accepted the special gift and gratefully took a long drag, letting the sweet tobacco smoke fill his lungs, then he exhaled slowly and stopped moving.

"Save the arrow, then put him on the wall," Jones commanded, his face a mask of control.

"Yes, Baron," the corporal replied, and the grisly task was accomplished without further conversation.

Accepting the arrow, Lady Veronica loaded it into her crossbow and reached out with her mind to find the original owner. There was a faint tug from the direction of the fuel pumps, and she instantly fired. With a strangled cry, a sailor stumbled into view, the arrow buried deep in his left eye. Blindly, the man staggered around, going straight off the dock and into the lagoon. He hit with a splash, and the blaster in his hand sank out of sight.

"Thirty more like that, and we win," Jones muttered, scanning the smoky exterior with his blaster at the ready.

"Doing my best," Lady Veronica replied, notching

another arrow into the crossbow. "How is the digging going?"

"There's no way of telling," the baron said, then jumped back with a curse as several snakes wiggled around the wall of corpses and into the tunnel. Shitfire, that mutie Carlton had summoned an entire nest of cottonmouths! Their poison was ten times more deadly than the venom of a jumper.

Retreating quickly, the sec men kicked dirt at the snakes, trying to herd them together. Firing an arrow at a cottonmouth, and missing, a sec woman swung down her crossbow and caught the snake on the rise, crushing the head flat. As it dropped lifeless to the ground, the other snakes converged on the sec woman, hissing and trying to bite her legs.

Letting loose an arrow, Lady Veronica got one snake through the middle. Pinned in place, it could only lash around madly, hissing louder than ever and snapping at anything nearby. A sec man cursed as the fangs scored a deep scratch across his arm. Quickly, he backed farther away, pulling out a knife and a butane lighter.

Uncoiling his bullwhip, the baron lashed the knotted length of leather forward and cut off the head. As the other two turned on him, he did the same. He coiled the bullwhip and returned it to his gunbelt. "Here, use this to save the poison," the baron directed, tossing over a paperback book. "Then smear it on the arrowheads." The sec men rushed to obey.

Huddled against the rocky wall, the bitten sec man played the flame of the lighter along the edge of his knife. When the metal started to change color, he slashed the wound and started sucking hard, turning his head to spit out the poison.

When the spit ceased to have a greenish tinge, the sec man weakly stood. "I think that did it, Baron," he grinned, just as another boomerang spun into the tunnel. Everybody ducked except him and the man's brains splashed onto the rocky wall.

"Son of a mutie slut!" Lady Veronica snarled, swinging up the MP-5, but then slowly lowered it against her will. The whole point of Carlton sending in snakes was probably to make them use up the last of the brass.

As if in response to her thoughts, the sailors opened fire with a fusillade of blasters, the hot rounds smacking into the barrier of corpses with meaty whacks and ricocheting off the rocky walls of the tunnel.

Suddenly a sec man charged out of the gloom from deeper inside the tunnel.

"We're through!" he whispered, a smile splitting the layers of grime covering his face. One hand was wrapped in bloody strips of cloth, but the man radiated a sense of victory.

"About damn time," the baron grunted, slapping the man on the back. "Good work! Send through some scouts, then the wounded. We'll take the six."

"But Baron!" the sec man objected.

"Obey your baron, arnsman," Lady Veronica commanded, using the ancient title of a loyal guard.

Stiffening at the honor, the sec man raised both hands in silent agreement and started arranging the exodus.

"You next, my love," Jones said, pulling a half stick of TNT from his left boot. He had been saving it in case the sailors mobbed the tunnel. The blast would chill them all, granting him revenge and saving his beloved wife from a gang rape that would never end.

Lady Veronica started to object, then saw the raw determination in his face and relented. Kissing him briefly on the sweaty cheek, she crawled into the hole and out of sight.

Waiting a few seconds, Baron Jones lit the fuse with a butane lighter, stabbed it into the soft dirt alongside the hole, then dived in and started scrambling for distance.

A few seconds later the half stick detonated, the confined explosion blowing out the corpses like a shotgun blast and shattering the support columns. With a stentorian groan, the roof collapsed and the walls folded to completely fill the underground tunnel, clouds of dust and dirt billowing out to mix with the woodsmoke from the burning *Moon Runner* until the roiling atmosphere of the lagoon turned as black as midnight for several minutes.

When the sea breezes finally cleared away the smoke and dust, the tunnel in the cliff was gone, as if it had never existed.

Chapter Twenty

Guiding the cumbersome barge into the calm water of the little inlet proved to be surprisingly easy for Ryan, and the man briefly wondered if he was a natural at steering a boat or if sailors had been trying to make themselves sound important for centuries by pretending that a relatively simple task was incredibly difficult. Then an unexpected wave hit the barge and Ryan suddenly knew the hard truth as he temporarily lost control of the craft and Jak went tumbling over the gunwale.

"Thanks," the teen sputtered, standing waist deep in the shallows.

"Sorry," Ryan shouted, lashing the wheel into place and running over to the side of the vessel to toss down a rope.

Climbing out of the water, Jak scowled at the man, then flinched as the salt water finally reached the open sores on his back from the ricocheted scattergun buckshot.

Understanding the source of the pained expression, Ryan grabbed a bucket of rain water from a peg and sloshed it over the teen.

"Thanks," Jak said, this time giving the word an entirely different tone. Shrugging off his jacket, the teenager hung it on the peg to dry.

"You two done fucking around?" J.B. shouted from the shore through cupped hands.

"Almost!" Ryan yelled back, giving a half smile.

On the shore, the rest of the companions stood patiently waiting near a spitting campfire. There was no sign of the two horses, and the air smelled of freshly broiled steak. In the distance, a large patch of the pine-tree forest was burning out of control, thick plumes of smoke rising high.

Wearily, everybody climbed on board, setting down their backpacks with grateful sighs.

"Trouble?" Jak asked, looking over the tired people.

"Nothing we couldn't handle," J.B. replied, easing the bulky nuke battery to the deck with a dull thump. The laser was strapped across his back, the cable still connected to the battery for instant use.

"I'll bet," Ryan said, noticing that Doc was carrying the munitions bag, Mildred the shotgun and Krysty the Uzi.

"Well, a swarm of stingwings aced both horses, and we've been on the run ever since," J.B. admitted, massaging an arm. "Dark night, this thing gets heavy after a while. It's like hauling a LAV on your back."

"Someone sent people to harass us with sniper fire," Mildred added, brushing some sand and nettles off her pants. "We couldn't find them in the treetops, so…" She glanced at the raging inferno on the nearby hills.

"Set fire ace snipers?" Jak scowled in disbelief.

"Well, it seemed like the thing to do at the time," Doc demurred, sounding slightly embarrassed.

"How about you two?" Krysty asked, removing her bearskin coat to drape it over a sandbag.

"Pretty much the same," Ryan stated with a grimace. "The captain sent some of his gunners in canoes after us. When they started shooting, Jak riddled them with the Fifties, and from then on we've been left alone."

Just then, an echoing roar sounded from the direction of the hills, and everybody spun with a hand on his or her blaster to see a mountain of mottle-colored flesh begin to rise above the forest fire. Soon, a single great eye was revealed to stare hatefully at the tiny people standing on the barge.

"Bastard!" Jak cursed, spinning to race for the closest .50-caliber machine gun.

Bellowing in unbridled fury, the colossal kraken began to slowly haul itself sideways along the hill, its thick tentacles grabbing onto the trunks of pine trees just outside the rampaging conflagration.

"Quick, John, use the laser!" Mildred shouted, pumping the scattergun. "On land we stand a chance, but we're doomed if it reaches the water!"

"Tell me something I don't know!" J.B. replied with a snarl, shrugging off the laser and dialing the controls to maximum power.

As the kraken started crashing through the greenery, J.B. sent a deep blue beam into the trees, the juicy nettles exploding like thousands of firecrackers at the touch of the power ray. Startled, the kraken recoiled, then the tree trunks whooshed into flames.

Roaring in frustration, the giant mutie began dragging itself in the other direction. But J.B. quickly set every tree in sight on fire, the flames forming an almost solid wall of fire between the behemoth and the shoreline.

"At this rate, the fire will die soon," Doc said in a deceptively calm voice. "And without any horses or wags…" There was no need for him to finish the sentence.

Aiming for the eye, J.B. tried to blind the mutie, but the billowing smoke threw off his aim and the laser merely scored a gash across the creature's forehead. Yellow blood gushed out, but not very much.

Changing tactics, J.B. narrowed the beam to its tightest focus, then swept the laser across the top of the mutie. The crown of the beast came off, pulsating gray brains swelling into view, and a torrent of piss-yellow blood gushed from the ghastly wound.

Howling louder than thunder, the kraken surged into the flames, uncaring of the pain, intent upon reaching the norms at any price. Holding down the button, J.B. swung the laser back and forth across the beast, cutting off tentacles and hacking off huge chunks of flesh.

Bursting out of the flames, what remained of the kraken slumped onto the sandy ground, the tentacles lashing to find any purchase to drag it into the life-giving ocean. But the laser removed the ropy limbs, then burned into the snapping beak, slowly traveling upward, boiling the eye a solid white, until coming out the top of the oozing brain.

A split second later the laser sputtered and died, the housing gushing smoke and sparks as melted circuits dribbled out of a vent like silver blood.

Still fighting to move forward, the kraken convulsed, then fell apart, the two sections spurting golden gore, the few remaining tentacles whipping around mindlessly before the dying mutie shuddered and went still.

IMPATIENTLY WAITING for the fleet to arrive, Captain Carlton suddenly went pale and stopped pacing the dock. A wave of incalculable pain flooded his entire being from the psychic backlash of having a creature under his mental control perish, and the man doubled over to noisily retch into the lagoon. Gurgling as if about to die, Carlton fell over sideways, gasping for breath, his limbs thrashing wildly.

WITH THEIR BARON and his lady safely in the middle of the group, the sec men of Sealton ville moved warily through the long dark tunnel, the only illumination coming from their butane lighters and one tallow candle that spit and popped constantly.

They had been afraid that the tunnel might lead to a lava tube and end in a sulfur pit, dooming them all to a slow chill. But the air was remarkably fresh, although reeking with the smell of old corpses. Clearly, there had been a major fight in the tunnel, and not that long ago.

Coming upon a crude barricade, the sec men checked the bodies on the ground, first to make sure they were aced and then for anything useful.

"Baron, these…these are cannies," a sec man growled, lifting a skinning knife into view. The handle was wrapped in human skin, a tattoo clearly visible.

"Any weapons?" the baron asked, holding his Ruger ready in case one of the bodies was actually alive. Cannies often played corpse to lure in their victims.

"Plenty, Baron," a sec man replied, not quite sure if he was happy about that or not. "Nothing that takes brass, but flintlocks by the pile."

"Any flints?" Lady Veronica asked suspiciously, a finger resting on the trigger of her MP-5 rapidfire.

"Pounds of them!" a sec woman exclaimed. "And more black powder and shot than we can possibly carry."

"Then arm yourselves, but watch for traps!" the baron commanded, keeping his back to the wooden wall.

"What do you think happened here, my love?" Lady Veronica asked, scowling at the murky figures on the floor. In the candlelight, they almost seemed to move, and the effect was unnerving.

"Something came down this tunnel, and they died trying to hold it off," the baron said slowly, then bent to pick up a shiny golden object. It was a brass cartridge with a tiny dent in the side, marking it as having come from a rapidfire.

"The outlanders," Lady Veronica stated, glancing at the darkness behind them. "They nuked the cannies to jack their boat, but tangled with Carlton instead."

"Doesn't sound like they work for him, after all," the baron said, shifting his grip on the Ruger. "I'm starting to believe the fight at the volcano was a mistake on our part, and they were just in the wrong place at the wrong time."

The woman merely grunted at the possibility, not quite ready to relinquish her hatred for the witch with the red hair.

When the sec men were fully armed, the group continued deeper into the tunnel and soon entered a spacious dining hall full of decomposing bodies. The reek was horrible, and they moved past the room and into another tunnel as fast as possible. Some of the bodies appeared to have been gnawed on, which meant that either there was no avenue to the surface or the cannies had tangled with their worst enemy, their own kind—screamers. At the realization, a dozen sec men cocked the stone-tipped hammers on their blasters into firing position.

"Anything moves, shoot on sight," the baron commanded, feeling the tension among the troops increase.

A breeze was blowing along the subterranean passageway into their faces, forcing the wretched stink behind, and they gratefully savored the flow. The air carried a faint aroma of growing plants, as if they were near the grasslands once more.

Abruptly calling a halt, a sec man crawled forward with a knife and soon stood holding a pipe bomb. "Whoever planted this knew his trade," the man stated, tucking the explosive charge into his belt.

More bodies were found along the way, but already carrying a full load of shot and powder, the sec men ignored the corpses, aside from thrusting a knife into them to make sure the decomposing piles of flesh weren't a threat.

"Any spears or axes?" the baron asked.

His broken arm in a sling, a corporal nodded. "Yes, sir. Plenty."

"Then strip the dead," Lady Veronica ordered brusquely, "and make some torches from their clothing."

The grisly task was done. The group continued onward through the subterranean labyrinth, but the mood
improved, as did their speed.

Passing by several prison cells, the sec men sighed at
the sight of sunlight streaming in through ragged holes
in the ceiling.

"We're almost out," Baron Jones said confidently.
"Let's find the front entrance and go back home."

"The first round of shine is on me," Lady Veronica
added. "And no wall duty for a month!"

Both of them tried not to smile when they saw the
grim faces of the sec men ease at the thought of anything other than fighting and chilling. Tired men made
mistakes, and they weren't out of this stinking rad pit
yet.

Taking a corner, the group paused as the lead sec
man knelt to disarm another trap. Then they became
aware of a soft glow at the far end of the corridor. The
smell of greenery was much stronger, but it was oddly
tainted with the smell of fresh animal droppings.

Advancing carefully, the group went stock-still at
the startling sight of a large patch of sunlight streaming
down from a colossal hole in the ceiling. Lying in the
pool of light was a sleeping thunder king, surrounded by
the partially consumed bodies of some cannies. Behind
the giant mutie was a flight of wooden stairs leading up
to a set of wooden doors, sunlight streaming through
every tiny crack.

Nobody spoke, but a sec man panted at the tantalizing sight, and the eyes of the king snapped open at the
tiny sound.

"Fire!" Baron Jones bellowed, triggering the Ruger.

The terrified sec men opened fire with their stolen blasters, and the king lurched forward, its horn goring the first man. With a shake of the head, the creature tossed aside the body and lumbered forward, trampling the next man and crushing another between the wall and its own armored body.

"Die!" Lady Veronica screamed, emptying her weapon into the face of the thing. The barrage of 9 mm rounds took out both eyes, but the king merely grunted in annoyance and bent to start eating the still living sec men, their hideous screams going completely unnoticed.

"Nuking hell, this is a trap!" the baron snarled, firing the Ruger. "Carlton wanted us in the tunnel to escape this way and get fed to his bastard pet!"

As the creature began to regenerate, a sec man threw a pipe bomb. The blast shook the beast hard, but it went on eating and repairing itself. A sec man darted into a prison cell and barred the door from the inside while another sec man tried to get past the king to reach the stairs. Never pausing in the grotesque feasting, the king merely shifted its bulk sideways for a moment, smashing the man against the wooden wall, pulping his legs and splintering the planks. He dropped to the ground with a weeping sob, and the beast chomped off his head, chewing the skull like a cow did soft cud.

"Retreat!" the baron commanded, grabbing the hand of his wife and taking off at a full run.

Frantically reloading their black-powder blasters, the sec men were right behind their baron.

"Where?" Lady Veronica asked, squeezing his hand, knowing it was probably for the last time.

"Here!" the baron said, unexpectedly stopping at an intersection to point at the wooden support beam. "Arnsman, seal the tunnel!"

Quickly the sec man planted the explosive charge as everybody else moved to a safe distance farther down the tunnel.

"That won't hold it off for very long," Lady Veronica said pointedly, looking at her empty rapidfire.

"Every minute of life is worth it," the baron replied curtly, dropping his revolver to pull out his bullwhip. "If this is our day to buy the farm, then we'll take that big bastard with us to hell. Right, boys?"

Knowing that was pure crap, the sec men cheered in response anyway. Their job was to protect the ville and the baron's family, with their lives if necessary. They had no fear of getting chilled, only of getting chilled uselessly.

"Ready!" the sec man shouted, holding a butane lighter and a stubby fuse.

Just then, the king walked around the corner and rammed its curbed horn into the side of the man. Dropping the fuse, he screamed wildly and beat the creature with a fist. Jerking its head, the king tossed him aside and started slowly toward the others, as if knowing full well that they had no place to ride or hide.

As her husband and the sec men cut loose with their useless weapons, Lady Veronica closed her eyes tightly and tried to extend her mind to touch the thoughts of the other witch. She didn't think it was possible, but there was nothing to lose in the attempt. The woman knew that she was already aced, but there was the slim possibility of revenge. That would have to be enough.

He can talk to animals! Lady Veronica mentally screamed, the words echoing inside her head. *Captain Carlton! Mind-talker! Animals! Beware!*

Then the blasters stopped shooting and the screaming commenced.

Carlton! Mind-talker! Animals! Beware!

Suddenly the king was upon her and the universe became filled with crushing pain, but only for a few moments.

Standing her turn at the wheel, Krysty suddenly reeled backwards as if physically struck, her hair tumbling down her shoulders limp and lifeless.

"What's wrong?" Mildred demanded, rushing over while J.B. lunged for the abandoned wheel.

"In…my mind…a death call," Krysty whispered, shivering hard. "Veronica…the wife of Baron Jones… the man we called the giant…" She paused as the physician forced her to take a drink of water.

"Are they coming to attack?" Ryan demanded, sliding the Steyr off his shoulder and working the arming bolt.

"No, they're aced…both of them," Krysty panted, her hair slowly starting to stir once more. Then the woman looked up, her face grimly determined. "Veronica died warning us about the captain, Carlton."

"He come?" Jak asked, scowling.

"Worse, much worse," Krysty said, rising unsteadily to her feet. The woman felt ill, as if she had been kicked in the brain. Not the outside of her head, but the bare tissue of her living brain.

"How can it possibly be worse, dear lady?" Doc asked, sliding a wooden box forward for her to use as a makeshift chair.

"Carlton is a Talker," Krysty said with conviction, massaging her temples. "He can command animals with his mind. Horses, dogs, eagles…even muties and bio-weps."

"Like krakens?" Ryan asked, glancing over a shoulder.

She nodded.

"Fireblast! J.B., head for shore," Ryan commanded, slinging the longblaster again. "Until he's chilled, we can't chance crossing the deep waters."

"How do that?" Jak demanded. "He baron of fleet, got dozen war ships. Mebbe more!"

Briefly, Ryan explained the plan, the details falling into place as he did.

"Dark night, that's one bastard gamble," J.B. said, angling the barge into the flow of the waves. "But with the laser aced, I can't see any other way of settling this mess that doesn't end with us feeding the fragging fish!"

"Yeah, I know," Ryan said, tugging the bandage covering his face tighter into place. "So we better get it right the first time."

"Or else," Krysty muttered.

Chapter Twenty-One

By the time the fifteen-ship fleet arrived at the cannie lagoon, Carlton had recovered from the death of the kraken and was seething for revenge against the hated outlanders. The ships were mostly a collection of fiberglass-hull pleasure craft recovered from the ruins of the mainland: yachts and sloops, equipped with gasoline engines, but also rigged with sails to use the wind, and now, fortified with sheet metal and cannons.

Almost out of control with rage, Captain Carlton sent the fleet to check every river, every bay, every inlet to try to find the outlanders and his stolen boat, and then they were to look along the coast of the mainland. He sold sulfur to most of the coastal barons, and they knew the *Tiger Shark* by sight. If the outlanders were stupe enough to make landfall at one of their villes, the baron would have captured them alive to sell back to Carlton for an uncountable cargo of sulfur. The captain knew it was a long shot, but the seas were vast, and all any good sailor had to guide his way were the stars and his gut instincts. Most likely the thieves had sailed off south to escape his wrath.

Carlton was astonished when the *Tiger Shark* was found, less than a day later, rammed onto the beach at the bottom of Nixon Falls, near the Cesium Mountains, on the island of Malibu. However, the barge was empty, crossbows missing and vital parts removed from each of the engines. Without those parts, the formidable *Tiger Shark* was now only a derelict, little more than ballast.

Surrounding the volcanic island with his fleet, Carlton used rowboats to send in an assault force of a hundred sailors to scale the cliffs to retrace the path of the LARC back into the steamy lava tubes, reluctantly assisted by the new baron of Sealton ville, Digger O'Malley. After ruthlessly chilling a lot of his former friends, Baron O'Malley had assumed iron control over the ville, and didn't want to leave Sealton on this blood hunt. But debts had to be paid and promises kept, sometimes, even by a baron.

After days wandering aimlessly in the lava tubes, the best hunting dogs of the fifteen-ship navy still couldn't follow the tracks of the hated outlanders, so Carlton summoned a couple of thunder kings. Waggling their hypersensitive tongues in the steamy air, the creatures easily detected the minuscule traces of mil rubber smeared high on the walls of the lava tubes, and retraced the smudges past a strange spherical depression in the ground, and all the way back to a massive black wall.

Sending the kings off to a side tunnel to await his commands, Captain Carlton walked slowly toward the titanic slab of metal, surrounded by his entire crew of heavily armed sailors. They scowled uneasily at the black wall, which smacked of predark tech to them, mil tech at that! But Carlton was fascinated. The tire tracks went straight to the wall and disappeared, as if it were actually a door. But how could that be possible?

The thing was enormous, dozens of feet high, and set directly into the volcanic rock. He had never seen anything like it before on the entire island.

Hesitantly reaching out a hand, Carlton fingered the air, trying to gauge if there was any heat radiating from the material. Mebbe it was some sort of barrier to block off lava? However, there was no sense of heat radiating from the black material. Taking a risk, the man briefly touched the metal, then boldly laid his palm flat on the surface.

Incredibly, it was cool, as if the volcano rumbling inside the mountain wasn't hot enough to affect the bizarre stuff.

"What in the nine hells is it?" Digger whispered, resting a hand on his matlock. "Some sort of bomb shelter? Or mebbe a crashed subbie?" They had all heard the legends of submariners, sailors whose boats went under the waves instead of over. Nobody sane believed such drek, of course, until now.

"The descends of the crew of a crashed subbie," Carlton said softly, unable to tear his eyes off the dark metal. That would explain their fancy blasters, and how they had beaten his men. Who else but a sailor could ever match a sailor in battle? Lubbers were good for target practice, and not much else.

"We could try to blast our way in, Skipper," Godderstein said, rubbing a partially healed scar on his arm. "We got enough black powder to blow open this mountain!"

"And trigger an eruption that would melt the sub and destroy everything inside," Carlton snapped, suddenly positive that this was a predark sub. It had to be. What else could it be? There was no other logical explanation.

Approaching the door...*no, the hatchway* once more, Carlton ran a hand across the satiny metal. It was unscratched, as smooth as the breasts of a teenage gaudy slut. Just on the other side of this hatch were the treasures of the predark world waiting for him, as well as the outlanders and the stolen engine parts. He would grant them a swift death as fellow sailors, but only after they had told him all of the secrets of their beached vessel. *A submarine buried underground.* Packed full of blasters, brass, wags and fuel. Enough for him to conquer the coastal baronies, and then the mainland itself, and finally the entire fragging world!

"Sir, I...well, okay, we found a thing over here," a sailor said, lifting the armored lid to expose the alphanumeric keypad. "Want us to try busting it open?"

"Touch nothing!" Carlton roared, a smile expanding across his face. So, he had been right, this was a hatch! There had been something similar built into the wall safe of the captain's quarters on board the *Tiger Shark* when he had first found the wreck. The rows of little buttons were a kind of lock, like a padlock, only it used numbers instead of a key. He had never been able to figure out the code for the wall safe on the *Shark,* and had eventually smashed it open with a sledgehammer. But this key lock seemed to be made of the same material as the door, and he felt sure no mere sledgehammer would breach this U.S. Navy doorway.

Reaching out with his mind, Carlton probed inside the beached submarine, trying to find any kind of an animal that he could use to trick the hatchway open from the other side. Dogs needed to visit the bushes, especially in a sub! Almost instantly there was a response to the mental call, strong, fast and nearly overwhelming.

With a low rumble of working hydraulics, the blast door began to cycle aside and out flowed the three Cerberus clouds.

Instantly they converged on Captain Carlton, surrounding the invader. Shrieking in unimaginable agony, the captain was dissolved from three different directions, until only his spine remained. The bloody length of white bone and throbbing ganglia dropped to the rocky floor with a clatter. Then the diligent clouds also consumed that small biomass before going after the rest of the intruders.

Attempting to flee, the sailors opened fire with their blasters, crossbows and black-powder grens, but none of those did any damage whatsoever to the nebulous guardians of the redoubt. In mere seconds, they were gone, and the sparkling clouds went after the thunder kings. The terrified bioweps lasted longer than the norms, but not by very much. Soon, the steamy lava tubes were empty once more, and the Cerberus clouds flowed back inside the redoubt to wait for further orders.

HIDDEN INSIDE the jungle across the bay, the companions watched as a single frightened man climbed the ropes hanging down the cliff alongside the rushing waterfall. As he staggered along the beach, the handful of sailors guarding the rowboats rushed to his aid. But as he shouted and waved his arms, they raced into the rowboats and left the island, their oars a blur of frantic motion.

As the crew in the rowboats reached the nearest

armed yacht moored offshore, the news spread, and the collection of homemade warships rapidly took flight, heading off in different directions, each determined to get away farther, and faster, than the others from the death clouds. Carlton was aced, the fleet was no more. Now, it was every ship and crew for itself.

In less than an hour, the azure Cific Ocean was clear of any vessels, and there were only the gentle waves cresting on the black volcanic sand of the deserted beaches.

Stepping out of the jungle across the bay, Ryan used his telescope to ensure the coast was clear, while the rest of the companions came out of the bushes, their clothing covered with leafy vines, added as crude camouflage.

"Well done, sir. My compliments!" Doc boomed, a hand resting on the LeMat. "To be quite honest, I really was not sure that your plan would succeed, but it has. It has, indeed!"

"Love comes goes. Hate always reliable," Jak drawled, hitching up his gunbelt.

"Sad, but true," Krysty agreed, her hair waving and flexing in harmony with the clean ocean breeze.

"Okay, let's go," Ryan declared, compacting the telescope and dropping all of his belongings to the black sand, aside from the panga.

Swimming to the other shore, the companions looted the remaining rowboats for anything useful, then replaced the missing engine parts in the *Tiger Shark,* reclaimed their possessions across the bay and sailed due north, then north-by-northeast toward the nearest redoubt.

* * * * *

James Axler
Outlanders®

CRADLE OF DESTINY

The struggle of the Cerberus rebels stretches back to the dawn of history…

When millennia-old artifacts are discovered in the Middle East's legendary Fertile Crescent, they appear to belong to one of Cerberus's own. It's not long before Grant is plunged back through the shimmering vortex of time, forcing the rebels to lead a rescue party across a parallax to destroy a legendary god beast—before Grant is lost forever.

Available February 2011 wherever books are sold.

TAKE 'EM FREE

2 action-packed
novels plus a
mystery bonus

NO RISK

NO OBLIGATION
TO BUY

GE10

AleX Archer
RESTLESS SOUL

The relics of the dead are irresistible to the living...

A vacation spot picked at random, Thailand ought to provide relaxation time for globe-trotting archaeologist Annja Creed. Yet the irresistible pull of the country's legendary Spirit Cave lures Annja and her companions deep within a network of underground chambers— nearly to their deaths.

Available January 2011 wherever books are sold.

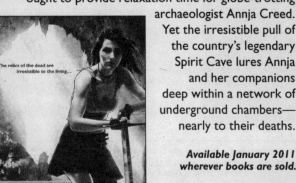

www.readgoldeagle.blogspot.com

GRA28